MY SIDE OF THE STORY

MY SIDE OF THE STORY

Will Davis

BLOOMSBURY

Published by Bloomsbury USA, New York
Distributed to the trade by Holtzbrinck Publishers

All papers used by Bloomsbury USA are natural, recyclable products made from
wood grown in well-managed forests. The manufacturing processes conform to
the environmental regulations of the country of origin.

LIBRARY OF CONGRESS CATALOGING-IN-PUBLICATION DATA HAS BEEN APPLIED FOR.

ISBN 1-59691-294-4
ISBN-13 978-1-59691-294-6

First U.S. Edition 2007

1 3 5 7 9 10 8 6 4 2

Typeset by Hewer Text UK Ltd, Edinburgh
Printed in the United States of America by Quebecor World Fairfield

Huge thanks to Mum, Dad, Tamsin and Seraphina for all their support. I am exceptionally grateful to my agent Peter Buckman, at whose prompting this book was written, and to Anne-Marie Doulton. Great thanks to everyone who offered helpful/tactful advice, especially Dawn, Eunji, Murielle and Sarah. And a big thank you to my editor Michael Fishwick, and to Alexandra Pringle, Trâm-Anh Doan, Chiki Sarkar, Emily Sweet and everyone at Bloomsbury.

1

I'm gonna start with one of those disclaimers like you get at the end of films where some writing comes up to tell you that even though it's all based on a true story the exciting bits might not really have happened. So you're all like, What was the point of even making it then? Not that there's much in the way of exciting bits to come, I'm not gonna lie to you. In fact, that's the disclaimer. I was gonna go further and do some spouting about not wanting to be some hotshot and trying to get people to love me for being this totally wonderful narrator, but then I figured that's just a waste of everyone's time. And if that's what you really wanted, and you see it as a reason not to read any further than this, then you can LIC GAS. Which stands for Like I Could Give A Shit.

So I'm gonna like, give you a brief rundown and then just launch right in. This is what you need to know: My name is Jarold, but everyone calls me Jaz, which is a damn sight cooler I think you'll agree. I know that everyone hates their names blah-blah but mine is really bad so it's lucky it abbreviates to something with a bit of cred. I'm sixteen (just) and I have two remarkably undivorced parents, along with a sister and a grandmother, and we all live in the same house together just like in a TV show. I've just started my A levels too, which me and Al are planning to fail, which is our way of saying Fuck You to the British educational standard.

Al's my best mate, by the way. She's sixteen too and she's totally into politics, which I'm like, totally not. And yeah, she's a she. Her real name is Alice, which doesn't exactly rock but is still a hell of a lot better than Jarold. Weirdly, like there's some perverted logic that says people with dull names can only get crap abbreviations out of them, hers turns into Al, which means that people always think she's a dyke, which she finds offensive (the word, being political and all). I reckon it's pretty appropriate though, because if anyone was ever destined to be a dyke it's her.

Anyway, I'm gonna do this now, or else you're still gonna be wading through bullshit ten pages later. I'm gonna start with the hassle. There's actually masses and masses of hassle to come, but this is pretty much where it all begins.

I'm just going up to my room after having some toast because I was literally starving and Mum's got this new Feed Yourself Rule for weekdays because she says me and Teresa (my sister, alias The Nun) are old enough now to boil our own eggs (it's like, what the hell is that supposed to mean?). So I come round the corner and find both my parents standing there with their arms folded. I mean they're literally blocking my way up like The Guardians of the Stairs.

I'm like, Hello?

Jarold, your father and I want a word, says Mum in her business-bitch voice. She's a lawyer, which as you can imagine is great for me. Dad's a chef, which makes this rule about feeding yourself seem doubly cruel. She says he shouldn't have to cook for us because he cooks all day; *he* never complains though, so it's just another classic example of her bulldozing over everyone else in pursuit of self-satisfaction. And she's one of those people who is never satisfied. Like, ever.

Anyway, I consider rushing them, but they look pretty serious, even more so than usual, plus their bodies are too close together.

Well, what is it? I say since I'm on a meter here. I've got to finish my reps in the next ten minutes, before *Bad Girls* starts, and I've still got sixty to do. You have to wait at least thirty seconds between sets of ten (push-ups, press-ups, sit-ups, whatever), but it's easy to overstep the mark and I really don't wanna miss any of this week's episode because Al texted me that the evil one snuffs it.

In the living-room, says Dad, like his voice actually carries weight around here. No one moves, not even him, so Mum roars Now! in commando-lawyer mode and we all file in and sit down opposite each other on the stupid armchairs. I sit next to Bilbo, our cat, who claws everything and who Mum's always shouting that she's going to skin alive, but who she secretly calls Cutey when she thinks there's no one around.

I wait for them to speak and there's this stupid long pause which is infuriating. They're both biting their lips, too, which looks really silly. As if to piss me off even further they give each other this special glance like they've got some secret code of communication going on. If I wasn't in a hurry I might think it was funny, but since I am I go, Are you gonna *tell* me what's going on or are you gonna mime it to me?

There's more silence so I make like I'm gonna stand up. This seems to panic Mum into talking.

Look Jarold, she says in this tense, this-is-a-big-deal kind of a way, We know what you've been up to.

I'm like, Huh?

We know where you've been going! cries Dad, still operating under the delusion that someone cares what he

3

thinks. You've been frequenting some gay bar and picking up . . . men!

He whispers this last word like it's some kind of mortal sin or something, rather than the logical thing you'd expect somebody to do in a gay bar. He's gone all white from the effort of being a parent, and it looks almost like he's gonna faint. Mum takes his hand and gives it a squeeze. He squeezes back like they're pillars of support for each other or something, and then they both look at me, hand in hand, like they think this display of marital harmony is gonna magically turn me straight or something.

I'm like, And?

Dad's like, Don't you want to say anything?

That's a tactic he learned off Mum, and if there's one thing I really hate it's when people can't be bothered to think up their own style. I just shrug, because that's all it deserves.

First things first, says Mum, seeing Dad floundering, and assuming control like a sergeant. It's OK if you think you're gay. You're young and you might grow out of it. But it's OK and you need to know that.

She watches me closely. I'm like, So now I know. Thanks.

But it's not OK for you to lie to us about where you're going and what you're doing! she says quickly, mega-emphasis on the *not* part. This is pretty maddening, because a) everyone lies to their parents because that's what they're there for, and b) it's not like I'm gonna go, By the way I'm off to the club to do some guy tonight and by the way *is that OK*? I mean, this is clearly like, a ceremonial talk you get from your parents, so I probably have to have it and everything, but couldn't someone at least have thought about what they were gonna *say* to me first?

So I'm like, So from now on I'll just tell you everything.

Don't try to be smart. You're not an adult yet, says Mum,

4

which is like offering round an invitation to come back at her.

I'm like, Mum you're embarrassing yourself. I stand up.

Sit yourself back down this minute! she screams, giving Bilbo a nasty surprise. Who the hell do you think you are?

Look, what is this? I say in a last stab at trying to be reasonable.

This is you sitting down and listening to someone other than the bloody CD player for a change! she goes.

I'm like, the definition of fuck off. Next thing I know Mum's screaming her head off like an ambulance, coming up with all this random stuff like it's just occurring to her on the spot and spilling out her mouth. She screams so fast it's hard to make much sense of it, but I get the gist. It's pretty disturbing, let me tell you. It's like you can just scrap that stuff she said about it being OK that I'm gay if this is anything to go by, because if it is, OK is like, Far From. Dad's looking at her all scared while he tries to unprise his hand from her grip (without success). Bilbo makes a break for it and gets away. Lucky him, I think. Neither me nor Dad know what to do so we just watch and wait, and eventually Mum winds down and drops her head between her knees and starts sobbing into the carpet. Dad uses this opportunity to take his hand back, which is now like, a totally different shape.

Maybe you should apologise, he suggests after a few minutes of us moronically watching her.

Are you serious? I say. Can't you see the woman has issues?

That sets her right off again, a bit like an alarm clock, only this time it's much worse and she goes on for much longer. It's quite impressive because she doesn't even take any breaths. To give you an idea, though, I'm not even

5

gonna try and get it all down: YOU'RE GAY AND I
DON'T UNDERSTAND WHY YOU DIDN'T SAY ANY-
THING TO ME THOUGH AS IF YOU WERE NORMAL
TO BEGIN WITH I SHOULD HAVE KNOWN IT WHEN
YOU WERE BORN IT'S ALL MY FAULT NO IT'S HIS
FAULT (Dad's) HIM AND MY MOTHER SHE NEVER
COULD UNDERSTAND WHY I MARRIED SUCH A
LOSER AND I DON'T KNOW WHY EITHER I WISH
I'D NEVER MARRIED NEVER HAD CHILDREN
NEVER DONE ANY OF THIS CAN'T YOU SEE
YOU'VE SUCKED UP MY LIFE WHY CAN'T I JUST
BE LEFT IN PEACE SOMETIMES I JUST WISH I WAS
DEAD! Seriously, no breaths. It's like, she should totally
have been a diver.

Anyway, I'm like, Suits me.

She opens her mouth for another blast but it's too much
so she just stares at me and twitches while Dad looks
around the room like he always ends up doing, as if he's
looking for an escape hatch. It's like, *You wish.*

So after a bit more mandatory painful silence she jerks
her head towards the door, as if she's dismissing me. I don't
need telling twice.

Upstairs on the landing I pass The Nun, who's opened
her door so she can hear Mum's ranting. She's sitting at her
desk and she gives me this smug look and all of a sudden I
know exactly who their informant was. Like it could have
been anyone else.

You really let the family down this time, she goes, with
this exaggerated shake of her head.

I'm like, Why don't you eat some glass?

Poor Jarold, she sighs, *So* terribly misunderstood.

I consider going in and tearing out some of her hair but I
decide, Later, and continue towards my room, which is

right at the top of the house. Grandma opens her door as I pass and we exchange looks. She doesn't know about me being gay or anything like that, of course, but since Grandpa died and she moved in we've become like, conspirators together, 'cos when Mum's not yelling at me she's usually complaining about her. I shrug to her as if to say, What can you do? and she shrugs back as if to say, Nothing. Then I go on up the stairs to do my reps. Unfortunately, after their 'word' with me Mum and Dad hole up in the living-room, so I can't watch TV and I miss Atkins' asphyxiation. I end up just doing reps for two hours in front of my shrine to Orlando Bloom.

OK, let me do some more explaining. First of all I do actually give a shit, believe it or not – I don't want you to think that I don't. I just figure that you've got to be mature about this sort of thing, and Mum may be an adult, but mature isn't something I'd ever call her. But to be fair I guess it must've come as a bit of a shock. Mother Teresa probably had a ball. I can just picture her telling them at breakfast this morning, which must have been when she did it 'cos I had mine at Al's. She would have waited till Mum was holding something probably, for the added drama of some breakage. And Dad probably spent all day smoking at the back of his kitchen (Mum famously told him once that she'd leave him if he didn't give up, which is one of several things I've got on him if ever I need to use it).

The thing you need to understand about Mum is, she's mental. We're all kind of used to it and so we don't say anything, but it's pretty obvious that she's a bit more than your average highly strung neurotic. And when you get subjected to this sort of thing every week you get desensitised to it pretty fast. She really does have some condition, by the way – I'm sure of it. Sometimes I think Grandma knows what it is, but she's keeping her mouth shut. Then again, it could just be that she's brain-damaged. All kinds of weird shit goes on in the brain, like maybe she's got some clot of blood in some gland that secretes like, logic, and that's why she's all screwed up.

As for Dad, he's like Mr Passive, unchallenged title-holder ten years running. I mean, he gives a shit if I'm a fag, of course, but what's he gonna do, give me electro-therapy for it? Throw me out? That's like a big joke, because he's the most ineffectual man I've ever met, which is what my answer'll be if he ever starts wondering about whose side of the family I get it from.

So it's not that I don't care, it's just that there's nothing I can do. My position is kind of wait-and-see, plus it's way bleaker for me than it is for them, you've got to admit. When I said Mum and Dad are remarkably undivorced they're also remarkably unmurdered – by each other. Seriously, they're like a surreal, toned-down, middle-aged version of Sid and Nancy, minus the heroin. Only Mum's Sid and Dad's Nancy. How they sleep in the same room, let alone the same bed, is beyond me. Thing is, they say your parents are supposed to set an example for you, but the only example my parents set is how not to end up, which is why I've sworn to Al that I'm never gonna get married. I used to think I was pretty safe there, but more and more gays are doing it these days, and though Al says she's against it on principle (neo-nihilist) she reckons it's the way the future's going. But I reckon it's bullshit and I'd rather be the bride of death.

Mum comes up to my room just as I'm about to lie down and have a rub. She's got like, this sixth sense that makes her automatically come and seek you out the second your thoughts turn impure, and there's been a fair number of

8

times when I've had to suddenly sit down because she's appeared in the room. Once you do that you're good as dead, because if you don't make a fast exit Mum'll go on and on and as we've seen she's one of those people who just doesn't ever get dehydrated.

OK, she says firmly, walking right on in.

I'm like, Didn't they teach you to knock in mother school? as I hurl myself under the bedcover to hide my hard-on.

Jarold, she says, ignoring me, I've discussed the issue with your father. We've decided to try and be understanding. But that doesn't mean we don't have some ground rules.

She always refers to stuff as issues. I'm an issue, Teresa's an issue and Grandma's an issue. It's something to do with being a lawyer, I guess.

She's like, Firstly, no more going out without our permission.

What is this, Auschwitz? I say.

No more lying.

I'm like, Yeah right.

And no more . . . activities.

I'm like, Do you even know what you're talking about?

She's like, You know perfectly well what I mean! No more doing things with men! I don't know what you've been getting up to and I don't want to know. But you're not old enough and that's final.

At this point I can't help smiling. I don't know what it is with smiling and me but I often have this urge to smile when someone's trying to be serious with me. Usually that's Mum so it doesn't matter so much, but it's happened once or twice with teachers and got me into loads of trouble. I feel it creeping up my face now like a worm or something. I'm

9

going all red and Mum's giving me her death stare, the one she usually reserves for jury members.

She's like, If you don't start taking this seriously I'm going to cut your allowance. Completely.

The way she utters this threat you'd think it was the same thing as being castrated. I get twenty-five pounds a month, and that's supposed to cover me for everything – clothes, CDs, shoes, face soap, even haircuts. Mum and Dad pay for books and uniform, for which I have to provide a receipt. Like most things, it's just pure encouragement to be devious. It's not exactly hard to get around – I just get other people to give me their receipts. But it would be a whole lot less hassle for everyone if they'd just give me more money. The Nun gets an extra five pounds just for being born with a vagina.

But money's money no matter what, so I keep quiet and turn my face to the side so it's hidden from her as much as possible. Mum looks at the wall, right into Orlando Bloom's eyes, and I can tell she's suddenly wondering, How did this sign get past me? because it's something I've often wondered too.

I know this is hard for you, Jaz, she says. I think about my hard-on and how right she is. Why can't she just leave now? But instead of doing that of course she goes on and on about how she does love me but how I'm always so closed up, and how she knows it's complicated and sometimes she doesn't know what's got into me but she wishes I'd open up a bit. The woman's like, a serial innuendo. I do my best to nod and make my sniggering sound like coughing, but finally she says, I just want my little boy Jarold back again, in this soppy voice and by this point I just can't take it any longer. I'm like, Please just get over it now, and she tells me I'm heartless but at last she gets the message and goes. Then of course I find that my hard-on's gone too and so I send Al a text saying OMIGOD PARNTS JUST FND OUT IM GAY! WWW.LAMECITY.COM – TELL U 2MORROW J and turn out the light. Half an hour later, just as I'm about to fall asleep, I get one back saying TELL ME T M T M (RPT!!!) + DID YOU DO UR ESSY? As is the way with these things I end up having a whole textothon with her in which I relate all the gory details and so I don't actually get to sleep till like, two.

2

I blame Al for what happens the next day. It's her fault for not shutting up about stuff. We're on the bus and she keeps asking me all the same questions she asked me last night. I'm really sleepy and wondering how she manages to stay pert all the time and if it's, like, a gene only born politicians inherit. Then this boy from our school who's sitting in front of us overhears her and turns round to check us out.

I don't know if it's the same all schools over, or if some schools are more liberal than others and ours just happens to have a higher percentage of sad rejects, but at St Matthew's it's like the eighties never happened. No one ever says they're gay, even if they're like, the definition of it. You always say you're confused. Once you go public not only do you end up forced into endless counselling sessions where some daft humanitarian tries to like, kill you with their empathy, but you also become like, target practice for the rest of the population (particularly the sports sect). It's such a cliché. And quite frankly, who needs the hassle? Yeah, so it shouldn't be like that 'cos we're all supposed to be democrats, whatever that means, but the fact is that it is, so you just have to deal with it. Up until now I'm the only 'confused' kid in our year (so far as I know), and I'm quite fine with it, since as far as I'm concerned everyone in our year can go blow.

But today, thanks to Al's big fat mouth, Fabian overhears us. Fabian the freak is like this Nazi-goth punk amalgam – one of those losers who has this reputation for being all extreme and dangerous. Most of it comes from this one time he allegedly tried to attack Mrs Bolsh in art class with a pair of scissors, and got expelled for it. Then it turned out he had behavioural problems, which must be like another way of saying it's OK to attack an old woman with a pair of scissors after all, because the school let him come right back (although he's not allowed to take art any more). What's really weird though, is that back in year one, which is like, eons ago in terms of a school life, me and him used to hang out. That was before he went all Against Man and I shrugged him. Nowadays he has no friends at all, and usually hangs out round the toilets showing off biro tatts of swastikas to impressionable molestables from junior school.

Who's gay? he growls at us, interrupting Al mid-flow.

Of course Al's not phased by this. She's not afraid of Fabian. She's like, Mind your own business, twat face.

Fabian looks between us and cackles like the Wicked Witch of the West. He goes, Watch it, corner shop, or I'll carve out your eyeballs and your little faggot friend's too.

Here I feel called upon to provide a contribution. I'm like, Go fuck a chainsaw why don't you?

Fabian gives us both this comic-book evil look that he probably perfects in the mirror and then flashes his tongue stud.

You better learn some respect, boyo, he goes, Before I decide to teach you a lesson.

Al's like, Get a purpose, and thankfully he seems to decide to do just that because he turns back and leaves us alone. Luckily it's only Fabian, so it's not like anyone's gonna listen to him if he starts spreading it around. But all the rest of the journey I have this uneasy feeling which later on turns out to be perfectly justified. I'm kind of psychic like that.

Me and Al split 'cos she's got politics first period and I've got English. We're studying (surprise, surprise) Shakespeare, which is so not the reason I opted for English. I thought it would be more of those cool books we did for GCSE, like *The Catcher in the Rye*, which I thought was the best book ever. The way this guy just cruises around and everyone he meets turns out to be phony – it's totally like reality, and the fact that he ends up in this loony bin is so sad because he's like, the only one who can see through all the shit around him. He even talks like a real kid does, or at least how a kid would have talked back whenever it was written. But there's one thing he doesn't get right, which is that the worst thing about people isn't how phony they are, it's what a complete bunch of cunts they can be. And the worst people aren't adults, they're other kids. Sure there's the odd cool one here and there, and you have to excuse a few of them on the grounds that they're deformed or orphans or something, but by and large they're all cunts.

Anyway, when I sit down I find that on the back of my bag there's this yellow Post-it with JAROLD IS A FAGGOT written on it, which goes some way towards explaining why people kept sniggering behind my back as I walked past. It's like, how retarded? It wouldn't be such a big deal though, were it not for the vast shadow of Bull Face (nicknamed so for obvious reasons) which falls across me at this precise moment. Bull Face's real name is Joseph, which is pretty ironic considering he's the sort of kid who must have grown up pulling the wings off of butterflies and throwing cats out of windows, before graduating on to torment other mem-

14

bers of the human race. He was suspended last year for punching some poor guy who accidentally made the mistake of trying to fight back. Probably he gets beaten by his own parents or something, and just needs a bit of love and compassion, but it's hard to have much compassion for someone who's got a face like a bull. I feel compassion for his parents. Standing behind him are his goons, Nick and Nathaniel, who are known as Tweedle Dum and Tweedle Dee (also nicknamed for obvious reasons). What any of these cretins are doing an English A level for is anyone's guess. What I find scary is that it means that at some point they must have passed some exams – although Al says it's only because GCSEs are so easy now that twelve-year-olds can do them.

Oi, Bull Face barks at me loud enough so that everyone stops what they're doing and turns to look. Wot's this about you being a poof?

It's pretty unusual for them to be hassling me, since usually their attention is undividedly focused on Sam Gibbons who's got this accelerated growth syndrome, which means his head's twice the size of anyone else's. He probably needs it to be that size for his enormous brain, but even he knows there's nothing much you can say when someone with Bull Face's IQ (which naturally I'm assuming to be low) and his goons decide to start laying into you in front of the whole class.

Anyway, it's not like I give a shit about what anyone thinks of me or anything, but you've got to consider your self-esteem, which when you're a kid is fragile and easily bruised. If everyone thinks I'm gay I'll have to endure their chronically lame remarks for the rest of my school life, and like I said, kids can be total cunts – just ask Sam if you've never experienced this (though if you haven't, you must

15

have been like, beamed into life or something). There's only really one way to protect yourself against it all and that is to just rise above it and not get drawn in.

So I'm like, Fuck off.

He's like, Maybe you didn't hear me. I said Wot's this about you being a poof?

I'm like, Maybe you didn't hear me because I said Fuck off!

Ooooooh, he goes, which is the sound dumb arses like him always need to make in order to give themselves time to think of something better. Behind him Tweedle Dum and Tweedle Dee make obscure grunting noises that might have resembled laughter in some more evolved species.

Looks like he's being a smart guy, observes Tweedle Dum (which is actually pretty astute for him).

Bull Face leans in even closer, so I get treated to a full blast of his death breath, which is his other special power next to brute force and chronic ugliness. Many's the time I've seen the faces of kids from year three contort as they teeter on the verge of suffocation while snared in one of his headlocks. When he smiles, which is pretty rare, you can see that his teeth are all yellow because he never brushes them. He's like a walking fungus.

Are you telling me to fuck off? he breathes. I'm itching to make a reply but I just keep silent and pretend to be fascinated with the contents of my bag. You get to know when to quit. Take it too far and you're just inviting trouble.

Jarold, Jarold, Jarold, says Tweedle Dee in this pansy voice, unable to think of anything actually cutting to say (mind you, repeated use of my lame name can actually be quite cutting).

Bull Face is like, Fucking poof.

He kicks the table and practically makes the whole room reverberate. Fortunately after that he and the Tweedles retire to their designated slacker spot at the back of the classroom, leaving me to wonder if this is one of those experiences that's gonna scar me for life. Like I said, I don't give a shit what anyone in this hole thinks about me, but when you're picked on, it hurts, and it still hurts no matter what you tell yourself. The best thing is to blame someone else, so I decide that it's all Al's fault, which means I bawl her out next period while old Fellows is delivering some lecture on organic farming (bawl in this situation = whisper with angry intensity). I tell her what a stupid ho she is for talking about it so loud on the bus.

Al tries to take the moral line in order to defend herself. She's all like, But you shouldn't feel ashamed! It's a part of who you are and that means you've got to come to terms with it and be yourself no matter what anyone else says.

I'm like, Spare me, sister. It really bugs me when she talks like this, since it's not as if she's knows what it's like. She reckons she does 'cos she's Asian and a woman, and women have been oppressed for centuries and so have Asians. But it's hardly the same thing since it's not like anyone ever had to come out about being a woman or an Asian, is it?

Al's like, But you can't hide from what you are!

I'm like, Get over yourself.

She's like, But you've got to be strong! It's up to you to do your bit to make things OK for the kids of future generations. You have a responsibility!

I'm like, What is your trauma?

For some reason she decides to get all offended and her whispering gets a bit over-incensed. Next thing Fellows has overheard and is stopping his lecture to suggest she share with the rest of the class whatever she has to say, since it's

17

clearly much more interesting. I give her a look in which I am basically saying, If you dare I will kill you.

I'm waiting, says Fellows. He's one of those youngish old teachers, if you know what I mean. The sort who weren't born quite long enough ago to completely miss noticing that there was sexual revolution going on – though it's pretty hard to imagine that he took part in it.

Of course Al keeps silent.

Oh dear, says Fellows with a feeble smile. Do you mean to tell me that it's not more interesting than my lecture after all?

Al's clearly pretty tempted, but she shakes her head.

Fellows makes this elaborate tutting sound as if he suspected as much. But he resumes, and so we're forced to spend the rest of the lesson gazing out the window at Freedom, trapped inside with nothing but Fellows' voice, which is like, the reason for the word Monotony. At the end of the sesh (when the bell finally rings and wakes us all up) he stops us on the way out the room.

I've noticed that you two don't seem to be taking your studies very seriously these days, he says, standing before the door with his arms folded like a prison matron.

In unison we're like, We're sorry.

The munchkin thing doesn't work on Fellows. He's like, Perhaps it would be a good idea if from now on you don't sit together.

Al's like, But sir that's a violation of our basic rights.

Unfortunately Fellows is pretty much immune to Al's smart talkback thing, which most of the staff seem to find so endearing. I suppose for them it's like discovering you've got this undercover ally on the other side. But Fellows gives her this look like, Who can be bothered?

I mean it. No more sitting together, he goes.

On our way out of school, just as it's looking like I'm actually going to get out without being rained on by shit, this voice whispers Faggot! right in my ear. I turn round to see who it is and who should be standing there but Fabian, Lord Freakzoid himself.

You're a retard, I tell him, and he gives me a crazy smile like this is a cool thing to be, and reaches out and flicks my shoulder. It's almost affectionate the way he does it, which is just plain weird.

I'm like, Can you go away before you give me a neural infection?

You just wait, he goes, You just wait. He smiles ominously and does his wicked-witch cackle before following the others out of the building to Freedom.

I'm like, the definition of whatever, but I give Al a glare anyway to show her that I still see it as all being her fault. She does one of her sighs like she's ready to wash her hands of humanity, which from what I can see feels much the same way about her. Al doesn't have any friends apart from me. She reckons it's to do with being Asian and refusing to see herself as a sex object, but to be honest it's probably just because she's Al.

So all in all it's a shitty day, and the cherry on top when I get back is the sight of The Nun dancing around the kitchen because she's won some stupid award while Mum and Dad toast her with celebratory cups of tea. Grandma's sitting at the table watching them with this expression on her face like she's thinking, Why am I still on this planet?

Dad's like, Guess what, Jaz! in this super happy voice he always puts on when he's not trying to act mad.

I'm like, Yeah?

The Nun's like, You're not gonna believe it!

I'm like, You've found a new home.

Mum's like, Jarold, don't you dare start an argument! If you spoil this I swear I'll give you the biggest slap! I mean it.

Grandma's like, Give the kid a break, he just got in.

Don't you start! Mum snaps at her like a wolverine, This is Teresa's moment and no one's spoiling it for her!

Teresa's moment turns out to be some award she's been given for the ultra-important life skill of having good spelling, and Mum's got it into her head that this is one of those wonderful family moments that time makes immortal or something, despite the fact that Teresa enters and wins these sorts of competitions practically every other week because she's one of those lame-Os who thinks it's a cool thing to do. While I'm enduring the sight of her making Mum and Dad all proud I suddenly remember that I still haven't ripped her scalp off for squealing on me, so I decide to get something right today and go upstairs to wait for her in her room. I slide myself behind the door and plan my assault.

The Nun's room is one of those horrible pink and white bedrooms where everything's all frilly and girly. She's got this massive stuffed panda that with sparkling wit she calls Panda. More freakishly, she keeps her room immaculately clean, and even more freakishly than that, she has this silver crucifix nailed to her bed-board. However, her worst crime against humanity is the two posters she has of Ronan Keating and Westlife. She's only a year younger than me but as you've hopefully gathered we couldn't be any more different if one of us had been brought up in an incubator. I mean, *Ronan Keating?*

She comes up about ten minutes later, all pleased with herself and holding against her heart the stupid envelope that congratulates her for not having a retarded grammar.

20

Second she walks in I flip the door closed and grab her by the throat, squeezing hard to minimise the sound of her screaming. Once I'm sitting on her and she has a clear view of my handful of her hair and can see that I mean serious business she stops trying to scream and says OK in this calm voice, like she knows the game is up. The thing about Teresa is that this is what she's like. Behind the do-gooder syndrome beats the brain of a computer. She's the sort of person you can imagine would have absolutely no qualms about executing someone if she thought she'd get something out of it.

I'm like, You're in deep shit.

She's like, Jaz be reasonable. I was thinking of you.

The Nun never calls me Jaz and so this feeble attempt to try and be my friend merely enrages me all the more. I pluck out a couple of hairs and she winces.

I'm like, Thinking of me, were you?

She's like, Please Jaz. I only want the best for you. Someone's brother at my school saw you at that club and they started teasing me about it. I was so shocked and hurt. You can't imagine! You've never given out any sign you were like that!

I'm like, Like what?

The Nun looks flustered. She's like, Can't you see that I was just reacting because I didn't know how to react?

For this crap I take out three more hairs, all in one go. The Nun's body goes deathly still and she closes her eyes. I recognise this tactic and prepare myself. She makes a sudden attempt to free herself by twisting her body to the side so I almost fall off the bit of it that I'm sitting on. It's a cunning manoeuvre but not cunning enough. I dig in my ankles and hold tight.

Jaz, please! I did it because I care about you! she cries.

21

No you didn't! I go, You did it because you're a fucking evil bitch!

It's true too. And The Nun's pretty much everything but she's not stupid. I watch with satisfaction as her face changes like the little girl's in *The Exorcist*. It's really horrible for people who don't know her to see her getting angry, because it's like the devil taking control. But I know it's just the real Teresa coming out.

Fine! she snarls, Maybe the real reason I told was because I don't agree with it! I think you're sick and I'm disgusted to be related to you! You ought to be ashamed of yourself.

She glares at me and for a second I'm tempted to take out her eyeballs, but instead I content myself by dribbling spit over them. She rolls her head from side to side but resistance is futile because I just follow it with my dribble.

You're gross! she cries, and then lets out this sob. I'm stupidly taken aback by this, and catching me off guard she manages to give off the most bloodcurdling scream known to man before I have a chance to cut it off at the windpipe. I leap off her as footsteps hurtle up the stairs. The Nun bursts into tears just as the door opens and Dad and Mum struggle against each other to enter the room at the same time like a pair of comically inept vigilantes.

What the hell's going on? demands Mum, her hands jumping to her hips (one of her elbows pronging Dad quite hard in the stomach as she does it). Dad puts on this fierce expression like this is exactly what he was just wondering.

He was trying to kill me! wails Teresa between two massive sobs. He's jealous of me!

Mum gives me her look of death. I hold up my hands but there's no avoiding it.

I'm like, Just shoot me and get it over with.

She's like, Get to your room this second.

In my room I do some reps while I'm waiting for Mum to come and do her nut. I get bored after a while so I end up just sitting on my desk and waiting. We've got a careers session the next day in which we have to show we've thought about a future for ourselves, and so I try to take my mind off my impending ordeal by thinking up answers. Just as I've hit upon Suicide Bomber, capital punishment arrives, and I'm surprised to see that it's Dad who's been given the holy mission of telling me what a disappointment I am. At least he has the decency to knock first, before coming in and plonking himself down on my bed and sighing deeply in this way so you know he's experienced a major disappointment he might never get over.

We're very disappointed in you Jaz, he goes, like maybe I hadn't got the message already.

I'm like, Oh really?

He's like, We just can't understand what's got into you lately. We don't know what we're supposed to do. Why are you being this way?

I'm like, Probably because I'm a teenager.

Dad looks a bit stumped by this. Sometimes it's as if he and Mum forget that actually you're a thinking human being. I notice how uncomfortable he looks and how he keeps fidgeting. Mum must have sent him in here saying that she's sick of being the bad guy, but it doesn't matter because you can see he's just some kind of sub-lieutenant and the only reason he's come is because she's made him. He never does anything out of his own initiative. Sometimes I get scared that he's secretly having all these murderous thoughts and one of these days he's gonna like, kill us all or blow up the house or something. The man just has no self-respect so there's bound to be tension mounting. Remembering this gives me a brilliant idea.

23

I'm like, I just wish someone would talk openly to me about what men do when they're in bed together.

Dad starts changing colour instantly. He's like, the definition of Help Me. After he's gone through the whole rainbow, I decide to let him off the hook and say that I'm tired now and maybe we can resume this conversation tomorrow, at which point he practically runs out of my room, leaving me to think how ridiculous it is that I don't have a lock for my door.

Later on I hear Mum shouting at him. She usually lets off steam this way at least once a week. But it's kind of like, Hello? Some people are trying to sleep here. But I figure it's pretty useful since it's good Bad Mother ammunition for the next time she starts shouting at me for inhaling the wrong way or something. You're probably thinking it's no wonder I'm fucked up, because that's what I think too sometimes when I hear them. It's not like I care or anything, but it can't be good for my sensibilities.

3

I probably wouldn't have bothered putting in that bit about my chronically lame teacher Mr Fellows were it not for what happens next, because it has like, total relevance. This I like to call the Love Scene. It's easily the best bit as far as I'm concerned – it all goes downhill after. OK:

So I'm in the club. Of course Mum and Dad said no more nights out, but they can't exactly chain me to my bed and I do have legs and a front-door key, so no surprises, I'm back in Starlight (the club) three days later.

I'm here with Al and we're a couple of drinks towards a good time. She can sneak out of her house any time she wants since her bedroom's on the ground floor, and she's wearing this full-length floral gown – which we both keep tripping over – 'cos she's convinced the nineties are coming back. I don't have any money since Mum decided suddenly she was being too lenient and withdrew it all the day after the Word, so I'm totally sponging off Al, who's not totally OK with it, and is letting out that she's only here for my sake (like she's got something better to do). It's totally time for me to try and get us drinks off one of the geries who prop up the bar, which is dead boring because then you have to talk to them and simultaneously ward off their ancient fumbling mitts.

Al's going on about how the future should be non tax-deductible or something and just as she's launching into a really yawnable bit about insurance fraud it happens. I see The Guy. We're talking lightning striking, like, multiple times. Heart palpitations, shivers, butterflies, nausea, the works. He's just gorgeous, and totally the opposite to what I usually go for. He's got this dark skin and big jaw and slanty, angry eyes. He kind of floats, if you know what I mean. Well, if you've ever had it bad for someone then you will, and if you haven't then you've got something really special to look forward to, assuming it ever happens for you, 'cos if it doesn't then you're probably doomed to end up like my parents, and I pity you. Deeply.

So I'm like, struck dumb; meanwhile Al, bless her (and just like the nineties neo-conservative throwback she is), doesn't even notice. She starts accusing me of not listening to her and saying she's gonna go, by which she really means it's time for me to prostitute my company for a drink.

I tell her, Fine then, which throws her off track a bit.

What's wrong with you? she wants to know.

I'm like, Are you like optically challenged or something?

She turns and looks. She's like, Who? Him? Seriously?

Like I said, Al's destiny is to be a big fat dyke. It's written in her aura and there's no escaping from it, so I don't know why she doesn't just accept it and move on. She's got about as much clue when it comes to men as Dad does.

Anyway, I've like, got to meet this dude, so I shake Al off and walk forward, only to be nearly decapitated by him as he turns and gestures to the guy he's with (who, incidentally, is from Librariansville and is No Competition).

Sorry, my vision says to me, managing to catch my arm as I stumble backwards. I regain my balance and try to shrug it off.

No problem, I say, but I can hear my voice quavering, which pisses me off no end, I can tell you. I've had crushes before, but this one struck in a matter of seconds with enough force to wipe out all the tourists in Trafalgar Square.

Hey, aren't you a little young to be in this sort of a place? he says with a smile.

I don't know if this smile is a could-be-persuaded/fuck-me kind of a smile, or an I'm-a-licence-inspector/police-officer kind of smile, so I give him a freezing look and step away like I don't want to get contaminated. The librarian he's with looks me up and down and likes what he sees.

Come on, he says in an unexpectedly deep voice. Let's buy him a drink.

I'm OK with that, of course, so a couple of minutes later I'm drinking a Bacardi and Coke (I know, I know) and chatting to this guy. Or listening to him anyway. And it's the librarian, unfortunately, since The Guy turns out to be one of those brooding types. I like this, 'cos in my book it makes him way sexier, but it's annoying 'cos I have to nod along to Mr Chaucer beside him, who's giving me the deluxe literary edition of his life story. God knows what happened to Al but I start praying that she'll come and rescue me.

Just as I'm preparing myself for one last gasp before I die of this fish-man's voice (his name's Cod or Plaice or something), The Guy actually deigns to say something, which is, So where are you from?

OK, so it's not like, an award-winning question, but it's a break and it's from him so I ain't complaining.

London, I say. I realise that's pretty obvious, so I add Shepherd's Bush.

Now when I was a kid, or more of a kid if you like, Shepherd's Bush was a rude thing to say, and the sniggers it produced were of the lasting variety. So it's pretty weird to

27

tell this guy I'm from there and not get so much as a smile, which I figure must be a sign of class, which is alarming but kind of cool. 'Cos The Guy just nods.

What about you? I say.

I'm from Brighton, he says.

Now that's definitely cool. Everyone who's anyone knows Brighton is the place to be these days. I'm planning a trip down there with Al at some point this summer, though chances of it happening without me running away are infinitely smaller now that Mum's got insider info.

I'm like, So what are you doing in London? and he explains that he spends half his time here and half his time down there, since a friend lets him stay here in his flat while he's away doing photo shoots or something.

So how old are you? he goes. That fateful question. Let me tell you so you don't ever make this mistake: it used to be a bit of a faux pas to ask an old lady – well now it's most definitely not something to ask a person in a bar if you're anyone who's not the barman.

Forty, I say. You?

Twenty-two, he says, smiling. Cod the librarian is grinning manically, and I think he thinks he's in with a chance, which is like, so not the situation. Like I'm gonna go for someone with goldfish-bowl lenses and a mullet (which isn't even ironic). But this guy, whose name hasn't even cropped up yet, is killing me. He's completely drop-dead, and it's kind of hard to understand why he's not fending off guys on all sides in a dive like this.

You sound really young, he says, still harping on about the age thing. I don't know, maybe gorgeous people just shouldn't talk. No one's ever invented the talking billboard, have they?

I'm like, What is this, an inquisition?

28

Sorry, he says, finally seeming to get that all this talk about my age is offensive. I look into his big brown eyes and forgive him. In fact I practically melt. Then he goes and spoils it by saying, I remember what it's like when you're young. It's tough dealing with who you are.

This is so not cool. I'm like, Did you ever?

Give him a break, says Cod, mercifully. I have a quick look round for Al while he crunches up The Guy for me. Regrettably, I'm concluding that this is a no-go state of affairs. This guy might have me in the woods physically, but when it comes to chit-chat it's Antarctica.

It's pretty obvious that I'm offended and about to leave. The guy looks sorry and tries to say something about it, but I'm like, LIC GAS. I make as if to go, since it's seriously looking like Al's deserted me, but then The Guy touches my hand. Fireworks ignite on the inside. Look, he says, I'm sorry. I didn't mean to insult you. Really.

I'm like, super-conscious of his skin against mine. I can feel the blood rising to my cheeks so I try to play it cool. I'm like, Do you mind? You're invading a chakra.

He's like, No really – I meant it in a good way. You should be glad. I wish I could still pass for . . . seventeen! He laughs and I pull my hand free.

I'm like, I just remembered something better to do.

And I'm about to leave, but then he stops me . . . and I don't know quite how this happens, except that he's leaning in to say sorry once more and I'm leaning in because I'm like, magnetically drawn to him, and the next thing is we're kissing. Hello. I'm not complaining one bit, even though snogging in front of the old-timers at the bar isn't really my thing. Cod's pissed off I think, since I hear sighs from behind The Guy (whose name I still don't know), and there are also a few annoying whoops from the geries.

29

It doesn't last long. With stonkingly bad timing, Al reappears in my life like the fairy of chastity, and yanks me away, saying we've got to go 'cos she's got a headache. She always makes up shit like this when something's wrong. I turn to The Guy, but he's getting grilled by Cod (joke, ha ha). I decide to leave Cinderella-style and then instantly regret it because I don't even have his number or anything.

As soon as we're outside in the freezing cold I'm hissing at Al What the fuck does she think she's doing? I was like, *in* there.

I saw Mr Fellows, she says, her lower lip wobbling like it's engine-powered.

Which is ridiculous, and at first I think she's just having me on. But then I notice that away from the multicoloured disco bulbs she's got this mega-freaked-out expression and pale yellowy skin, and I remember how Al's never been much good at faking with me.

What – in there? I say. State of shock.

She nods, and then a giggle erupts out of her turbo-trembling lip and she starts laughing hysterically, and so do I, even though I'm actually kind of disturbed, since Fellows is kind of gross and definitely not someone you want to run into at a club, especially a gay one. Then something occurs to me and I stop laughing.

Did he see you?

She shakes her head in between bursts of laughter. She sounds a lot like a dog that's been hit by a car. We make our way to the night bus desperately huddling against each other for bodily warmth in the vicious cold. It's annoying, because even though I've just met this amazing vision of a guy, all I can think about is Mr Fellows. Al's the same, 'cos she keeps bursting into laughter all the way to her stop, and I can see the other passengers looking at her like they wish someone would come along and put her down or something.

The thought of Fellows snogging another man is what does my head in, though when I reconsider, the thought of him snogging a woman is just as bad. Some people just shouldn't bother, plus he's old. The strangest thing will be seeing him the next day and trying to keep a straight face. I secretly curse my decision to do geography. Then I figure who gives a shit since it's not like I'm gonna be turning up for it much longer anyway.

Mum's waiting for me at home, about as cheery as death. No sooner have I walked in than she pounces on me like a cobra, fangs bared, ready to swallow me whole – it's not even one o'clock yet. I don't get it, so maybe if you're reading this and you're like, over thirty, you can help me out. What is the deal? I mean, what's so bad about the concept of having fun that causes people to practically eat their own brains in fits of total mad rage? I just don't get it. And from what I can see everyone seems to stop having it at some point in their mid-twenties so I'd really appreciate the opportunity to make the most of it while I still know what *it* is.

Anyway, short version is I get threatened with psychiatric care or something, which, being a lawyer, Mum knows all about. I tell her if she keeps on at me I'll probably need it, which is just guaranteed to get her really pissed off, and then, as per usual, she launches into hypersonic mode (remember?) and I run for the cover of my room, feeling sorry for the neighbours.

Just as I'm about to fall asleep I get a text from Al. It says STILL CN'T BELEVE MR FELLWS = GAY! DO YOU THNK THE SCHOOL NOS?

I'm about to text her back when my door opens and Grandma glides in. It totally freaks me out. She's lit by

31

nothing but the moonlight from the window and she's wearing just her nightdress and has this silly smile on her face that looks like it's plastered on. But the worst thing is she's staring straight ahead without focusing on anything. She looks like one of the zombies from *Dawn of the Dead*.

I'm like, Grandma? What are you doing?

She looks at me and makes this low humming sound in her throat, and for a second I think she's flipped out and is probably holding a kitchen knife behind her back and has come to kill me. I start making a mental note of all decently solid objects close to hand that I can throw at her head should I need to. But then it occurs to me that maybe she's just whacked out from too many amphetamines. It happens once every now and then, usually at Christmas when she forgets what pills she's taken and ends up having this drug and sherry cocktail.

I get up and switch the light on and this seems to bring her back to her senses 'cos she looks around blinking like she's never seen a room before. She's like, Why do you have all those posters of that young man on your wall?

I'm like, Now is not the time.

I take her by the arm and lead her back down to her bedroom. I think it's sad that she's old and a bit senile. I know it's something that has to happen and all, but I hope it never does to me. I reckon they should freeze people after sixty and wait until they've got like, some formula to stop it before they unfreeze them again.

I put Grandma to bed and just as I'm leaving she starts making her humming sound again, but I figure let her hum if she wants to, maybe it's just a really like, contemporary piece. Before I turn off the light I send Al a text saying OMIGOD. MY GRAN —> OFF DEEP END.

32

When I get back from school the next day it turns out Grandma's had a stroke and is now in hospital. Mum says she's OK but it must have happened some time during the night. I keep my trap shut about the whole wandering-into-my-room thing. Mum makes us all clean the house which is what she does when she feels guilty. You don't have to be a shrink to see that it's like, a representative for her conscience, and the cleaner it gets the less guilty she's supposed to feel. By the time we're done with the kitchen the floor's like lick-your-food-off-it sparkling, and Mum looks a bit less tense and says we'll all go visit her at the hospital on Sunday and why don't me and Teresa make her a nice card? The Nun dashes off to her room to do exactly that but I'm like, What is this, *Blue Peter*? and Mum tells me that sometimes she just despairs of me. I'm like, Welcome to my world. Just move on to the living-room, Mum goes.

4

OK, the whole thing with Grandma and Mum is pretty old, but you kind of need to know some stuff which at the moment you like, don't. So I'm gonna rewind a year (which is quite a lot in terms of my life) to this thing that happened when she first moved in with us after Grandpa died.

So it's one of those wonderful freak afternoons where school's given us all this time off to revise for our mocks. Me and Al are upstairs in my room, which is now in the attic 'cos I've had to relocate for Grandma, something which did prejudice me slightly against her at first. We're supposed to be studying but instead we're reading this porno I managed to nick from the local while Al distracted the shop attendant with her views on the minimum wage. Al's quite impressed by the content but I'm not – but then, of the two of us I'm the only one who actually has any experience, even if it was just a drunken fumble in the toilets of this club we dared each other to go to. The rest of my experience happens over the course of the coming year, which is when we start realising that actually there is a life out there to be had.

There's a knock at the door and we just about manage to shove the porno under Al's skirt before Grandma comes into the room with two glasses of OJ.

Grandma's like, Who's this lovely young lady then?

Al blushes 'cos she's like, chronically bad with compliments and I'm like, Where? Al slaps me on the wrist (yeah, she used to be one of those).

I'm like, What do you want?

Grandma's like, Look what I brought you.

So I look. Al's like, Thanks very much, and Grandma gives her this solar smile like her whole life's been given a meaning and starts asking her all these questions and basically getting the low-down on her like she's thinks she's looking at her new daughter-in-law (no offence, Al, but it's like, even if I wasn't, *as if*). I'm like, oozing the vibes of Leave Us Alone.

After about ten minutes of mind-numbing small talk she finally seems to get the message and goes, OK, I'm going to give this house a bit of a clean. You two make sure you don't work too hard. She gives me this impressively un-subtle smile and thankfully exits.

Al's like, Your Grandma is So Sweet, which is the sort of thing only people whose grandparents died long before they got to know them ever say. Anyway, sure enough the Hoover starts up (we used to have one of those ones that sounds like you're trying to vacuum up the whole world) and so we try to ignore it and read a bit more of the porno. Then I start to get switched so I say I have to use the toilet and dash off to have a lightning fast one. But on the next floor I rapidly wish I'd resisted, 'cos just audible over the sound of the Hoover is this other sound which is blatantly Grandma crying.

Since this is back in the days when I still had a conscience I feel duty-bound to go and see, and I find her in Mum and Dad's room sitting on the bed and making it all wet while the Hoover's on full blast and leant against the wall.

I'm like, Are you OK? which is about the dumbest thing you can say because it's so obviously like, No.

Grandma jumps in surprise (or at least stands up quite quickly, this being an old woman we're talking about) and goes over to turn the Hoover off. Then she quickly starts smoothing down the bedspread like it's her vocation or something.

She's like, Dear me, I didn't hear you come in!

I want to say, There's a pretty good reason for that, but instead I'm like, What's the matter?

She's like, Oh, I'm just being a silly old sod, that's all.

Then she bursts into tears again and starts going, I miss him so much! Why am I still here? Why did he have to leave me? and so on. This is when I start to feel an iota of sympathy for her, because up until this point she and Grandpa were just this annoying monthly visit where me and The Nun got paraded around the living-room like man-sized dolls and forced to recite what we were doing in school to choruses of Ahs and Oohs.

I give her a hug and she practically squeezes the life out of me for a few minutes and then sits back on the bed and says, I wish I was dead. I shouldn't be here, Jaz. I should be up there with him. Or wherever he is.

The idea that she thinks Grandpa might be somewhere other than up there is pretty disconcerting but I try to smile and start coming out with all this bland shit like It's going to be OK and You've still got us blah-blah-blah. But then she starts telling me all this stuff about how Mum hates her and has never forgiven her and how it's never gonna work out her living here and why haven't they found her a nice home or something? I'm like, without a clue here. Why would Mum hate you? I say.

She's like, It's complicated. Sometimes relationships between older people are very, very . . . complicated.

While I'm trying to figure out how to process this she

36

starts crying again and in between bouts of rain is like, I'm sorry Jaz, I shouldn't be bothering you with this, you're still young, you've got your whole life ahead of you, etc., which is the daft thing old people always say, like they think you don't know what a problem is.

Anyway I spend like, an era calming her down. I say she just has to give it time. She nods and says I'm wise beyond my years, which is pretty funny because actually I don't think this is a good idea at all when you're old but I don't really see what else there is I can suggest. When I finally get back to Al she's like, So how was it? I try to explain where I've been but she's like, Yeah right, what do you think I am, born yesterday? I'm like, Seriously! all annoyed and I explain. Eventually Al pretends to believe me. We read some more from this story about this guy and his amazing long willy, and then there's the sound of the keys in the door downstairs (sounds really travel in our house, and they kind of congregate in the attic), which means Mum's home. Given the whole situation Al decides to go so we hide the porno under my rug and she skedaddles.

Left alone I finally have a good old jerk and wipe it up with some old school report (which I reckon is both poetic and economising). Then I feel hungry so I go to get something to eat but just when I'm about to enter the kitchen I hear Mum and Grandma talking in there so I press myself to the wall and eavesdrop instead.

Grandma's like, I just need to know that you've forgiven me.

Mum's like, Forgiven you for what? I have no idea what you're talking about. Is this about Dad?

There's a long pause and then she goes, Did you take your tablets?

Grandma's offended. She's like, Don't try and blame this on tablets!

Mum's like, What the hell's got into you? Can't you see I've had a hard day? Look at the state of you! This is the last thing I need when I come home.

Grandma's like, That's right, just tell the old woman to keep quiet and die quickly.

Mum's like, How dare you?! You have no right to say that! Would you stop and listen to yourself? I brought you here to live with us when I could have just shoved you in a home – what more do you want from me?

There's a long pause with tumbleweed blowing through it. Then Grandma's like, I just want you to stop resenting me.

Another desert pause and I can hear two sounds: Grandma's sobs and Mum's breathing. Then Mum goes, It's a bit late for that, isn't it? and then I hear her clippity heels coming my way so I quickly slide behind the door because if she caught me listening at this point she'd probably disown me on the spot.

I go into the kitchen and Grandma is sitting at the table with this heavy face. She's sees me and gives me this smile which is like, totally bitter about life.

Well. That's that, she goes.

After this scene from *EastEnders* Grandma starts to ignore Mum. It just gets worse and worse. She never says a word to her apart from stuff like How was your day? or other questions which can be answered by just grunting. This is pretty horrible really, but I don't know how else to describe it: Grandma just starts to fade, and before you know it she's not much more than a piece of furniture which moves now and then all by itself. Every so often Mum has a go at her, but most of the time she complains about her behind her back, which makes you feel really sorry for Grandma since it's not like she can't hear the way sound travels in our house (even if she is old).

So by the time Grandma has her stroke, there's a pretty good reason for Mum to feel guilty. Try translating that guilt into house-cleaning and you'll see we had our work cut out for us.

By the way, there's also like, more to the porno thing. Mum finds it three weeks later 'cos it stayed hidden underneath my rug for all this time and she comes across it collecting up washing. Luckily she was in one of her I'm-of-the-understanding-variety-of-mum phases, and if you can believe it she looked at it and said Uh-huh in this knowing way and opened my desk drawer and put it inside. At some point the next day she changed her mind or the phase must have ended or something, because when I looked for it after school it simply wasn't there. The other theory is that Dad got hold of it.

5

Major fast-forwarding now. I'm skipping ahead to the next time I see The Guy because it's way more interesting than any of the other stuff that happens right after Grandma's stroke. It's also when I see Mr Fabulous Fellows in the flesh too, and it all takes place in the same club. Only difference is Al's not there this time since her parents found out about us going out the other night and, like, latched her window shut. Amazingly enough Mum's stopped bothering about me – it's a new tack she's trying (I overhear her talking to one of her judge friends about it on the phone). The idea is I'll stop 'rebelling' if there nothing for me to rebel against. She turns out to be so wrong.

So I'm in Starlight, on my own, feeling a bit of a muggins to be honest since no one wants to talk to me except the geries and no one's even dancing yet so I can't do that either. I wouldn't have come except that it's Saturday night and I'd rather spend it anywhere other than listening to Mum shouting at Dad or watching crass TV with Bilbo and The Nun. But it's turning out to be pretty shit and I'm just about to start communing with my depression when He walks in, also alone, and I think to myself, Right, OK, here we go.

A quick word on the sex thing, by the way, since you'll probably need to know sooner or later considering what's coming. At this point I've not done it up the arse yet. I know it's like, what gays are famous for but it just hasn't happened with any of the guys I've been with. OK, I'll admit that there've only been three, and the first two were just fumbles in the dark (the first time a guy came in my hand it was pretty awkward, actually – I mean, it's like my fingers are dripping with his cum and I don't know where to put them). But hey, I'm ready to be taught.

So I walk up to him and do the whole Hey, how're you? thing. He looks blank for a second and I'm terrified he's not going to remember me, even though it was only a week ago. But he does. His face lights up adorably – he has these really cute cheeks that sort of puff in and out when he smiles. He seems to have forgotten about the whole offending-me thing though because the first thing he says is, If it isn't the young buck!

I'm like, Like whatever.

Still, he buys me a drink, and we go sit down in the corner and start chatting, and he turns out to be a pretty cool guy. I get his name too – it's Jon. I know: Jaz and Jon, it's not good. In fact it's the stuff of a PA's nightmare, but what can you do? He's a windsurfing instructor and he teaches on this massive pond to rich university students. It's cooler than anything I can tell him, though I have a go. I say that I'm a trainee chef at this big restaurant, Breeze. That's what I always say, 'cos it's where Dad works, and I can talk about it at length if they decide to find it fascinating. Fortunately this guy doesn't, which is totally to his credit 'cos neither do I. There's like, other things . . .

Pretty soon we're kissing again, and boy am I exploring the inside of his mouth. Maybe that's a gross way of putting it, but what I'm trying to tell you is that this is the business. I am hard down below and light up above.

Then, with the timing of a fanny fart, Mr Fellows

suddenly arrives. It's almost enough to make you believe in God because sometimes it seems as if someone has to be watching over me and picking out the choicest moment to fuck everything up. Well, this time he gets me a diamond. Fellows actually pulls us apart with his hands.

Jarold Jones! he says in his stern voice. What in heaven's name do you think you're doing?

I'm like, Oh shit.

Jon's like, Who the hell are you?

Mr Fellows is like, Jarold, come with me right now.

I'm like, Please . . .

But there's no talking sense with an angry teacher. I don't know what it's got to do with him anyway, since it's not like I'm here during school hours or anything. But somehow it's wrong, and I have that feeling like when you know you're wrong and you have to do what you're told. So I follow Fellows out of the club, leaving Jon looking like a sour lemon, probably thinking Fellows is either my Dad or my lover, both of which are pretty grim prospects.

Outside Fellows is like, You've got some explaining to do.

It's like, what's to explain? But he stares at me like this silent volcano just waiting to erupt. I know he's going to give me one of those coma-causing lectures you get when you've done something that's really against the rules.

So I'm like, Do me a favour and get it over with.

He immediately goes all stiff upper-lip and taut cheeks. He straightens and twitches in a freaky sort of a way, like Norman Bates or something. I consider bolting, but suddenly it's like I've realised that I'm not really that scared of him actually. I'm kind of more intrigued as to what he's doing in this kind of a place. Well, picking up obviously, but hello? He's like, totally mature.

42

Look, he says, I don't want to make trouble for you. But you're too young for that kind of thing. Too young, understand?

I'm like, What are you, the gospel on age?

He's like, Don't make this into a big deal. I don't want to have to tell your parents.

That kind of has me laughing, and maybe it's because of the whole clichéd soap-opera situation, but suddenly Fellows starts laughing too. He's got this high-pitched squeaky laugh, which sounds like it doesn't get much airing and suits his personality down to the ground. We're laughing about different stuff though – I'm laughing at the thought of Mum's face when she gets his phone call and Fellows is laughing because he's embarrassed.

So I'm like, What were you doing in there? Patrolling for schoolkids?

He's like, properly rumbled at that, and totally stops. He goes all serious, and get what he says next, 'cos I'd give anything to have a signed copy:

My lifestyle choice is a perfectly valid option.

Sorry – I've heard some funny things, but coming from a geography teacher this is as good as it gets. He watches me emptying my sides of oxygen for a minute, and then pulls me back upright and slaps me. Big mistake. Teachers don't slap and I'm not one to take it lying down. The words Look I'm sorry have hardly got past his lips before Bam! – Fellows down. My fist hurts from the impact, which I'm sure must be the sign of a good one. Actually for a horrible minute I think he isn't moving, and worry that maybe he hit his head a little too hard and now, in the space of one hot second, I'm a murderer. It's not so bad, I think, since my defence is all sorted, what with Mum being a lawyer and all. But it soon turns out

43

he's not dead, because he starts groaning and crawling around on the pavement.

I hover over him for a minute like a moron. Then it occurs to me that there's not much more to be said here so I take off.

I meet Bilbo at the front door so I take him in with me. Mum and Dad are in bed when I get back, which is a godsend, so I go straight to the bathroom mirror. Bottom line, he chooses to talk then I'm talking too, and I've got a big red mark across my cheek to prove it. I'm just regretting that once again I've been whisked away from Prince Charming. At this rate I'm gonna have to start fucking frogs, or maybe Bilbo.

I send Al a text: I MET SEXY GUY AGN! NMES JON + NRLY GT IT ON WTH HIM! BUT I GT RMBLED BY FELLWS!!! HE WS IN CLUB 2 + SAW ME X-ING HIM! HE HIT ME SO I PUNCHD HIM BCK + RAN AWY! J

Her text back is, like, the definition of disbelief, and I've got to admit it does all sound a bit hectic for a single night out. It takes ages to get to sleep but when I finally do I have a wet dream and it's really something, at least until I'm woken up at silly o' clock in the morning by a strange smell which turns out to be Bilbo washing his arse right next to my face.

6

I guess it's about time to give you the story of my second shitty day which happened earlier on in the week. This takes place the day after Grandma's stroke. It started off with me thinking I might be able to get a couple of days off school out of it, and trying to act all upset, but Mum saw through that right away and started ranting about how I deserve to have a stroke too so I know what it feels like. Meanwhile The Nun's set up this vigil in her room and when you pass by you can sometimes hear her praying, which you'd think would be far more alarming than anything I could ever do or say, but it slips right by Mum unnoticed.

The day starts off bad because of Al's parents. Without bothering to ask for my permission, which she claims not to need in her own home, Al went right out and told them everything they could possibly not want to know about me. Apparently she was hoping they would offer her some advice on how to persuade me to be openly out or something. Trouble is, when it comes to this sort of thing, Al's parents are about as enlightened as lumps of coal, which you'd think is something she'd know about, being their only child and all.

So I knock on the door and instead of getting Al I get Mrs Rutland, who's like, the opposite of her daughter and is tall and thin and always dresses like she's expecting the Queen to drop by. She looks positively aghast at the sight of me, and raises both hands like she thinks I'm going to attack her or something.

I don't know that they know yet, so I'm like, It's OK, it's not contagious like, jokingly.

Mrs Rutland lets out the fakest laugh known to man. Slowly read out loud the words ha ha ha and you'll have an idea of how it sounds. I start looking around to check that I haven't like, accidentally entered the Twiglet zone or something, and Mrs Rutland goes, You surprised me! which is like, totally obvious. I can kind of see that something's up, but before I can put my finger on it Mr Rutland appears behind her at the door.

Who is it? he says and then sees me. His face undergoes the exact same changes as hers did – like, Jim Carrey style.

Hi, Mr Rutland, how's the job? I say, since Al told me he had this job placement thing lined up which was really important. He runs a furniture factory that produces sofas for Habitat in a colour range consisting of various shades of beige.

Mr Rutland like, totally ignores this. Oh, hello there, Jarold, he goes. I'm going to drive Al to school today.

I'm like, Huh? since me and Al always catch the bus in and out together. Can I speak to Al please?

Mr Rutland's like, I think she's in the bathroom right now. I'm sure you'll see her at school. Best be getting on, hmmm?

I'm like (really gently in case someone died), Is everything OK?

He lets out an identical copy of Mrs Rutland's laugh. Of course, of course, he goes. Now hadn't you better hurry along before you're late for school?

Just then Al appears behind them both with her bag. She

looks between her parents like she can't believe it and then she mows through them like they're nothing more than feathers in her way.

She's like, Let's go, to me. I note how she turns and gives them a chilling glare before we leave. Mrs Rutland shouts out after us, Don't be late back!

I'm like, What the F?

Al's like, They are such Neanderthals. I told them you were gay and they totally freaked out. Now they want us to stop hanging out after school.

I'm like, You told them what! You'd better be pulling my leg!

Al's plays it innocent. She's like, No, it's true. Why?

I'm like, You're sausage meat, sister.

I prepare myself for a full-on hair-pulling/dribbling extravaganza, but it turns out that Al genuinely doesn't have a clue she's done anything wrong. I try to explain it to her, but she's like, Why do you even care about what they think anyway? They're so ignorant! I don't understand how they manage to persevere with such ignorance in today's society . . . She launches into this sermon about human rights before I get the chance to respond, and my anger gets totally killed under the tidal wave of boredom that follows, since when Al really goes off on one there's no point in even trying to get a word in edgeways. It's like, sit back and hope exhaustion sets in soon. She goes on the whole bus journey to school. When she finally comes to a conclusion (right before our stop) I make a last-ditch effort at getting her to see it from my perspective.

But the point here is from now on your mum and dad are going to see me as this queer freak who's corrupting their daughter.

Al's like, Didn't you hear *any* of what I just said?

47

I'm like, Yeah, I just didn't listen. I still can't believe you told them!

Al's like, Not everything is about you, you know!

I'm like, Fuck you, because this is!

Al's like, Fuck you, no it isn't! These things have far-reaching implications—

This is where I lose it. I'm like, Just fuck off!

Al's like, You just fuck off!

We have to get up for our stop. There's all these other kids from school standing there too so we squeeze in beside them and I hiss at Al, Loser bitch. She shakes her head and mutters, Pathetic, and that's it. When we get off she immediately starts pretending I don't exist so I decide to let the bitch stew and stalk out of Freedom wanting to kill someone (clue: Al). It's only when I get inside that I realise this is a Serious argument we're having. I know because I'm literally panting

But what's weird is that this is like, the first time we've ever argued seriously. Like, *ever*. We text-row a lot but that's just taking the piss out of each other. I can't even remember the last time we had a fall-out. I started hanging out with Al in year three, back when she was an overweight thirteen-year-old with a pudding-bowl haircut. Now she's an overweight sixteen-year-old with a pudding-bowl haircut (supposed to be ironic but I've got my doubts) and the worst we've ever done is bicker.

I spend first period feeling like life has let me down, which is topped off by Bull Face mouthing Faggot at me as I walk in. When Mr Pond laughs at me because I ask him why everyone always gets hitched at the end of Shakespeare plays I have this urge to start weeping which I only manage to distract myself from by twisting my watch all lesson so the reflection of the light keeps getting in his eyes.

After English I get stalked down by Mary, this chick who's, like, totally infatuated with me despite the fact that in a moment of exasperation I've even admitted to her I'm confused (some people just don't get it). She's always trying to get me to do stuff with her, like go hang out after school or meet at her house for some private candlelit study session for two. She stands between me and Freedom and gives me her dazzling perfect smile – her father's an orthodontist so she dealt with the whole brace pony-trap scenario thing the rest of us have all just been through (except for some poor metal-mouths who are still going through it) when she was like, a first year.

She's like, Hi Jaz, how's it going? – so obvious. It's like, get some self-respect.

I'm like, Hi/Whatever, 'cos I can't be bothered with her right now.

She's like, You are coming to my party, aren't you? like I've made a blood oath to her or something, when it's the first I've even heard about it.

I'm like, What party?

Turns out she's organising this party (wouldn't ya know) in two weeks' time and I'm like, the guest of honour or something. The thing I should explain about Mary is that she's one of those blonde, blue-eyed sorority types. To complete the stereotype she's even got cheerleader boobs, which stick out from her stick-thin body like Jessica Rabbit's. Al's like, madly jealous of her and totally hates her, but of course all the boys are totally obsessed with her, which makes it like, a hundred times more awkward for me when it comes to putting her down. Thinking of Al and just to spite her I'm like, Yeah, sure, why not? even though I'm pretty sure that a house party organised by Mary will basically involve watching one half of the school pairing up with the other half, like a mass pukatorium.

Mary's face lights up like a Christmas tree. While she's all elated from my unexpectedly easy affirmative I quickly tell her I've got to go and I slide past her before she can spout any more embarrassingly obvious garbage simply to be in my presence.

To try and cheer myself up about the day so far I decide to smoke one of Dad's cigarettes which I keep in the pocket by my heart for emergencies. I head for the traditional place of refuge, which is the bike shed. Behind this old shack it's like smokers' central and I don't know why the school doesn't just set up a CCTV camera or something unless it's due to some like, secret unwritten teacher–pupil alliance that stretches all the way back to the very first school ever.

Anyway, I've just sparked up when who should appear but freaky Fabian. I'm like, Oh brother. He doesn't see me at first because I'm wedged in between the bike racks, so I keep quiet and watch him light one up and start turning his hand round so he can admire his latest biro masterpiece. But sooner or later I have to exhale. He spins round like he's expecting the Gestapo or something. When he sees me he smiles in his comic-book evil-villain kind of a way and goes, Well, well, well, if it isn't the faggot.

I decide I can't be dealing with The Freak right now. I'm like, Did your neck just throw up or what?

Fabian's like, majorly incensed. You better be careful!!! he goes in this ultra-shrill way, like something's just bitten on his balls, You better be careful what you say to me, man! Faggot!

I'm like, Why, 'cos you'll burst a blood vessel?

Then, to my total horror, Fabian produces a knife. It's one of those ones that you press a button to make the blade click out. Fabian does this and holds it up against his cheek where he rakes it across imaginary stubble in like, homage to Clint Eastwood or something. He gives me a Nazi smile.

I'm like, Woah.

He's like, Want to find out what it feels like to be knifed in the chest?

I'm like, No!

He's like, Are you sure? as if there were a genuine chance of me changing my mind. He throws down his cigarette and steps on it really deliberately as if to say, Any second now this could be you.

It's one of those situations where there's just no point in bothering. On the one hand I have this weird sense of calm, 'cos I figure being stabbed would kind of fit in with my shitty day, and you have to just roll with these things. But there's another side of me which isn't exactly thrilled at the prospect of a painful death, especially at the hands of a loser freak with behavioural problems.

So I'm like, Just chill out, man.

Fabian's like, all menacingly, Oh I'm perfectly chilled, my friend. The question is, are you?

I'm like, totally not. Just put the knife away! but he just stands there grinning and stroking himself with it. He's like, practically masturbating here. Panic rises in me 'cos this is turning into a scene from the *Texas Chainsaw Mascara*.

I'm like, Listen – you're sick.

Fabian appears to be quite flattered by this 'cos his eyes positively gleam. But to my relief he flicks the blade back and puts the knife away in his pocket.

Just remember, I'll be watching your faggoty arse from now on, he says. Don't tell anyone or I'll cut you.

At this point I'm like, literally saved by the bell, so I grab my bag and run for it, half-expecting him to stick it in while my back's turned. It's like, a clear case of serious harassment and this freak obviously needs be locked up and lobotomised or something, but to be honest there's not a whole lot you can do. I don't know if it's like a code of conduct all kids are born with, or if it's just because the idea of treating any of the teachers in this school like people who are there to help you brings up, like, bile, but I just can't quite bring myself to tell anyone (quite apart from the fact of me smoking would most definitely have to come out if they followed it up). I figure the best bet is just to hope Fabian decides to cut his own throat with it instead of mine or anyone else's.

Second period is geography and that's ultra-weird now for two reasons: Al and Fellows. Al and me see each other coming up opposite ends of the corridor and immediately we both start pretending like the wall is the most interesting thing ever and when we both reach the door at the same time Al pretends her skirt needs seeing to so she doesn't have to go through at the same time as me. It's like, how juvenile?

Fellows is at the board and has his plans for today all chalked up in bright green and pink. I've virtually forgotten about Al's seeing him in the club (this is before the whole fist fight so ho-ho-ho – little do I know what's coming!) but it all comes right back. When I tried to picture it before the idea of this guy in tweed dancing to cheese in Starlight was like trying to imagine Dad married to Grandma. But looking at him now, everything seems to be a possible indicator, from the tweed to the curly writing. But it's only when he nods to a couple of the spectoids at the front and starts sharpening his pencil that it becomes like, painful. He's totally like, gayness personified.

He notices how me and Al are sitting at like, opposite sides of the room and obviously interprets it as us being conscientious and doing what he told us to do. He comes over to me with this pleased look like we've made his day or something.

Very well remembered, he says, Just try it for a couple of days and then you can sit together again.

I'm like, the definition of LIC GAS.

But funnily enough it's thanks to Fellows that this thing between me and Al resolves itself, because halfway through his narcolepsy-inducing lecture on the oil industry Al catches my eye and just like that the battle's over. We both start giggling like maniacs. It's the memory of Al's face when she told me she'd seen him that does it for me. Fellows doesn't stop talking, but he looks between us suspiciously like he's trying to gauge the likelihood of us both bursting into spontaneous fits of spluttering coughs at the exact same time. He decides to let it pass at first but it just keeps getting more and more uncontrollable and it's infectious too 'cos several other guys can't help joining in. It must be pretty hard to lecture a class when half of them have their hands clamped over their mouths and are quivering like a bunch of switched-on vibrators, but he manages it for a good ten minutes.

Unfortunately it's the kind of virus that just doesn't go away, and the second I let out a sound that could just possibly be identified as laughter he loses it and decides to put the blame all on me.

Wait outside! he barks.

I'm like, This is total discrimination, but as I've said before there's just no talking sense with an angry teacher so I end up doing what he says.

I hate being made to stand in the corridor outside. It's like, the most humiliating punishment 'cos all the moles-tables from junior school can see you through the window as they pass by on their way for elevenses or whatever. I end up standing there with my middle finger permanently stuck in the air for the next half an hour, bored out of my brain. But I'm relieved that at least the issues are over with Al. When the class is over all the pupils file past me, most of them giving me sympathetic looks. I'm expecting a lecture from Fellows but instead he just gives me this look that's like a weedy version of Mum's death stare. When I catch up with Al we have hysterics all through lunch hour and agree to disagree about her parents because, according to Al, that's the mature thing to do. We make plans to go to Starlight at the weekend (though as you know for her it doesn't happen) and then I tell her about Fabian. She's like, Stay away from that freak show from now on, like I need any telling.

So the day wouldn't have turned out so shitty after all were it not for this mind-bendingly stupid thing that I do on my way out of study period. Maybe it's just because it's the end of a long day and I've regressed to this younger version of myself, or maybe I've just lost all sense of proportion after my near-death experience with Fabian. Anyway, it's pretty simple. I'm walking towards Freedom and I happen to turn my head at the wrong point and find myself looking at this naff collage the molestables have put together to commemorate some field trip to a farm. It's massive and takes up half the wall, so even though it's the usual crap it's quite impressive when you think of the size of the people who worked on it like, in comparison. But directly facing me are two cows, one of which so closely resembles Bull Face it's like, uncanny. In my pocket my fingers touch upon my pen and it's like, destiny has spoken or something. The next thing I know the deed is done and there's a simple arrow pointing towards the cardboard creature with Joseph aka Bull Face written in a circle above. Then I turn round and find the genuine article standing behind me and pointing at it like he can't believe what he's seeing. He looks like he's just been flashed at. And before he has a chance to connect it in his brain with the sight of me standing there with the pen, and then like, have an appropriate violent reaction (which with Bull Face it has to be said is quite a long time), I start bolting for my life.

7

So all in all I'm not much looking forward to Monday morning. But Sunday happens first, and I'm going to give it to you so you get an idea of exactly what our family is like as a collective.

It starts off with me trying to sneak out to meet Al, but Mum's guarding the ground floor and catches me before I can get away, so I end up having to go with her, Dad and The Nun to visit Grandma. I'm not the only one who doesn't want to go. Once me and The Nun are stood to attention in the kitchen, Mum barges into the living-room where Dad's peacefully watching some football match. She switches off the TV and we hear her saying to him in this contradict-me-and-I'll-bite-your-eyes-out voice, It's time for us to go! Mum has no sympathy for when you're watching TV – the only programme she ever watches is Trinny and Susannah. Still, it seems pretty mean for her since it's one of the few pleasures Dad seems to actually take in life these days (apart from secretly smoking). He once told me that football is the last remaining tenet of true masculinity. I was like, Ahuh, and Did you not *see* Freddy Ljungberg in those underwear ads? but he just smiled like I would never understand, which is probably true.

The journey there is the worst bit. Dad's car radio doesn't work and it's actually one of those ancient bombs that don't even have a CD player. Mum's always on at him to trade it in or something, but Dad loves it like a third testicle and it's just about the only thing she hasn't managed to bulldoze him into doing. But I wish he would. The Nun alternates between humming snatches of hymns and the latest Westlife album, until finally I can take it no more. I'm like, You're giving us aural cancer.

The Nun's like, I can hum if I want to, and Dad's like to me, Leave her alone, trying to seem like he has a presence or something. A few minutes later though he comes round to my side and asks her if she wouldn't mind doing it in her head. I start sniggering and she mouths at me to get lost (Teresa doesn't swear, she thinks it's sacrilegious).

After a while, not used to being in such closed-off space with his entire family, Dad makes this chronically feeble attempt at having a conversation with us. First of all he goes to Mum, Do you think you've remembered everything for her? quite brightly like, given the circumstances it would be completely understandable if she hadn't.

Mum's reply is like a mousetrap snapping shut. Are you trying to make me even more nervous, Lawrence? she goes, Because if you are, you're doing a fantastic job!

Dad waits a few seconds and then tries with me. He's like, So how was school this week, Jaz?

I'm like, the definition of Don't ask. Finally he tries The Nun, who he asks if she still wants to be an actress these days, which is what she wanted to be back when she was like, still being breast-fed. But The Nun's all, like, jumping at the opportunity to talk about herself. She's like, Either that or a nurse, and then starts going on about how much she admires nurses and what an important job they have and how wonderful it must be to care for sick people blah-blah-blah. It's like, Go and be a nurse in a leper colony then.

Eventually I interrupt to ask how much further we've got

to go and Mum snaps back, Not very far all right? like it's this question I've been firing off every minute or something. I'm like, Fucking hell, I was only asking, and Mum's like, God damn it, Jarold! Is it so much to ask that you do not use words like that when we're together as a family?

The Nun's like, to her, And can *you* stop saying things like that *too* and have a bit of *respect* please?

Mum's like, Not now, Teresa! like religion's this annoying habit of hers rather than this chronic insanity she's got.

The Nun's like, Anyway, what I was saying about being a nurse is—

I'm like, Jesus fucking Christ.

The Nun crosses herself when I say that. I don't know at what stage it's supposed to become like, pathological, but if I actually cared I'd be seriously worried for The Nun. Someone ought to be, since it seems to be totally bypassing Mum and Dad that their only daughter's becoming this religious maniac, which is far worse than being gay. You'd think they'd take her to a correctional facility or something. But no, it's all about me. Every now and then in the evening Mum'll switch to Brady Bunch mode and say stuff like, Do you want to have a discussion, Jaz? in this scary happy sing-song voice. Of course I'm always like, No, I'd rather have AIDS or something, which I only say for effect because obviously it isn't true, but it makes Mum go all silent and shake like she's having a conniption, and is the only way I can get her to leave me alone. Meanwhile The Nun gets more and more out of touch with reality every day and nobody notices or thinks it's a big deal. It'll serve them right if she decides to go and have a full-on stigmata.

Anyway we finally get there, in silence of course, which is how we always end up travelling. I'm sure our family isn't more dysfunctional than other families, and I know I'm

58

supposed to be all lucky to even have one, but to be honest if Mum and Dad came along and told me I was adopted and they'd decided to swap me or something I really wouldn't give a toss.

Mum leads the way to the hospital reception, where we find out Grandma's ward. Then there's this era of corridors and elevators in which people in blue pyjamas seem to be randomly wandering, probably lost. The whole place is totally creepy, but The Nun's loving it and keeps smiling like an idiot at all the nurses who obviously think she's retarded or something because they all nod and smile back at her.

We find Grandma asleep in this contraption that looks more like a pony trap than a bed. But at least she's by the window, which is thankfully open, since the whole place stinks of decaying flesh.

About not wanting to come, by the way. It's not that I don't want her to get well or anything, 'cos I do. In fact this may sound arrogant but I actually think I care about her way more than anyone else does, 'cos I reckon I've got the most in common with Grandma. I don't mean being old and shrivelling up or anything. I mean 'cos it often feels like we're both not wanted in our own home. It's like I'm just waiting to grow up and she's just waiting to keel. I know that she wouldn't like to be cooped up in hospital, but I also know that the last thing she'd want to do is force me to be cooped up there with her. And sure enough the first thing she says when she wakes up is, You didn't have to bring the children, Lois (and yes, we've all got bad names in this family).

Mum's like, They wanted to come, in this voice that's, like, so unconvincing it's embarrassing.

We all kiss Grandma in turn and The Nun takes her hand

and sits there clutching it like this is supposed to provide some kind of pillar of support or something. If I ever end up in hospital and someone does that to me I'm going to squeeze their hand so hard I cut off the circulation and it has to be amputated.

Anyway, we all sit around making earth-shattering observations about how cold the weather's getting, and then of course we all fall silent. It's like, totally awkward, and Grandma looks like she wishes they'd come and put her back to sleep or something. Finally, after pretending to fix Grandma's hair for several minutes, Mum goes, So Jaz, why don't you tell us about school these days?

I find this pretty mean, since it's not my fault she can't think of anything to say and I don't see why I should be the one to suffer. But Grandma gives me such a look of hope I decide to make a stab.

I'm like, Well . . . we're studying Shakespeare in English and, er, oil in geography. And um . . . that's it really.

I run out of ideas. Mum glares at me with eyes that could fry. I hear myself continue, I can't understand why everyone gets married in *Twelfth Night* at the end. They do it in all his comedies and it just seems to me like it's a big white-wash.

I sound like this total reject but Grandma nods enthusiastically like it's the most intelligent thing she's ever heard. The Nun rolls her eyes like she can't understand how I've managed to survive this long.

I mean, why is that supposed to make everything OK? I go, It's like they've had all this fun running around and making mistakes and fancying each other, and then all of a sudden bang, someone comes along and says, time's up folks. Time to live happily ever after.

I look around but no one seems to have a clue what I'm

talking about or even to be listening, apart from Grandma. It's totally depressing. Then I look at Mum and the next thing I know is there are tears slipping out of her eyes and falling on to Grandma's hair. At first I think she must be, like, moved by what I was saying, but then Grandma looks up to see where the shower is coming from and Mum goes, I really thought I was going to lose you, in this wailing voice like she's just taken a breath of helium.

Grandma's like, No, not this time, Lois, in this wise voice like the old master in *Karate Kid*.

Mum turns away and goes to the window, where she presses her forehead against the glass. It's like she thinks she's trapped in here with us, whereas it's like, so the other way around.

She's like, We need to talk.

Then there's this moment in which the whole awkwardness of the situation seems to be like, making the air thicken or something. Then Dad, in this like, paranormal display of initiative, comes to the rescue. He taps me on the shoulder and nods his head towards the door like we should probably step outside. Since The Nun's totally immune to subtlety he practically has to prise her hand off of Grandma and like, personally escort her through the door.

We hang out in the corridor playing dodge with this constant stream of fat nurses pushing tea trolleys and ga-ga patients in wheelchairs around. Dad looks like he's having the life slowly sucked out of him and I'm almost tempted to offer him one of his cigarettes. The Nun's like, It's so nice that Mum and Grandma are bonding over this. Then she decides she's thirsty so Dad sends her off with forty pence to look for a drinks machine.

I'm like, What is the deal here?

Dad sighs deeply, like he's holding up the world or

61

something. He's like, It's complicated. Your mother's one of those unfortunate people who never got on with her parents very well, so it was a real shock for her when your grandpa died and Grandma had to come live with us.

I'm like, Why didn't you just put her in a home? but he just shakes his head like I'm too young to understand. I'm properly curious now, and I kind of feel like it's all this big game of Cluedo and if I could just put the scraps together I could figure out what's going on. At the same time I'm kind of annoyed, because it's like, why can't he just tell me? The only way to respond is to say LIC GAS, but it's kind of sad because it's not like I haven't tried to. That's what happens though when people treat you like you're only half a person. It's like my parents think I'm this interesting experiment they've had together and are waiting to see if it'll work out. Maybe it's the same for everyone, I don't know, but I think it's pretty dumb.

We don't go back in again so the whole trip was pretty much a waste of time as far as seeing Grandma was concerned, since we only saw her for about ten minutes. When she comes out Mum's got tears in her eyes still, and she says Grandma's asleep. On the way to the car Dad puts his arm around her and surprisingly she doesn't shove him away. She even leans into him a bit, and I give The Nun a glance to see if she's noticed, but she's far too busy concentrating on being a saint.

But for a second it's actually like they're working together as a team, like the sort of team two married people are supposed to be, instead of these two arch-enemies who've been like, handcuffed to each other all their lives. It's kind of sad that by the time we get home Mum's feeling more like her real self, because just as she's about to get out of the car she looks around inside and goes, Lawrence, your car is absolutely filthy these days. If you're not going to trade it can't you at least give it a clean? and Dad's like, Why can't you just let me look after my own car? and Mum glares at him and they both go to opposite ends of the house. Which just goes to show that losers will always be losers.

8

Anyway, this section is all about Fellows. We're fast-forwarding a bit: it's a week after our visit to Grandma's, and also a week after my fight and make-up day with Al, and also a week after I saw Fellows and he slapped me and I punched him, and also a week after I drew Joseph aka Bull Face above an arrow pointing towards one of the cows on the junior-school collage in full view of him. So in case you haven't got the message yet, it's a week after all that.

First things first. I've started meeting Al at the bus stop instead of her house, since the idea of another freak sesh with her creepy parents isn't much of a turn-on. She says she's working on their education, but she's not having much luck now they've found out about her sneaking out and have decided I'm like, spawn of Satan or something. It's lucky our parents don't get on 'cos otherwise I bet her mum would have called mine and then the shit would be really flying.

Second thing is that at school I've been playing like this cat-and-mouse game with Fuck Face (which is what I rechristen him with Al after telling her about what happened). It's pretty freaky stuff, 'cos him and the Tweedles have been leaving me notes with stuff like U R DEAD MEET and FAGS GO TO HELL creatively written on them. But he can't get me in class so long as I turn up right after the bell and leave the second it goes at the end, and I'm watching

64

out like a laser for him and being especially careful round corners. Meanwhile someone's torn down the bit of the collage I wrote on (I wonder who) and, almost as though whoever did it was a large graceless beast with the co-ordination of a total spaz, they also tore down most of the rest of the collage in the process. The school's supposed to be launching an 'investigation', whatever that means. In our Monday morning assembly the headmaster, who's this ultra-fat blimp who tries to make up for it by acting like every single one of us is his very best friend, went off on one and called it a 'heinous act of barbarism' on 'what was a shining collective work of art'. When he said this last part the whole hall was full of people choking on their own tongues, and even some of the teachers sat behind him were studying the floor in a desperate effort to restrain themselves.

The third thing is another person I'm avoiding like a virus is Fabian. Every time we see him me and Al end up walking in this massive circle so we don't have to cross paths. He looks kind of put out when he notices, which makes me wonder if I was supposed to think his whole freak show with the knife was cool rather than an indication of raving-mad loony disorder.

But the biggest issue is Fellows.

He arrives on Monday with this circle of dark blue on his face, inside which his left eye sits blinking like a target or something. Cue the usual jokes from the front-row lame-Os about him rescuing damsels in distress or secretly attending Fight Club. But of course I recognise my handiwork. He didn't ring my parents, which is a good thing, but neither does he make eye contact with me, which means when I sit there in class (back beside Al) it like, redefines the word awkwardness. To be honest I feel ever so slightly guilty. It looks painful, man. But he deserved it. You don't hit kids. Full stop.

At least that's what I think to begin with. Then I speak to him a couple of days later. This is, like, a sappy bonding scene.

It's after class, and I'm increasingly in guilt-ridden mode. I don't know if it's got something to do with the fact that Fuck Face might be lurking behind every corner waiting to blast me out of this life with his death breath, and if I've got like this subconscious urge to tie up all loose ends or something, but I decide the man *has* to be spoken to. He just looks suicidally unhappy of late, and his face still looks like he's been attacked by an eye-shadow-wielding maniac. I didn't know that I'd have that much effect, but still he won't look me straight in the face. Instead he lectures the class all lesson with this dry voice, which now sounds all cracked and like the hope's been liposuctioned out of it. Meanwhile he stares into the distance as if behind the far wall of the classroom there's this wonderful thing he can never have. He looks well depressed, and the fact is it's as killing for me as it is for him.

Anyways, everyone has gone, 'cept for me and Al, and I eyebrow Al out of the room, like she needed telling. She's another reason I'm talking to him, since she reckons there are bridges to be rebuilt, and that otherwise this will come back and haunt me when I'm older. It's like, get a foothold.

So I go up to the front desk, where Mr Fellows is shuffling his papers and doing a pretty foul job of trying to look busy.

I'm like, Look, I'm sorry, OK?

He looks up. I guess he thought I was going to say something else, or blackmail him or something, because the relief in his eyes is pathetic, but touching in a weird sort of way. I smile a little and his whole face lights up even more, like his skeleton's gone fluorescent under his skin or something.

That's OK, he says. I shouldn't have hit you either.

Yeah well, I begin. But it doesn't seem right to harp on about it, so I just shrug like as if to say who gives a fuck.

He's like, I was trying to be helpful.

I'm like, Oh right. Um . . . thanks.

He's like, I know. I screwed it up. I was shocked that you were even at that place. It's for . . . older men. He pauses and looks at me closely, as if he's trying to put together a puzzle. Jarold, do your parents know? he says in this soft voice like he's afraid of waking some sleeping demon or something.

I'm like, About you?

No. About you. About your . . . sexuality? He's gone red as a beetroot.

Kind of, I say. He's making me want to laugh, but I know from our last experience I should keep this urge to myself at all costs.

Kind of?

Yeah.

He looks all sincere, and I have this sudden desire to tell him about that night when they found out. Then, without even realising it, I find that I've started talking. I give him a pretty condensed version.

I think they're hoping it'll go away, I tell him, realising that it's the first time I've really considered it, and it's true – they are hoping it'll go away, like the measles or chickenpox. Either that or they think that maybe it'll develop into something healthier, like heterosexuality.

Mr Fellows takes what I say very seriously. He positively bristles, and I remember the comment he made about his

67

valid choice that started the whole punching business in the first place.

Do you want me to speak to them? he goes very gravely. I could give them a call and arrange a meeting. Would that be helpful?

I'm like, Er, no. I can handle them. Plus I know when Mum goes supersonic down the phone it's a real killer on your eardrums.

I'd like for you to think of me as a friend, says Mr Fellows, I'd like for you to come and tell me when you have any problems.

At this point he oversteps the mark and things get a little too cutesy-poo for me, so I'm like, Sure. Whatever. Bye.

And that's that. Only next time I see him Mr Fellows doesn't look any happier. Or the time after that, though this is Thursday now and his bruise is hardly visible any more. I kind of realise that maybe I was being a bit arrogant to think that *I* was the problem. In fact, it's obvious what the real problem is – the poor old git's lonely *as*. I notice that he never really talks to any of the other teachers, which I wouldn't want to do either, but *hey*, this was his choice of profession. He eats his sandwiches alone in the classroom after we've all gone, and trudges off after school all on his lonesome.

Me and Al watch him all week. I mean, he's kind of fascinating. We try to figure out which of the other teachers know. Fatty, the headmaster, blatantly can't – It's just not possible, I say – though Al reckons he must do. Fellows is open with everyone, she says like he's this super dude she aspires to one day be. Actually it's funny, 'cos Al really starts to like Mr Fellows, almost in a creepy stalker sort of a way. She gets this thing about him being unhappy, and she makes a point of always saying hello to him in this ridi-

68

culous bright voice every morning. He says hello back but looks totally freaked out by this greeting, which is understandable since it's a totally weird thing to do. I tell her to stop speaking to him when I'm around. In fact I start to wonder if she doesn't have a crush on him. It's like, impossible, but I don't know how else to explain her behaviour. Trust Al to get a crush on someone with whom she'd only stand a chance if she had a lot of surgery and he had a lot of alcohol.

It's Friday morning, and we're having a cigarette behind the bike shed. Al's sucking on the butt while I keep a careful watch at the corner for anything shaped even vaguely like Fuck Face.

So I'm like, What is your deal with Fellows?

Al's like, Nothing, I just think it's really sad that he doesn't have anyone. It must be really hard to get a man when you're in his shoes.

I'm like, Like whatever, since it can't be any harder for him to get a man than it is for someone like Fatty the headmaster to get a woman, but I don't see her bursting her guts with sympathy for him.

But Al's like, I feel seriously sorry for him.

I'm like, Brother.

Then she goes, You ought to as well, as though I've got this special connection with Fellows now or something. It's like, Return to this planet, please.

She's like, He probably just needs a push in the right direction. We should totally go and offer him our support, in this sugary voice which she does when she gets all romantic.

I'm like, Vom.

We *should!*

And little do I know it but seeds of this terrible plan start

69

germinating in her brain, and it's not long before she's worked out this whole scheme for getting us into serious trouble. That comes this evening. But before that comes Fabian, who must have been watching us from a bush and waiting to ambush me, because the second Al heads off to buy us some gum he materialises behind me like a ninja assassin. He actually comes up behind me and puts the knife against my neck and goes, So how's my favourite faggot today?

At first I'm, like, totally gobsmacked, but then I feel kind of annoyed. Thing is, maybe it's because of the whole nicotine rush but I kind of know he's not really planning on cutting my throat. And having Fuck Face the hulk after me kind of makes Fabian seem about as scary as a mutant gerbil, even if he does have that stupid knife.

So I'm like, Just fuck off, you freak!

Fabian's like, Brave words. Brave indeed, but will they save you? in this old-world style of speech, like he's impressed at me actually using my mouth or something.

I'm like, What are you, Yoda?

He's like, You've got a smart mouth. One of these days someone's gonna have fun cutting it all up.

The freak then takes the knife off my neck and goes to the wall of the shed where he sets to work on carving out a swastika. While his back is turned I consider running, but it's like that would be an admission of defeat or something, and I can't be doing with that so I decide to stand my ground. I stare at his back, trying to see if I've inherited Mum's superpower of making stuff burst into flame by looking at it hard enough. Maybe it works a bit, 'cos Fabian turns round and gives me a funny look before going back to his swastika. Then he starts singing this totally stupid song that sort of goes like, Fuck the blacks, Fuck the whites, Fuck

70

the women, Fuck the men, Fuck the cripples, Fuck the faggots, etc.

I'm like, You should totally kill yourself.

Freaky's like, You're just jealous 'cos I do what I want to do. People like you just do exactly what you get told. You're so fucking lame. You and that brownie bitch you hang out with are so *fucking* sad.

This is like, the worst insult ever coming from someone like Fabian, considering the Nazi-punk thing is, like, a total throwback and he's, like, a total loser. I'm about to argue when Al arrives and saves me from wasting more saliva on him. She looks between me and Fabian and goes, Hey let's go, to me.

Just as we're edging our way around him, Fabian suddenly turns back and goes, So, uh, are you guys going to this party of Mary's? in this ultra-casual way that freaks like him just aren't able to pull off.

Al's like, straight in with the, What's it to you? You're not invited anyway, which is pretty rich since she's not invited either and the only reason she's able to go is 'cos she's like, totally latched on to me. In fact, she's the only reason I'm going. Fabian just scowls at her and there's this series of clicks which means he's thrashing his tongue-piercing back and forth against his teeth. He looks like he's about to start spewing and so I begin preparing myself for the spray.

Fuckers, he suddenly goes, in this voice that's like, the definition of bitterness and the next thing he's dashed off, knife and all.

Al's like, What the hell just happened?

I just shrug because I have no idea. I have this sudden memory of me and Fabian when I first started at school and how he used to spit in the test tubes in chemistry. Anybody

71

should have seen his total descent out of this galaxy coming. Then he goes and attacks Mrs Bolsh with a pair of scissors and all of a sudden he's got behavioural problems. Like, Doh! And now he's allowed to roam around freely with his knife and fuck only knows what he's gonna do next.

9

So Grandma's just got out of hospital the day before and Mum and Dad have gone out to some local council meeting or something, which is probably Mum's idea of them spending quality time together. Since they're out I've been left in charge this evening, but I'm hiding with Al in my room. Al had to lie about where she was going so she could hang out with me. Her parents are pretty sure I'm going to turn her gay or something and so we're not supposed to see each other any more. They're like, total fascists.

The reason we're hiding is that The Nun's got The Order over. These girls are all the same as she is: die-hard humanitarians. You'd think that kids in a convent school would be a pretty wild and exciting crew just because they'd want to rebel against all that religious crap they have to deal with, but Teresa's posse are just the opposite. They're like this ultra-fucked-up version of the Brady Bunch. They have these study parties where they'll all sit around the living-room watching *The Sound of Music* and, like, test each other on it and stuff. It's kind of hard to believe until you see it. Me and Al reckon they must hold secret ceremonies as well, like, where they all dance around the cross naked and smear themselves with the blood of Christ and chant psalms and stuff. That would be almost kind of cool actually, but I've yet to catch her doing anything like it.

Right now they're down there practising their vow of chastity or something.

So anyway, me and Al are just hanging out and trying to de-weird ourselves from the latest adventure with Fabian. I'm sitting on the bed cutting out photos from *ID* magazine for my altar to Orlando, and Al's trying to plait a piece of cotton into her hair, Christina Gorilla style (despite my patiently explaining that this is only beautiful for five-year-olds). We've got the radio on and it's the ad breaks, and all of a sudden Al stops midway through another never-ending rant about how old Fellows just needs some joy in his life or something and starts hopping around screaming. In fact she literally jumps on me.

I'm like, Are you having a hormonal surge or what, sister?

She's like, Shhhh. Listen!

So I listen. There's this totally fake woman's voice which sounds like she's overdosed on Prozac or something, going Why not look out for our special Maker Date agents – because they're looking out for you!

Al's like, This is a sign!

I'm like, What the huh?

Can't you see it? she says as if we've been stranded in the middle of the Atlantic on a raft for days, and now dry land is like, right in front of us.

I'm like, No.

This is how we're going to find Fellows a fella! she goes.

Now this is a joke, right? 'cos there's not much else it could be. Al's still leaping around joyously as if she just invented the vibrator or something, meanwhile I'm groaning in horror, 'cos Al's like a politician in this respect. Once she gets a plan in her head, trying to get her to forget it is like trying to get a dog to forget about the bone they've got

74

wedged between their jaws. One of those little snappy ones that never lets go.

Are you for real? I say, though unfortunately I know the answer.

Oh, come on! It'll be doing everyone a favour, and he deserves it. It's not his fault he's lonely. He's probably too shy to even talk to anyone.

I say, LIC GAS. What is this? *Clueless Two* or something?

Come on! she insists. He probably hasn't had sex for years! Maybe never!

I'm like, How the fuck do you know? He could be screwing someone right now. He could have a whole basement filled with bodies for all we know.

But Al's having none of it. She's totally attached to this idea that it's like, our duty or something to find Fellows an eligible bachelor. I know what you're thinking, 'cos I was thinking it too. Like, how the fuck do we do that? Well, good old Al's right in there with an idea (she must store plans up for a rainy day, because she always knows what to do, even at the shortest possible notice. I can be, like, I didn't do my homework – what am I going to say? and she won't bat an eyelid before going, Just say your parents are taking you to anger-management counselling).

Maybe he doesn't want our help, I suggest in a last attempt to preserve us from the inevitable chaos I just know is gonna result from this.

She's like, He totally needs it.

And she proceeds to tell me her elaborate scheme. I'm like, Give me a minor role, please, and Al's like, No problem. Next thing worth knowing is we're tiptoeing our way out the house and off to Starlight. (I know, it's like, can't we ever go somewhere else for a change?) The plan is we're going to hunt down a man for Fellows by pretending we're Maker Date personnel – or at least Al is. I'm just going to be assisting her. Unfortunately, before we can reach the front door a girl with like, multiple chins who I recognise straightaway as this witch-friend of The Nun's with a broom permanently shoved up her anus, not to mention a degree in eating, comes bounding out of the living-room. She practically throws herself in front of the door and stands there with her arms out wide across it like she's protecting it from us.

She's like, Where do you think you're going?

I'm like, None of your business.

Actually it *is* my business, she goes in this superior voice that makes you just know she's a prefect at school, Because you're supposed to be supervising and you know perfectly well you're not allowed out!

It's like, who the hell is this? Al sizes her up and steps forward. She's like, Get out of our way before I kick your—

The fat girl cuts her off by screaming out, Teresa! Your brother and his Indian friend are going somewhere!

Before you can blink the hall's filled with The Order, like this locus of dumpiness. Seriously, you've never seen so many squat-faced girls crowded into such a small space before and neither would you have believed there were so many unflattering clothes in the universe. It's like they're *trying* to look ugly. It must be something they drum into them at the convent school. I don't have anything against ugly people, by the way – I've got a lot of sympathy for them actually. But it's like we're being assaulted by unattractiveness here, because they kind of cluster in front of the door in this squadròn or something, with The Nun up at the front, all facing us with these super-fierce expressions like we're the definition of sin.

I'm like, Get the fuck out of the way!

The Nun's like, You can't leave the house! Mum's forbidden you to go out and you know it!

There's like, a hundred ways to respond to this. If it were The Nun on her own I'd start scalp-ripping, but there's no way I can take on The Order. We're talking like, seven of the butchest teenage girls in da hood. I end up just going really lamely, What the fuck do you care anyway?

The Witch who first started this goes, This is about doing what's right! We've heard all about you. How you're a gay. You should ask for forgiveness.

There's this whole minute of silence while The Order all simultaneously nod their heads up and down like a bunch of ducks. The witch sticks out one of her chins as if to say we can just bring it on because she's not going to back down if we've got Lucifer himself working for us.

I'm like, Learn to masturbate.

The Witch is like, How dare you?!

The Nun's like, Just ignore him, Joan!

We stand there facing them for a further minute. It starts to seem a bit comical really, since we're basically under house arrest here because of a bunch of Jesus freaks. At this point I remember that there's a back door, and I'm about to signal to Al to follow me into the kitchen when I suddenly think that actually maybe this isn't such a bad thing after all, since at least this way I don't have to enter into Al's stupid scheme to get Fellows a date. But to be honest there's another reason I want to go out, and it's got nothing to do with Fellows. I'm thinking about The Guy of course, who I've been having wet dreams about all week. Every time we go out there's this thin chance I might run into him again, so any excuse is a good excuse as far as I'm concerned. Then Al suddenly pushes in front of me and stands there facing

The Order like she's preparing to take them all on at once. She's like, By refusing to let us pass you're breaking the law and if you don't move aside I'm calling the police!

There's this like, collective gasp. No one's expecting this. You can see The Nun wrestling with it on her face, since the idea of breaking the law is second only to blasphemy for these girls. Then she like, steels herself.

She's like, *You* can leave, but Jarold is grounded.

This is too much. I poke Al in the back and shout, Back door now!

We race into the kitchen, pursued by The Order – which is fucking scary, let me tell you. As we pass the kitchen table I grab the back of a chair and throw it backwards without stopping, Indiana Jones style. I hear the sound of a crash behind me and one of the girls cursing and then being told off for it by The Nun. Al's at the door and is frantically unlocking it. I reach her as she opens it and we launch ourselves into the safety of the back garden. Knowing they've lost us, The Order stand on the step and glare at us as we scale the fence, shaking their heads in this one synchronised motion of disapproval. Once we're over I look at Al and then we both turn and give them a simultaneous up-yours sign.

Al's in full-on *vive la revolution* mode. She shouts back at them, Burn in hell, bitches!

We watch as they display signs of righteous horror at this before disappearing from sight out of the kitchen, probably to go and pray for our souls or, like, a lightning bolt to strike us or something. We both start giggling, although the truth is I'm a bit weirded out by being mobbed by my own sister and her friends. I'm kind of hoping Al will have forgotten about her crazy scheme and we can just go have some fun but no such luck.

Right, let's do this – she goes, all super-serious.

As soon as we get inside the club I'm cringing, because Al's taken off her coat. Underneath it she's wearing this bright pink T-shirt and a sparkly tiara she nicked out of Mum's dressing-up drawer. I'm wearing black by the way, for extra sink-into-the-crowd-ability.

Hurry up, I hiss at Al. This is the plan: she does the rounds of all the tables and has a quick word, meanwhile I'm supposed to scan the bar to see if I can't find someone who looks desperate enough to go for old Fellows. And if I should run into Jon, well . . . I've got eyes for me too. Assuming he doesn't think I belong to some mental institution round the corner now or something.

So Al goes off even though this so isn't going to work. I mean, her opening is going to be: Hi, I'm a Maker Date agent and we're looking for someone special to participate in our new programme – would you be interested? It's like, so not going to happen.

Which is a shame, 'cos if there was anyone in the room who might actually be Mr Fellows' type, I can't help but reckon it would be this tall, thin guy standing on my left. He's got glasses, but not too unfashionable, and he's not bad either, though he's a bit on the bald side (that can be only good if you're a Bruce Willis lookalike. Otherwise you want to invest in some miracle formula, pronto). The more I look at him the more I can kind of see him having dinner with Mr Fellows – you know, in one of those polite English restaurants that uppity homos go to. I can see them chatting away about the oil industry and income tax, and the state of Antarctica or whatever, and I can see them getting all cosy over dessert . . . Don't ask me why I'm even thinking these things, but it's kind of addictive, and Al seems to be having success over at the far table, and is noting down the details of all these beefy queers on her glittery pad.

I'm on the point of actually signalling to Al, when Jon turns up. With a guy. I'm like, properly gutted, and I sink into the shadow of the jukebox wishing the ground would swallow me up. Naturally, the first thing they want to do is select some music, despite the fact that everyone knows your song only ever comes on as you're leaving.

So here's me like, cowering behind the jukebox while watching their shadows and thinking that if I get discovered I'm gonna be like, frying with embarrassment. Meanwhile, Al's been surrounded up by a small crowd of excited men who want to be part of her stupid made-up programme. I bet you're thinking what I was thinking, which is all I need now is to encounter Mr Fellows and my night will be complete.

Enter Mr Fellows, dressed in shocking leather trousers (I mean like, shocking on him). Thankfully he doesn't see me, but he does see Al, who's walking right in his direction with some man at her side. Straightaway he's over there and bearing down on her like the phantom menace. It must look a bit weird. I crane forwards, and I can just about hear them.

What the devil are you doing? he demands.

She's a Maker Date agent, says the guy she's with innocently. Al smiles at Mr Fellows like an angel, but of course it doesn't wash.

She most certainly is not! he snarls. Alice Rutland, you're coming with me right this minute! He takes her arm and starts leading her off like a prisoner of war. She shoots a quick glance round behind her, looking for me, so I give her a little wave, at which point . . .

Hey? says Jon, looking at me like I'm a moron.

There's no point in pretending, so I'm like, Yeah, hi.

I come out from behind the jukebox and scope out the

guy he's with. I'm jealous even though he isn't even cute really. Just average and No Competition. Jon's looking at me expectantly, so I say, That guy from the other night – long story.

Jon's like, It's OK. Exes can be hard work.

Inwardly I'm like, shrieking in horror at the word ex, but I don't let on. Instead I say, This must be your brother.

Oh. He looks at the guy, suddenly uncomfortable. I give him this real sarcastic look.

He's just a friend, he says, like I could care less.

Sure. Whatever.

But I do kind of believe him, and not just because I want to. I know you might find this pretty sappy, since it's not like we even know each other, let alone own each other or anything, but I feel this real connection with him. And to be honest, I don't give a toss if he is here with this guy, since I've never got this whole hang-up everyone has about being with one person all the time. I think he feels it too, even though he's older. Actually I left out the bit where I lied to him last time about being twenty, which is important. You let on that you're underage and most guys'll evaporate before you've even finished your sentence.

Anyway, I can't stay of course, since Al's probably waiting for me with a slip that says detention for life in her pocket. But this time I at least have the sense to get his number, which he gives me on a little card with a printed pair of flippers on it.

Cute, I say and leave.

As predicted, Al is waiting outside. So is Mr Fellows, who's obviously twigged that I'm here too, and catches me as I come out. He shakes his head at me, like he's some kind of old sensei that I've failed.

Jarold, I'm very disappointed in you, he says to me.

I'm very disappointed in you, I say, looking at his leather trousers. He sets his jaw rigidly, like a fighter-jet pilot preparing to dive.

I'm not going to warn you again about this, he says. Either you stay away until you're of age or I'll have to contact the authorities.

I'm like, so Oh brother, since being banned from the one gay club that lets you in without checking for ID is the last thing I need. I drop my head and join Al in a chorus about how sorry we are and that we'll never try to have fun again or something. All I can think is how shit it is since in a way we were only here to do him a favour. Well, Al was anyway.

He's like, OK. Get lost the pair of you. Mind yourselves on the way home.

Al's pretty sorry on the way back. She says he tricked her into letting him know I was there. I'm not angry though, since when I put my hand in my pocket I can feel the edges of this little piece of card that makes everything all right.

Everything stops being all right once I get home. I go through to the living-room and find The Nun sitting beside Grandma, who's asleep on the sofa, watching over her in this totally freaky way, like she's been appointed to make sure she doesn't suddenly pass away or something. The second she sees me she's like, You are in *deep* trouble, in this super-smug voice.

I'm like, Go fuck a crucifix.

The Nun instantly goes Regan.

I hope they put you in a home! she shouts, but I'm already out of the room.

I go on up the stairs all cautiously in case Mum and Dad have set up like, motion detectors or something, but there's no sign of either of them so I open the door to my room thinking I've had a lucky escape. They ambush me. Seriously. Mum is sitting on the bed, and no sooner have I gone all indignant, demanding to know what she's doing in my room, when the door shuts behind me and I turn to see Dad standing between me and Freedom. He looks thoroughly not amused.

I'm like, Just put me out of my misery.

Stop trying to be smart and listen up, says Mum, in business-bitch mode. There's a few things we've got to discuss.

And we mean it, adds Dad, like he's even a factor.

I'm like, You mean there's a few things you're going to *tell* me.

Mum chooses to ignore this and continues: We've decided that you're going to stop going out. Full stop. She waits like she's expecting me to start whining or something. I'm like, Yeah, *and*?

And you're going to get counselling.

I'm like, Huh?

. . . and we're going to come with you, she goes. It's all precautionary, but we've thought about it and we agree it's for the best.

She takes a deep breath like this has all been much harder for her to say than for me to hear, and then goes, in a softer voice, What do you think? Will you do it for us?

I'm like, It's a great idea. You should both go. But leave me out of it.

Mum nods like she was expecting me to say exactly this. She's like, Look Jarold, you have to understand that this is hard for your father and me. We don't mean that we're angry at you. You are what you are, and we can both accept that. But we need time to adapt. It's your duty to help us understand.

It's like, duty? To these losers?

Dad's like, You can't talk with us normally so maybe a therapist can help. We just want to understand. He sounds like he's dying of thirst or something.

So they wait in, like, total anticipation while I sit there and consider, as if I've actually got a choice in the matter. But the truth is I really don't see what harm it can do. I mean, I'm not exactly gagging to be given the third degree, but there's no way anyone's ever gonna tell me I'm less sane than Mum and Dad, so what the hell?

I'm like, OK, but if they want to lock you up don't blame me.

Mum's face just floods with happiness. She's positively like, radiating, and Dad even goes so far as to put his hand on my shoulder, which is just totally unnecessary. I bear it for a couple of minutes, during which Mum launches into this speech about how we're going to be all right and how we're a strong family, and then I lose it, and I'm like, OK, can you go now?

That shuts her right up, but they comply. Thankfully. It's a downright infringement of my privacy to get me in my own bedroom, I think, which everyone knows is totally sacred to the teenager. I mean, they're probably scarring me for life, not that they can see beyond themselves. I send Al a text saying OMIGOD PARNTS + ME R GOING 2 HVE THERPY!!! She sends me one back that says GD. U NEED IT.

84

10

Anyways, to my surprise the therapy happens the very next day. Yeah sure, Mum, it wasn't pre-planned in the slightest. What am I? Retarded or something?

What's totally unfair about it is that The Nun doesn't have to come too, though actually I decide I'm rather glad about this because it turns out she *wants* to come, and when she gets told that she's, like, not invited, she starts whining like she's nasally challenged.

But this is a family thing so I have to come too, she goes.

Mum's like, This is between your father, me and Jaz. You don't have the same kind of problems.

Dad's like, We'll deal with your therapy next year, trying to make a joke out of it, but he can't pull it off so it hangs there in the atmosphere like a cloud of carbon monoxide. Mum gives him her death glare and The Nun decides that Life Is Not Fair and goes up to her room to pray or something.

So this is like, a big-deal family scene.

Our shrink is called Dr Higgs. He's about forty and looks kind of familiar. He has this neutral expression like, frozen on his face and when he frowns or smiles it looks like he's putting it on, which makes him seem like this human computer. He totally deadpan too, so it's a bit like having Morticia Adams treating you, but Mum and Dad seem really pleased when they meet him, and Dad's whole body relaxes when he shakes his hand. When Higgs comes to shake mine I make a point of giving his hand a really firm yank so he knows who he's dealing with. He peers at me like he's giving me some kind of classification already, which I find totally depressing. It's like, This Is Your Type And This Is How I Shall Act To Deal With It.

Mum and Dad get sat on a big white sofa while I'm sat apart from them on an armchair. Higgs shows us to the places, so it's blatantly deliberate, though Mum and Dad don't seem to notice. Quite what this arrangement is supposed to do is beyond me, but presumably the human computer knows what he's on about.

Once we're all settled (it takes Mum an era to get comfortable) Higgs asks me how I feel about being here.

I'm like, Yeah, this is totally what I want to be doing with my Sundays.

Higgs smiles in a kind of I-don't-know-if-that-is-supposed-to-be-funny kind of way and turns to Mum, who he seems to know instinctively is the boss around here.

He's like, So tell me what you've been experiencing.

I'm thinking, Oh shit, which is perfectly justified, since Mum launches into this intergalactic speech about Stuff. It's kind of like a toned-down version of her usual woes, but it goes on for ever, and by the end of it even the guy who gets paid to listen looks dazed. He kind of does his robot smile and says, Why don't we start right at the beginning? which makes me laugh, and then everyone looks at me, so I'm like, a multiple of What?

Higgs is like, Can you tell us why you laughed?

I'm like, Because of your face, which is the truth but it comes out sounding really rude, and Mum hisses, Jarold! like she's ready to slap me or something.

But Higgs stays calm and says not to worry it's a perfectly

normal reaction. I keep trying to decide where it is I've seen him before. So far he's mostly been addressing Mum and Dad, but each time he turns to me I try to get a good look and think hard. For some reason I'm drawing total blanks. Maybe it's just because he looks like what your conscience would look like if it took on human form, like in some *X-Men* episode or something.

Anyway, at first it's like the whole session's this total waste of time, since basically after Mum's rant Higgs just asks all these really dull questions that don't seem to be leading anywhere like, What's everyone's favourite hobby? and, What's the best holiday you've ever had? It's like, who gives a shit? At one point even Mum gets impatient, probably 'cos she wants to start talking about herself again. She's like, Is this really important? Shouldn't we be talking about our feelings towards each other? like she knows this guy's job much better than he does. That's her being a lawyer for you. But Higgs puts her right back in her place by calmly telling her that therapy isn't like some pill you can take that just makes everything OK again – it takes hard work and dedication.

I'm like, Maybe we should just go.

Everyone just ignores me, which makes me kind of mad, but a few minutes later Higgs goes to me, So you're not uncomfortable being here, Jarold? so I guess he must have heard after all.

I'm like, Whatever.

Higgs is like, Do you feel any resentment towards your parents for bringing you here?

I look at Mum and Dad, who both look down at their laps. It's kind of funny. That's when I realise I don't feel resentment so much as pity. It feels like an act of charity or something, me being here, because if I'm honest I guess I think that it's way too late for this sort of thing. There's fucked up and then there's just fucked, and that's what we are.

I'm like, No, not really.

Higgs doesn't look too impressed by my answer, but he can see that I'm not biting so he switches his attention to Dad. He surprises us all by asking him what *he*'s feeling. There's this pause with tumbleweed blowing through it. It occurs to me that I've never thought much about Dad as a separate human being from Mum. Apart from as an idiot, I mean. I look at him now and it doesn't seem fair, and I feel guilty, a bit like I felt with Mr Fellows after the fight.

Dad's like, Well, I don't know . . .

Higgs waits. Dad stares at his lap until it gets to hot for him to look at and then he looks at the far wall instead, where there's this picture of a load of black-and-white diagonal lines. It's a total cryptogram and once I've noticed it I soon find myself totally absorbed by it too.

Mum's snaps us both back to attention by going, Answer him!

Dad stutters a bit and then goes, I just want us to be happy.

Next thing I know is everyone's looking at me again. I realise I've started laughing – like, big time. It's obviously totally inappropriate, but it's like some kind of hysterical reaction or something. And then it turns into crying. Don't ask me why, because crying is not my style. It's like, the most un-ironic thing you can do. I don't know – maybe it's some kind of reflex response to cheesiness or something, like when you see *Titanic* and you cry at the end even though the stupid couple drowning is like, justice or something. Or maybe it's a delayed reaction from being exposed to the sight of Fellows in his leather trousers. In any event

Mum jumps up and rushes to my side (partly for Higgs' benefit, I'm sure) and thrusts her boobs in my face till I'm not crying but gagging instead.

I'm like, Get the hell off me!

Mum ignores this, or maybe she doesn't hear because my voice is, like, muffled by her chest. Of course Higgs finds it all extremely significant, and through the gap in Mum's silk shirt I see him staring at us and reaching for his pad like he's watching some never-before-seen display of mutant behaviour. He notes something down, meanwhile I attempt to prise myself free from Mum's mauling.

I'm like, Don't read into this. It's just a thing.

But why are you crying? goes Higgs. Can you tell us?

He sounds all smug and self-knowledgey, which pisses me off a bit, so I'm like, It's the dust, yeah? in this really sarcastic voice. Mum sighs and goes to sit back down next to Dad, who's watched all this with big fearful eyes that look like they should belong to Bambi, not some grown man.

Higgs is like, so thinking this is all deeply important. I don't know. Maybe it is. Maybe they've been getting to me more than I've realised.

To cut a long therapy session short, it turns out Higgs is on my side. He's like, Jarold is young and it's good that he's got a definite sense of who he is. You (Mum and Dad, who look pretty shocked at this point) need to support him and be there for him when the inevitable difficulties start to arise.

I don't know what the inevitable difficulties are, but Mum and Dad are silent all the journey home, whereas I'm sniggering like a lunatic on the inside, though on the outside I say nothing, since I figure they've got enough shit to deal with. By the time we reach our street Mum is actually weeping a little, and Dad puts his arm round her, and just like that time when we went to see Grandma at the hospital, for this one instant they look like just maybe they do bring each other some happiness from time to time. I suppose there must be a reason they got married in the first place. But then I get to thinking about it and it seems like it can't be right if the only time they're happy is when the shit hits the fan.

That night Mum actually kisses me on the forehead, which normally would have me going, What am I? Like Black Beauty or something? but this time I let it slide. Dad comes in to say goodnight too. He makes a sort of shuffling with his arms from across the room, which is about as close to a hug as we've come in the last five years. I don't know if this means the therapy is working already or if it just means we've reached a new level of screwed-upness. I get a text from Al saying HOW DID IT GO? I send her one back saying FCKED. DN'T ASK.

11

So this is my third shitty day at school. I know, it's like all I have is shitty days. Well, *yeah*. But it's especially shitty because it's a Monday, so I hope you can try and empathise just a tiny bit.

I get cornered by Fuck Face and the Tweedles outside the canteen. It's totally stupid of me, but it's been over a week since the whole writing-on-the-collage incident, and the school's stopped its stupid inquisition into who did it now, so I guess I figured maybe he'd have forgotten about it too, what with being thick and all. No such luck. I've totally let my guard down and me and Al have split up after lunch 'cos she's got maths and I've got a free study. I've got this essay due on *Twelfth Night* which I'm just dying to get stuck into, so I spend a while dawdling and reading the artwork on the wall (it's a total canvas here and the school gave up trying to keep it clean like, years ago). I'm just debating over a few improvements when there's this voice which goes, Well, well, well, like a pantomime villain, and I turn round to see it belongs to Tweedle Dum. Fuck Face and Tweedle Dee are standing behind him like the definition of ugly.

Fuck Face is like, You got some nerve, poof.

There's no chance of me bolting but I give it a go just in case, and the Tweedles instantly span out to my left and right like sheepdogs penning me in. Fuck Face advances and so I look around for help. There's a couple of kids sitting on the wall truanting it not far away. But they're watching what's going on like it's a documentary on the Discovery Channel so you can just forget about relying on them for any help.

Tweedle Dee is going, You're in deep shit, boy, as if I thought maybe they were just going to ask me a few questions for some school project.

I'm like, Listen, it was just a joke, yeah?

Yeah? Trying to be funny were you? goes Tweedle Dum, I don't think old Joe here finds it very funny – do you, Joe?

Fuck Face's nostrils flare and these two great black holes appear in the middle of his face, like they should have a ring put through them or something.

Well, Tweedle Dum goes, We can be funny too.

That doesn't strike me as probable. I'm like, For fuck's sake! and the Tweedles launch into their specialised grunts, which is their way of trying to show contempt. It's like, they must have the most fascinating conversations. Then Fuck Face pushes me against the wall and gives me a full-on blast of his death breath. You've got to feel sorry for the guy, I guess, since he's been afflicted with this thing that means he's never gonna be able to kiss anyone, let alone pass on his genes.

Anyway, I'm like, practically dead already, but I can see he's just getting inspiration for whatever it is he's going to do to me. The Tweedles have a few suggestions. Tweedle Dee's like, Take his pants! and Tweedle Dum's like, Just kick the shit out of him.

So I'm like, preparing myself for the afterlife when salvation arrives in the form of Mr Fellows, who's on patrol duty, slacker-searching. He literally arrives just as the first blow is about to strike, and he's like, What's going on? in this special voice that even the most measly teachers can summon up when they have to. Fuck Face and the Tweedles sort of look at each other in turn like they're swapping expressions or something. The truant kids watching in the background beat a hasty retreat.

Fuck Face is like, Just having a laugh, Sir.

He drops his fist which was looming terrifyingly close and which looked a lot like the hammer of Thor or something.

Fellows is like, Jarold?

I just bow my head, because spragging at this point is totally unnecessary. He's caught them in the act. I'm not really expecting him to do anything much other than tell them to get lost or something, so I'm surprised when he launches into this rant that would have impressed even Mum. Probably he was just looking for some excuse, but boy does he let old Fuck Face have it. He's like, I'm going to call your mother and tell the headmaster and I'm going to be watching you from now on and if you set one foot out of line I'm going to come down on you like a Yorkshire shithouse!

It's always weird when a teacher swears, 'cos it's like supposed to be against their religion or something, except with the ones who try to be all cool, like Dr Head from the science division who's quite young (like, comparatively) and says bugger and shit a lot, like this is supposed to give him kudos (it doesn't – everyone just calls him Dr Dickhead). But when Mr Fellows swears it sounds like the wrath of God. Even Fuck Face, whose destiny is like, to drop out of school, is left trembling by it.

He goes, Sorry, Sir, in this tiny voice like he's been castrated.

Fellows is like, It's not me you should be apologising to.

Fuck Face looks at me aghast. I'm aghast too. Next time

there's going to be no escape, I can see that in his eyes, which are like, burning full of hatred.

He's like, Sorry, in this voice that's like, the opposite of sincere.

Fellows is like, Get out of here.

Once Fuck Face and the Tweedles have fled, I find out that the whole righteous-anger thing has all been for my benefit. Fellows pats my shoulder in this ultra-cringe-worthy, fatherly sort of way, which is downright freaky, not to mention totally unnatural.

He's like, If kids pick on you, don't let them get to you. You have every right to be what you are, Jarold Jones. Just you remember that. Every right in the world. Never let them make you feel ashamed and never let them tell you other-wise. Are you OK?

I'm like, totally not OK, but not because of Fuck Face. It's like, you can tell *him* to come right back and finish the job, because seriously this kind of talk is like being forced to drink milk and orange juice. It's enough to make you long for the good old days of fascism. Since my senses have sort of shut down in an automatic response, I give him a shrug. But Fellows hasn't finished with cliché-ising me yet.

He's like, I mean it. Jarold, I want you to feel you can come to me if you have any problems, OK?

I'm like, OK already.

Fellows is like, And I wanted to talk to you about the last time I saw you. In that club.

All hope of a swift end to this torture vanishes. I'm like, a deeper level of Oh brother.

The thing is, I do understand what it's like, he goes, Discovering you're attracted to other boys and not know-ing what it means. The realisation. And then all the nights lying awake wondering about yourself and wishing you weren't different. I've been through it all. I was young once too, you know.

He says this like it's meant to be a joke, rather than something that actually *is* quite hard to believe. It's weird, 'cos it is always kind of hard to imagine older people you know were once young. Like, trying to see them as teenagers, asking stupid questions and making stupid mistakes, and getting all interested in sex and making jokes about it. I've tried to imagine Mum and Dad when they were younger, but it's like trying to imagine having a third arm or something. It's easy to imagine them as screwed up, because they are, but not as screwed-up sixteen-year-olds.

It's a lonely life, goes Fellows like he's dispensing this blinding pearl of wisdom, But things aren't what they were. Times have changed. I remember how much harder it used to be. You're very lucky, to be growing up now. Thirty years ago you would have found it even worse. Back before Stonewall and the protesting, people like you and me hardly stood a chance.

Being called 'people like you and me' has me practically choking on my own vomit. Fellows clearly mistakes this as a sign that I'm riveted to his every word. I bear it for as long as I can stand and finally I'm like, Can I go now?

Fellows loses his sympathetic smile. He looks at me for a minute like he's not too impressed by what he sees, and then goes, Off you go then, like it was his idea.

Al thinks it's really sweet. We're stood in the corridor looking for loopholes in the scheduling that mean we can get out of doing sport on Tuesdays and Thursdays. We were taking debating, but they kind of cottoned on to the fact that we didn't actually debate ever, and now we've both been ejected. It's compulsory to do sport, but it's just another great example of how stupid rules are, because all the kids who don't like sports, like us, end up just standing around in a field or at the side of a tennis court wasting our time watching balls fly back and forth. It's like, what's the point? Fortunately they always have loopholes, like the debating society. Right now it's looking like our best bet's gonna be to sign on to do handball with Mr Reginald, who's like, a thousand years old and is only employed by the school because he's like, a fixture here and has been around since like, the beginning of civilisation. He can't even remember who he is most of the time, never mind who's supposed to be in his games set.

Anyway, I'm telling Al all about how Fellows saved me from Fuck Face earlier on, and she's going on about how it shows what a decent person Fellows is, instead of rolling her eyes or having any vaguely normal reaction. And when I tell her about the 'It's a lonely life' part, expecting her to at least have enough taste to make a barfing sound, she instead goes all dreamy like it's the most beautiful thing she's ever heard. I give up trying to make her see the light.

I'm like, Sister, you've got it bad for this guy.

Al's like, What are you talking about? She can be pretty stupid when she's not being political.

I'm like, You totally want to bone Fellows.

Al's like, Fuck off, Jaz! She always refuses to admit it when she's got a crush. It's no wonder she's never even come close to getting laid, 'cos she can't even admit this kind of thing to herself. Probably it'll be easier if she really does become a dyke.

At this point Mary shows up with her posse. She hangs out with these like, total clones, Kathy, Louise and Athena, who all have dyed blonde hair and wear ultra-thick eyeliner that makes it look like it must take a lot of effort to hold the lids open. Their look is kind of like rock chick meets cheerleader or something, but it just makes them all look the same. Seriously, it's only from the sound of their voices that you can tell them apart. Athena's got this super-strong Greek accent and a really deep voice, while Kathy sounds like a pipsqueak. Louise is somewhere in between.

Mary's like, Hey, Jaz.

I'm like, Hey.

Al says hi, but no one even looks her way, which irritates the hell out of her, you can tell. She always says hello when Mary and her posse are around, even though privately she's always like, the definition of contempt for them. I guess she's also always had this secret desire to be liked by them, which is pretty normal I suppose, although at the same time totally fucked up.

Mary's like, You still coming on Saturday?

I'm like, Yeah, sure.

Bring some booze! cries Athena in her thick accent, which sounds a bit like foreign neighing. Kathy gives a supersonic giggle and Mary puckers up her lips in this pout that's probably meant to be sexy. I want to tell her, You're wasting your time, darling, but girls like Mary never get the message. She'd probably think a limp dick during sex was just coyness or something.

Al's like, Yeah! We're really looking forward to it. It sounds like it's going to be wild.

This finally draws a response from Mary and the clones, which is four totally blank looks, like this bogey has just launched itself into the conversation. Al kind of simpers and tries to say something else, which just comes out as this mishmash of words and makes no sense whatsoever. It's pretty painful to watch.

Louise is like, What *language* is she speaking? to Kathy, who lets out another glass-breaking giggle.

Then Mary's like, So we'll see you there, to me and she thrusts her boobs out like she's going to do a trick with them or something, and then they all turn together and totter off down the corridor.

Once they've finally gone I'm like, Could someone please call pest control? to Al. But she's like, Shut up! as if I'm totally out of line or something. She's been really irritable lately. I guess it's because of her parents, who are, like, applying for a diploma in being anal. But I don't see why she has to take it out on me. Maybe it's because of her unrequited love for Fellows, though the very idea of them together is a complete gross-out.

12

Anyways, if you're even a tiny bit on my side, you're gonna be wondering about Jon. What happened next with him? you must be crying, shivering with anticipation. Well, I'll tell you.

I call him up the night before in my room, while Mum and Dad are vegged out downstairs, recovering from the shock of being told about their issues. It's a mobile, and it rings for a few and then:

Y'ello, says Jon.

I'm ashamed to admit it, but I'm like, so totally lame here. In trying to be funny I say Orange! which gets met with this big pause. I'm tempted to slam the phone right back down and spend the rest of my life being a monk, but I take a deep breath and go, It's me, Jaz.

I think I can hear him smirking. It's like this series of weird vibrations down the phone, like there's a poltergeist interfering or something.

Jon's like, Hey, what's that music in the background?

It's some impressively naff boy band The Nun's listening to, which she's playing on full volume. It's almost like she knows I'm doing something important, through some sisterly sixth sense. I go over to the door and kick it shut.

I'm like, Just get over it, OK?

More smirking sensations. He's like, So how's it going?

I'm like, Great, how's the snorkelling?

Windsurfing.

I know. Whatever.

He's like, You know something, you've really got a chip on your shoulder.

I'm like, Do you wanna meet up or what?

And he does, so we do. We make arrangements to meet on Wednesday night, at this club which I've never been to, but is supposed to be really underground. I try to drag Al along, but of course she's like, locked in these days. (Right after my phone call that night Mum actually calls up Mr and Mrs Rutland for a healthy discussion about our influence on each other, not suspecting that she was singlehandedly fucking up the girl's entire life – her parents both had, like, consecutive aneurisms when they found out she'd been going to a *gay* club.) Of course Al's perfectly capable of breaking a window, but she's like, determined to go to this lame party of Mary's so she's trying to play it safe this week. So when school is over I'm like, on my own. I figure to hell with it – either you do or you die.

I get into this club by the skin of my teeth – I'm right behind this punk with a blue mohican who throws this total hissy fit about having to pay to get in (it's like three quid, which even I can afford), but it turns out to be a good thing 'cos the girl kind of shies away from even looking at me, and the bouncer just jostles me along. So Bob's your uncle, I'm in.

This place lends new meaning to the word dive: it's like, artfully so. There's heavy metal coming out of the speakers from all sides of the room, while people are like, jumping up and down (it's so packed there's not much space, so I guess they have to dance upwards). It's basically this big mosh pit with trashed guys and girls with long black hair and lots of silver flinging themselves around, a bit like the zombies in

100

that vintage Michael Jackson video. I'm like, This so is not my scene. And I've no clue how I'm supposed to spot Jon in here. I'm looking down at my Levi's and T-shirt and thinking Shit – since I stand out like a hick in *Beverly Hills 90210*. I decide I'll give it one drink and fight my way to the bar, which is like going to war or something. The goth there doesn't even listen to what I ask her for, and I finally get served with this weird green stuff, which tastes of aniseed and actually isn't too bad. In fact, once you roll with it, the whole joint is kind of OK in an alternative sort of way. They're playing some Guns N'Roses track which I dimly remember listening to when I was, like ten, but that's kind of OK too. And at least I'm never ever gonna bump into Fellows here, which is a definite plus.

After a few minutes the skinhead on my right tries to chat me up, or at least shout me up, over the music. It takes me a while to figure out what he's saying. He's going, I'm so into your look – it's really unique!

I'm like, Thanks. I guess he thinks it's ironic. He's wearing ripped leather and has a skull pendant which dangles over his groin kind of amusingly. He grins at me and I'm thinking Oh shit man, leave me alone, since he's, like, so not my type. Fortunately at this point Jon appears. He's wearing this net thing which would probably look totally faggy on anyone else, but on him looks totally gorgeous. I rapidly start to feel better about this whole manoeuvre.

I'm like, Hey, is this your kind of scene?

He grins and shrugs, and shouts in my ear, I'm very adaptable! and then give me this sexy look in case I'm in any doubt as to what he means. I'm like, so there, man.

He orders a drink – of water, if you can believe it, and starts fiddling with the side pocket on his trousers. The skinhead sees this as an opportunity to move in again, and starts shouting in my ear some stuff about how he wants to show me his tattoo and will I come to the bathroom with him to see it?

I'm like, mouthing Help Me to Jon, who finally stops fiddling, licks his fingers and comes to rescue. He just leans forward, pushes this guy away and kisses me, and the next thing I know is his tongue is in my mouth, and there's something on it. Before I've even thought about what it is, I've swallowed. Then I realise. I'm like, so pissed off, and I shove him away.

Jon's goes, Hey, what's the deal? That's a good pill.

This'll probably make you snigger some, but until this point I've managed to remain a blissfully vitamin E-free zone. I tried a dab of coke in the toilet with some guy at Starlight (one of the fumblers), and weed is obviously always good for a rainy day, but this is totally new for me, and I'm not sure if I'm ready for it. Still, I didn't spit it out. I swallowed. Joke. Ha ha.

I'm like, Yeah, well thanks.

He's like cottoned on to my reaction, and looks a bit guilty. You don't do them? he says. I shrug, since what's the use of making a big deal out of it now?

Anyway, we shout at each other for a bit more over the music, and pretty soon we're kissing again, and I'm think-ing that this is totally the night for it when I start to get this little tingle at the back of my spine. It starts right at the bottom and gradually travels upwards, till it's at my neck, and all of a sudden I'm dancing crazy and so's Jon, and I can't stop myself. But it's great. I'm telling you, I feel like I'm flying through the stars or something. There's all these sparks of happiness just igniting all across my body and it's like I'm on this new level where everything's just fucking wonderful. Nothing can stop me.

We wind up back at Jon's. I'm going to be in so much shit with Mum and Dad the next day, I'm thinking, but who cares? It's like, three o'clock, and I'm still feeling good, though I've kind of got used to it now and maybe it's even starting to wear off a bit.

We get a taxi, 'cos the idea of the bus is a total turn-off. I pretend to be too wrecked to function when the time comes to pay, since I used up the last of my money on the aniseed alcopop, but then I come right around once Jon's dealt with that little situation. Turns out he's staying in this flat in Kensington, which is totally swank. He reminds me that it belongs to his friend who's out of the country. I'm like, What are they, royalty?

We go to the kitchen, which is so big you can like, run and it'll still be a few seconds before you reach a wall. Jon makes us some tea and I hang around watching his cute behind as he gets out the cups.

So what's the deal with the age thing? I hear myself asking him all of a sudden. I don't know why I do – it must be this like, self-destructive urge to spoil everything or something.

He's like, Just a thing I have. When I was small my dad was always seeing younger men, and I always swore to myself I wouldn't turn into him.

That totally shuts me up for the next few minutes while the tea brews. While he drinks it he goes into greater detail about his parents. Turns out they were totally fucked up too. He had this crazy gay dad who used to offer him speedballs, and this Barbie-doll mom who was, like, obsessed with plastic surgery and now looks like the Bride of Wildenstein. By the time he's finished I'm almost at the stage where I'm glad of who my parents are. Almost but not even.

We go to the bedroom and Wow. It's like one of those penthouse suites from the perfume ads where everything is impossibly perfect. The walls look like they're lined with silver and there are pillars, like, from a temple around the door and windows. There are red silk sheets on this bed that's, like, a mile wide, and on the ceiling there's this mirror so you can, like, watch yourself doing it.

Jon's like, What do you think?

I'm like, It's OK.

He thinks this is funny, and he gives me this affectionate poke which turns into a full-on grope. I give him one back and we kind of flop on to the bed, kissing. But then the weirdest thing happens. This great wave of stuff comes over me. Like, stuff. I don't know how else to describe it. I have all these good and bad feelings, like a total nostalgia overload. It's feelings about all these random people I can't stop thinking about. Like Fabian, and how we used to be friends and how sad it is that we don't hang out any more because he's this screwed up Nazi loser now. Like Mary and how she fancies me and how sad it is for her because she could have any boy in the school but she wants me and it's never gonna happen. Or Teresa (if you can believe it), and how maybe beyond the whole religious thing and beyond the whole spoilt-brat thing she's actually just this confused teenage girl and that's kind of a sad thing too. I even think of Fellows and how sad it is 'cos he does genuinely mean well even if he doesn't know the difference between his mouth and his anus.

So we're like, kissing and all that on the bed and I'm not feeling it. This should be really great. I've like, totally had a hard-on for this guy since I first laid eyes on him. He keeps moving his hand down to my cock, but it's just not working like it should. It's not stage fright either, which I've never had a problem with. It's just that I've got this woozy sensation all over and I can't seem to concentrate. The truth is this bed is so nice and big I just wanna shut my eyes and roll around on it.

Jon's like, Oh fuck, you're one of those.

I'm like, One of what?

Jon's like, You can't get it up on E.

I'm like, Oh. It seems to make sense, and in a way it's all pretty funny, since he was the one who tongued me with it. But he's horny, and he keeps trying to grab me. I give it another go, but all of a sudden sex is the last thing on my mind. I'm getting these ideas about what Mum and Dad are gonna think if they wake up and somehow discover that I'm not in my room. They'll either disown me or padlock all the exits, I think, which is stupid because all that'll happen is the same thing that always happens, which is that Mum'll go on a death rave and Dad'll stand there behind her trying to look like he matters. It's the drug that has me all bothered, I'm sure, but it's weird and I just can't stop thinking about it. I have this overpowering feeling that I need to be home, back in my own bed. Then, and this is like, *über*-weird, I find myself actually missing Mum.

Jon's like, totally stunned when I say I have to leave. He pleads with me not to, but I'm like, totally focused on this new mission. It's the E, it must be, 'cos it feels great to actually have this journey planned out ahead of me. To be actually going home.

At first he walks with me along the road to the bus stop, saying that he doesn't get it but he knows someone else who can't sleep in other people's beds and oh well he doesn't mind so long as I don't have any flatmates who are going to be annoyed by us getting in so early in the morning. He goes on and on, and it must be something about the E too

105

because I didn't know he could be such a talker. There's like, smoke coming off his jaw from so much use.

Once we're at the stop I realise I can't have him come back to Mum and Dad's. Without thinking I kind of go ahead and say so, whereupon his face literally gains another six inches as his mouth drops open. Whoops. Forgot about that.

How old *are* you? he demands.

I'm like, completely found out, but I tell him I'm seventeen to ease the pain a little. He looks like he's going into shock or something. He kind of drops to his knees and goes all foetal, and then starts rocking back and forth repeating Fuck, oh fuck! in this tinsey-winsey little voice like he's just found out that death exists or something.

Just chill, I tell him.

Don't you tell me to chill! he goes, and he sounds really like he's about to explode. For a minute I think I'm going to have a fight on my hands. Jon's quite big like, in terms of body weight, and there's no way I'd stand much of a chance against him (but just in case I prepare my fingers for Uma Thurman's eye-jabbing move in *Kill Bill II*).

I'm like, Listen, what's the big deal?

Jon's like, You're just a fucking kid!

I'm like, Get a clutch.

But he clearly has like, the issue of issues over this because there's no talking to him. All of a sudden he jumps up, spins round and punches the shelter, which I think hurts but he doesn't say anything about it. Instead he's like, I can't believe I gave ecstasy to a seventeen-year-old. I can't believe I almost screwed a seventeen-year-old.

I'm like, What are you, statistically challenged or something?

He just shakes his head, and meanwhile I'm starting to

think this is boring and that I just need to get back home and hug Mum and Dad or something. Then everything'll be OK. I wish I felt like this about them normally.

Anyway, at this point the night bus comes and I kind of leave Jon glowering at the stop and ride off into the night. I feel bad about this later, since I figure I've kind of killed off our relationship before it's even begun. I suppose it is pretty mean of me, but he did give me the E, even if he wishes he hadn't. Anyway, I'm like, totally dazed from that euphoric experience, and I've got to admit that now I see what all the fuss is about. Nice, man.

Back at home, no sooner do I get in the door than I'm falling all over the place. I can't seem to function properly, and pretty soon Mum and Dad have heard the noise and are like, surrounding me, and I guess it's pretty obvious that I'm not on my bestest, most normal behaviour.

Mum's like, Oh my God!

Dad's like, Jarold, do you understand what I'm saying?

I like, slur back at him, Yes, Dad, but it comes out sounding more like 'shag'.

Mum's like, We need to take him to the hospital right away. What if his blood starts boiling or his brain over-heats! which is exactly the sort of thing I don't need to be hearing. But I don't really care. I'm so glad to be home and to see them. I'm in full-on la-la land.

Dad stays quite sane while Mum goes to the side of the room to freak out big time. He holds me up and peers into my eyes like a doctor, at which point I throw my arms around him and tell him I'm sorry, and then Mum comes over and I give her the same treatment, and she goes all mushy too, and then we're in tears and hugging, and then Dad's the one backing to the side of the room, totally freaked by it. Mum like, carries me in her arms to the living

107

room and tells me what a wonderful thing life is and how she loves me and she doesn't care about who I am or anything so long as I stay her little boy.

I'm like, Of course, I'll always be your little boy, which is totally the E talking because there's no way I would ever say something as barfable as that if I wasn't utterly spasticated.

And that's the last thing I remember. I must have fallen asleep in Mum's arms. When I wake up she's sitting on my bed and leaning over me like Florence Nightingale, asking me how I feel in this tender voice, so I can tell instantly she remembers what I said. It takes a minute for the rest of it to come flooding back, and then I groan inwardly, because I know I can just kiss goodbye to fun from now on. Mum obviously thinks I've learned a Big Lesson from the incident, which is like, so not the case.

The Nun comes in to see me a bit later with a plate of cookies and a cup of tea. She acts like I'm a total invalid, but at least she doesn't try to pray over me or anything because I can't even be bothered with her right now. Later on in the day, by the time I'm feeling perfectly fine but am pretending not to be and wondering how long I can make this last for, Grandma hobbles up to see me.

She's like, Your mother says you've got flu.

I'm like, Yeah but it's OK, I'm feeling much better now.

Grandma smiles and nods. She sits there for a few minutes, still smiling and looking kind of daft, and it suddenly occurs to me that she really hasn't been the same since her stroke, and that maybe she's never going to be the same. This thought just strikes me as so awful that tears come to my eyes. Like I said, I don't cry, so it must just be an after-effect from the E. Grandma looks down at me and goes, What's the matter, Jaz?

I'm like, I don't know, Grandma.

She nods as if this were just the answer she'd expected and starts looking around the room.

Why do you have all those posters up of that young man? she goes, for like, the hundredth time.

13

So like, just because I can, I'm zooming this thing forward to what's going to seem like this completely random scene where me and Al are standing in the dark and freezing cold on a platform in Brighton station.

Al's going, I can't fucking believe this.

She's talking about our rations, which I'm supposed to be in charge of, which I have just left on the train, which is now long gone, and which we're staring down the track after like a couple of spastics.

I didn't mean to, I forgot! I'm whining, like that somehow means it wasn't my fault.

Al's yelling, How could you forget? That was our food!!!

I'm like, So we'll just get a burger somewhere.

Al's like, We're supposed to be on a budget! We're meant to be cooking noodles in the hostel. We can't afford burgers!

She chews me up for a bit longer until I finally lose it and go, Shit happens, Sister!

Not on my watch! cries Al.

The next shit thing to happen is that Al realises she's forgotten to book the hostel, which is now closed for the night (it's nearly two). We start yanking out the contents of our rucksacks, trying to find our guidebook for other hostels. But Saint Bastard is watching over us and so it's nowhere to be found.

You fucking idiot! I scream at her, You fucking get in a strop with me about the fucking food and then forget the fucking book!

Al puts her hands on her ears and sobs. I go on quite a bit, lots of fuckings, and I start getting quite emotional about it, and then Al suddenly starts screaming back, Fuck you, Jarold! You only ever think of yourself! I'm only *here* because of you! Because you wanted to run away so you can suck dick for the rest of your life without ever giving a shit about anything or anyone but yourself!

I'm like, thinking, Where did this come from? but I just start walking off towards the other end of the platform, which is a totally stupid place to walk to because it's like, where am I gonna go next?

I remember that I've got the cigarettes so I light one up, even though it means taking my hands out of my pockets and exposing them to potential frostbite. I'm trying to think of the best course of action, but the only thing I can come up with is throwing myself in front of the next train, which I've heard is a really gory way to go.

After ten minutes of standing at opposite ends of the platform, both stewing, Al finally walks over to me. We look at each other warily, kind of like WWF wrestlers assessing each other's stats.

She's like, Look, I'm sorry, OK.

I'm like, Yeah, me too.

We go and sit on the bench, balancing each other's heads on our shoulders and shivering in like, harmony.

Station's closing! calls this guy in a uniform. Everyone off the platform!

Al's like, We're gonna die, aren't we, Jaz? and just as I'm about to agree how we're well and truly fucked my hand touches upon this little piece of card in my coat pocket. I

111

take it out and look at it, and see that it's a business card with a pair of flippers decorated around the address. Al sees it and immediately understands. She can be pretty sharp sometimes, and if she doesn't become a politician I wouldn't be very surprised if she becomes like, a hostage negotiator instead.

She's like, Just do it. Call him and get it over with.

I'm like, Oh shit.

Since on our phones between us we've now got about enough credit for one text message (we both got new SIMS in case our parents decided to, like, trace us, but then kind of forgot about the other important thing), we go to look for a payphone. The one in the station looks like someone's kicked it to pieces, plus the guy in the uniform gives us this look like he wants to have us arrested or something so we have to go outside.

It's like one of those comedy disaster films where just when you think things can't possibly get any worse, they do. Somebody somewhere must actually have this hobby where they go round all the phones in town and wedge gum in the slots, probably hoping cold, hungry kids like me and Al will be the ones who suffer because of it, and end up getting sold into slavery or something.

We walk around screaming for a while, which is probably a good thing because it warms us up a little bit, though not much, considering it's like, the ice age or something, but after a bit we find ourselves out of phone boxes and walking down this totally deserted street.

After about five minutes of walking I look back and get the shock of my life because there's this figure in a long coat walking quickly towards us. It looks like Death is coming for us. I'm like, Oh fuck, and Al looks round and lets out a little shriek.

112

We pick up pace, which isn't easy considering the circulation has practically stopped in our legs, and turn the corner hoping to lose him. We find ourselves facing the cruellest wind known to man. Seriously, it's like, blinding and you literally have to run into it to get anywhere. But when I look back I get the second shock of my life. I see that the figure in the coat is now like, ten steps away from us. His face is hidden by this big hood and it's the scariest thing ever, like *Scream* or some horror film. At this point there doesn't seem to be any sense in trying to avoid him so we stop dead in the hope that he'll go on past us. He doesn't.

In this super-deep voice, like Sauron, the figure goes, Good evening.

Al's arm tightens around mine like a metal clamp.

I'm like, Hi, in this tiny trembling little voice that's hardly even there.

Are you lost? Do you need somewhere to stay for the night? says the voice. I'll tell you what. There's some space back at my place.

I'm like, That's OK, thanks. We're all right, literally shaking like a train.

Come on now, goes the voice, Why don't you let me help you out? It's very warm and comfortable.

He takes a step towards us. I whisper in Al's ear one word: Run. We throw ourselves into the wind and battle for our lives. Seriously, we're like, swimming against it here. And it's terrifying because neither of us can even bear to look behind and see if he's running after us, so we don't stop until we've reached the end of the road, which is like, the source of the wind and is like standing on top of a mountain. But when I dare to peek the figure's gone – thank Fuck.

We turn the corner before our faces get blown off, and find ourselves on yet another deserted street. It's like, where is everybody?

We need to get back to the station, Al goes.

I'm like, OK, though I don't really see why, unless she figures they'll have the most comfortable benches outside for us to sleep on.

She's like, Hey, I recognise this road, in this voice that's more like, hopeful than believable. I'm pretty sure I know how to get back and it's not how she thinks, but my mouth's too frozen to argue so I let her lead the way. Next thing we know there's this police car which has just materialised out of nowhere and is driving straight down the road towards us. Al's all for waving our arms and surrendering to them, but I tell her I haven't come this far only to be packaged up and sent back home all gift-wrapped for Mum to tear into pieces.

I'm like, You want to do that you go right ahead and do it. I'd rather freeze.

Al wavers for a second but then she walks with me into this alley which I figure the cops won't be able to follow us down. I figure it'll probably take us back to the main road where we started. But when we come out on the other side we're on a different road completely, and instead of turning back I keep going, and then pretty soon I realise that I'm totally lost. Al's like, We're going round in circles! You've got us lost! like she seriously had a clue.

This backstreet we're on is totally dark and dodgy, and the buildings along it are all messed up and falling to pieces. Al has the bright idea of trying to read her map, but she fumbles with it for ages since neither of us can hold it because we've lost all sensation. While she's getting her bearings I suddenly see this movement in the distance, and that's when I get the third shock of my life. It's The Figure again, and this time it looks like he's running straight at us. Like, *fast*.

I'm, like, the definition of Oh fuck.

Al looks up and sees him. She's like, Oh my God, he wants our kidneys!

We take off like crazy people, and then just keep running for the hell of it. I can't understand where all the people are, since I thought Brighton was supposed to be party central or something. It's deader than a graveyard, and totally eerie. We finally stop to breath and let our insides catch up and Al bursts into tears.

She's like, I just want to go home! like this complete baby.

I expected better from her. But to be honest I'm starting to feel the same way. It's like we've got two choices: either freeze to death or get murdered and have our organs sold by The Ripper, who's probably on our trail this very second. I can feel the urge to start crying too and I'm not the sort who cries. Like *ever*.

Then, just as we're about to lie down and like, die of hopelessness, the police car magically re-materialises. Even I'm glad to see it now. It draws up right beside us and the window rolls down. There's this middle-aged copper with cross eyes who looks like he seriously shouldn't be driving. He peers between me and Al and says, You kids all right?

I'm like, Yeah, in this thin little voice that's hardly even there.

His partner, who's obviously this hard-as-nails, by-the-book bitch, looks across at us like we're filth of the earth. What are you kids doing out so late? she goes, like she thinks we're prostitutes or something.

I'm like, trying to think fast, which isn't easy considering my brain's become this lump of ice inside my head.

We're trying to get to my uncle's house, I wail, But I can't remember the way.

Thankfully the policeman is one of those none-too-bright types, which might explain the cross eyes. Either that or he's just one of those people destined for a life of being taken advantage of, because I read him the address on the card all tearful like I can't believe this is happening to me, and just like I was hoping he goes, Ach! Just hop in the back and we'll run you over, it's only up the road.

We claw our way into the car. I give Al a nudge so she knows I'm watching her in case she was thinking of blowing my story. While we sit there thawing, Cross Eyes starts telling us about what a slow night they're having and how he's having trouble keeping awake. The Bitch beside him doesn't say anything at first, but I can see the reflection of her face in the window. She looks like the sort who thinks fun is something that happens to other people. After listening to her partner for a few minutes she brutally interrupts him midway through telling us about the contents of his lunchbox today by turning round and going, So what are your *names* then? like she doesn't believe we'll have any.

I'm like, super-fast, Richard and Judy (oh shit).

She's like, That's a TV show.

I'm like, Yeah, I know, we get it really bad at school.

It's just as well that Al sounds like a cross between a dying horse and a dying dog when she laughs 'cos otherwise we'd have been totally rumbled. Alarmed, the bitch looks at her and goes, Are you all right? and Al nods and tries to turn her head one hundred and eighty degrees to hide her smirk. The bitch looks totally suspicious now. I can see her

116

thinking of more questions to ask and I just know that what with my frozen brain cells there's no way I'm gonna be able to keep this up.

Here we are, chirps Cross Eyes, drawing up next to this swanky-looking place. It's got those modern sliding windows and a little patio balcony thing that's sort of a garden as well. I'm thinking that there must be some mistake but I see the number on the door and sure enough, this is it.

I'm like, Thanks so much, trying to get out of there as fast as possible. We'd better go 'cos he's gonna be worried sick.

The Bitch looks pretty sceptical and points out that all the lights are off. I pretend not to hear her and bundle Al out of the car. We climb the steps to the door and stand there debating. Because even after all this hassle I'm not sure if I can face just turning up out of the blue at this guy's place in the middle of the night.

They're waiting, Al hisses in my ear.

I'm like, Shit.

I reach out and press the buzzer, and hold it down for, like, twenty seconds. There are all these sounds from inside the flat and lights are switched on. The door opens a crack and this bleary-eyed face which just about resembles Jon appears in it. He takes in the sight of us with our backpacks and the police car behind us. His whole face like, lengthens.

I'm like, Surprise.

14

So I bet you think you can guess where all this is going, and if you happen to be right, just remember one thing, which is LIC GAS. But just in case you're confused, don't worry, it's all going to come together. Somehow. Maybe.

Anyway, this chapter is going to be dedicated to The Nun, aka my sister Mother Teresa. There's, like, this whole history between us as siblings, like you'd probably expect us to have, and also it kind of seems a bit unfair that I haven't really included her much so far, since she's always around – more's the pity. But there's also this thing that I go and do too, which you kind of need to make sense of.

Being only a year older, I can't remember when I first became aware of her or anything like that, 'cos it's like she's always been there. And 'cos she's only a year younger she doesn't really get treated differently to me, apart from being a girl, which for some reason qualifies her for more allowance and more sympathy (though like, I could care less about the sympathy).

But we didn't always hate each other either. Back when we were tots we actually used to get on. We even used to play together – we even used to take *baths* together, if you can believe it. I remember once devising this really cool game where I'd lie down on the living-room carpet with my legs up in the air with my feet together like this sort of platform. She'd sit on them and then I'd bend my knees and launch her into the air. I was always trying to get her to go splat against the far wall of the living room like a cartoon character, but I never quite managed to launch her far enough, and one time she landed on her ankle instead of her foot and started bawling. Mum put a stop to it right away, as she always did with anything the second she suspected it of becoming even remotely enjoyable.

The bath-times are this super-shaming piece of our history together which The Nun likes to bring up when the whole family's together, like we're all supposed to find it really cute and laugh about it or something. Probably it was cute back then, but seeing how Teresa's turned out the idea of it now is like, totally gross and weird. But in a way it's quite a sad story really, and of course the reason for it being sad is all to do with Mum. I remember our last bath together, which was when we were like, eight and seven, and how Dad let us use some of Mum's bubble bath and we were building things out of it, giving ourselves beards and stuff. Then Mum comes back from work after having read this magazine article on teenage deviancy. Dad's downstairs watching TV and she asks him where we are and when he tells her we're where we always are on a Tuesday night she has like, multiple paroxysms. I actually have the memory to cherish of her marching into the bathroom and pulling me out of the tub by my neck, like me and Teresa are having incest or something. So that's like, this massive rift in our childhood, and probably the reason we're so different and hate each other is all totally Mum's fault.

But I guess we really stopped getting on around the same time it became clear that Teresa was one of those freaks who actually enjoys studying, which prompted Mum and

Dad to enrol her in this prissy convent school up the road from us where she's seen as like, their star pupil or something. The one time I went there, which was with Mum to watch her perform in some crappy play, it was immediately clear to me that all the teachers and nuns have got like, major crushes on her. They kept running up to us and congratulating us for being like, related to her, and when she came on at the end to take a bow the Sister sat next to us was positively weeping with joy. Probably she's being molested or something, which is why she's all screwed up and religious now. You don't have to be Derren Brown to figure out the nuns there are basically just a bunch of lezzers in total denial of themselves. Plus you've already met The Order, so you know what her friends are like.

Anyway, once we started going to the separate schools we kind of stopped getting along too. All of a sudden she was coming back with these coloured ribbons for having like, the biggest vocabulary in her class or being able to braid her hair blindfolded with one hand tied behind her back or something, and meanwhile I was discovering that basically school is just a load of wankers, some of whom teach and the rest of whom sit next to you in class. So we kind of developed different outlooks and just got further and further apart until we were at like, opposite ends of the spectrum. We still had the odd moments of being civil though, right up until last year I guess. Like once or twice we'd share a joke, or Dad would say something lame or Mum would freak out about a piece of fluff on the carpet and we'd be like, united in pity for them. But then she refused to call me Jaz and I started calling her The Nun and then the Devil started possessing her and now it's like, if Mum and Dad ever do split up we're so not gonna end up living with the same parent. Probably we'd both make a beeline for Dad, but I'll settle for Mum if it comes to it.

About three years ago The Nun got this pet rabbit as a reward for acing her exams. I was offered the same deal but I couldn't be bothered and besides back then I wanted a PlayStation, which Mum refused to get me 'cos she said it induced violent behaviour, as if I was just this robot waiting to be programmed. What Teresa actually wanted was a horse, like every other teenage girl seems to want (there's, like, this gene for it or something), but she had to settle for this bunny. She spent ages trying to decide on what to call it. Eventually it got called Rabbity, which just goes to show that being clever doesn't also guarantee you'll be creative.

When she got Rabbity it was this huge deal. Dad called me downstairs to the kitchen to like, welcome this new member of the family. They gave it to her all wrapped up in this box in shiny silver paper, so the poor bunny must have felt like it was in a coffin or something. I think that's cruel. I'm not a vegetarian or anything, but I do think putting an animal in a small box with no windows is pretty cruel, 'cos it's kind of like being buried alive. Al's like, totally pro-animal rights, and sometimes she goes on about the poor foxes or minks getting made into coats and how would you like it if it was done to you? I say if you've ever seen a real live mink you lose sympathy for them pretty fast 'cos they're horrible animals, always wanting to get their claws at your eyes. You can make 'em into tea cosies for all I care. But I wouldn't be so cruel as to stick them in a small box covered with wrapping paper.

The rabbit sort of nosed its way out of the box, all suspicious like it didn't trust anyone. Teresa took one look at it and started leaping up and down a bit like one herself,

121

and screaming with joy. This was the first thing the poor rabbit must have seen, so it's not really surprising it retreated right back inside the box again.

Teresa was like, She's the cutest thing I've ever seen! She started poking the box, trying to get it to come out again.

Mum and Dad both had these ridiculous smiles on their faces like The Joker or something. They always get these smiles that look like they've been airbrushed on whenever we're together as a family and are supposed to be having one of those scenes which magazines and stuff tell you are meant to be timeless. They sure feel like it. But it's a load of bullshit really, 'cos it's all totally fake, and like I've said the only time Mum and Dad really look like they're genuinely glad to be together is when something fucks up and they have each other to hold on to.

Anyway, this rabbit finally got emptied out of the box and The Nun was all ga-ga over her and we all played pass the bunny and that was that. New member of the family recruited. But it's kind of funny, 'cos Dad got to hate that rabbit with a passion. It was winter and The Nun was supposed to be keeping it in her room but it started to stink the place out because it kept soiling the carpet. It turned out Rabbity could produce droppings like a factory. So in the end Mum told her she could bring it downstairs and let it run around on the kitchen floor so long as she promised to shovel up afterwards.

Dad couldn't stand it. This was before he became a chef at Breeze and he had this job where he was supposed to be assisting this writer by testing out her recipes for her. The Nun basically moved her whole life to the kitchen and whenever he was cooking he'd have to play dodge with this rabbit. It became like, totally normal to hear him shouting Ouch! or something even ruder if he was carrying stuff. It went on for weeks, and Dad grew to hate that rabbit like it was his own personal nemesis. He was always trying to get Teresa to trade it in for a nice quiet turtle or something, but of course she was having none of it because she thought of it as her baby or something and even thought the droppings were cute.

Anyway, so Dad was always tripping or getting burnt or something, while the bunny never got injured once, until this one fateful day when Dad dropped like this whole vat of caramel on it, which pretty much boiled the poor thing alive right there on the floor. It was kind of gross, 'cos there was all this congealed brown stuff all over its fur and it was all mangled and bloody in places. Plus it stayed alive all the way to the vet, who saw right away there wasn't much hope for it and put it down. It's a pretty horrible way to go. The Nun was traumatised by it, and Dad was like, guilty as. For the whole of the next year he was super-nice to The Nun and kept cooking little treats for us all and stuff, and she got quite used to this treatment and whenever she wanted something that she wasn't supposed to be allowed she'd just launch into tears about Rabbity. He probably would have even bought her a bloody horse if Mum hadn't put her foot down about it. That's how we ended up with Bilbo. To shut her up, basically.

But, and this is the important bit, right after Rabbity got stewed Teresa was so devastated she cried in her room for a whole week and refused to even look at Dad or talk to anyone else. Meanwhile we had this rabbit body decomposing in a black bag on the back doorstep. The vet had offered to dispose of it but Teresa had screamed at the idea that it might not get a proper Christian burial, so when her week of mourning was up it got taken out into the back garden and given this whole ceremony. It was still cold and icy and Dad pretty much bust his back digging out a trench for it to go in, which must just have made him hate Rabbity even more. He also had to shell out for this baby tree, which was The Nun's idea, which they planted over the top of it to like, symbolise its spirit or something. She took pretty good care of that tree though. Sometimes, when she wasn't talking to Jesus or God, she'd go and stand in front of it. Mum and Dad never knew, I think, but she was whispering stuff to it, like the tree really was Rabbity now. I know this 'cos I heard her when I was having a secret smoke behind our old shed this one time. It was pretty freaky, but maybe you'll find it touching if you've got like, a soft spot for girls who miss their fluffy dead pets. As far as I know she was still going out there to whisper her secrets to it right up to the point where I kicked it down.

Yeah. That's what I did. I don't know exactly why. I mean, I was kind of in shock, I suppose, over this thing that happened that day. I was kind of feeling all angry at her too, and my whole perspective was totally like, angular. I guess that probably won't excuse it to you, and I've got to admit it wasn't too lovely of me, but all I'm trying to say here is it wasn't like I did it because I'm evil or anything. I was just wandering back and forth in this straight line (our garden's pretty small so there's not much else you can do) and I was looking at this tree and feeling really mad at like, The World. And I kept thinking about The Nun and how she'd informed on me going out and how smug she'd been about it and how much I hated her. She just became like, this focus of everything that'd gone wrong, like *ever*. And then I noticed the tree and I just thought Fuck it and next thing I knew I'd given it like this full-on roundhouse, which I practise in my room sometimes and which I'm pretty good at doing. And then I was kicking it and kicking it for all I

124

was worth. After my fit finally subsided I looked down and saw that the tree was now just, like, a log and stump and I was in deep shit. But the worst thing was I didn't even care. It was like I'd totally lost my clutch.

15

So, stepping back in time here, Mum's got this new curfew thing going on, which is where she says I can go out at the weekend but I've got to be back before twelve. Also she wants this like, detailed plan of what I'm going to be doing and says she's going to call me halfway through the evening to make sure of it, which is like, lamest of the lame. Anyway, she knows all about Mary's party 'cos somehow it's become like, this legend at school and everybody wants to go to it (apparently), and even the teachers and parents know it's happening.

Al takes like, a century to get ready. When she finally comes downstairs after leaving me to deal with a total overload of awkwardness with her Mum (who spends the whole time gabbing about school and is super-careful not to come within a metre's distance of me), she's wearing this miniskirt and low-cut red top and has got blonde extensions clipped to her hair. She's even got *heels* on. It's basically just like the kind of get-up Mary and her posse totter around in.

Hi there, Al goes in this deep, throaty voice.

I'm like, What are you referencing?

She's like, I just felt like I'd try a change, all breezily like she's undergone some dramatic de-spectacle-isation scenario and emerged a beauty queen.

Darling, are you sure you should be wearing that top? goes Mrs Rutland nervously.

Al waves her off and then we leave for the party. All the way there Al's teetering like any second she's gonna do a forward flip. I'm sure it's going to be a total drag but she's all geared up, being the kind of kid who never gets invited to this gang's dos. Right at the last minute I go, Are you sure you want to do this? but she totally insists on it and tells me she'll never forgive me if I don't take her on this like, golden opportunity to be made to feel insecure for the rest of her life.

Mary's house is in Kensington and it's pretty posh. The second we walk up the drive you can hear the usual whoops and laughs and my heart's just sinking at the prospect of putting myself through this, but we've come this far so we keep on going. On the porch there're a couple of older kids I've never seen before drinking beer and smoking a joint while at the same time being like, bouncers or something. Seeing them makes me a little hopeful that inside there might actually be some vaguely cool people, so I chin up a bit. We're friends of Mary's, I go and they smile and nod and gesture for us to go inside.

No sooner have we got in the door than Mary is on top of me. She must have been watching at the window like some heroine in a Victorian novel or something. She appears out of nowhere with this smile which is totally blinding even without much light on it, and then like, welds herself to my arm. She's wearing this glittery black top which her boobs are like, overflowing out of. Straight away she starts propelling me in the direction of the music.

I'm so glad you came! she says, totally unnecessarily. Everyone's here! It's really kicking.

I'm like, Oh. Cool.

From behind us Al's like, Hi Mary, in this pipsqueak voice.

Mary looks over her shoulder as if she's just noticed the donkey that brought me here and then goes, Oh hi, in this total maybe-I-could-care-less-if-I-could-actually-be-bothered-to kind of a way, before immediately turning back to me. I can positively feel the vibes of fury Al is now transmitting. Good, I think, since it means we can go soon.

In the living-room the lights are all dimmed and the speakers are blaring some out some electro crap. Mary wasn't lying about the place being full, but of course her definition of Everyone is everyone from our school, which is a total let-down, because of course everyone from St Matthew's is some style of loser. It's like a zoo freak-show exhibit because here they all are, every like, subspecies of school attendee: the football heroes, the tennis preeners, the IT jerks, the Samaritan bitches and the redneck toffs. There are even a few spectoids, who've somehow slipped into the party unnoticed and now stand out like a clump of mutant bacteria in a petri dish. So it's like there's a representative for every demographic, and looking around it's so depressing I just want to curl up and cry. It's like I'm in the middle of this great human stew which is made up of all these types which everyone already knows, and which holds no surprises at all. It's such a total yawn. I mean it's like, can't someone just get a morsel of originality or something? I don't know, maybe this sounds totally OTT to you, and you're like, thinking, So what makes him such hot shit? But I never said *I* was special or anything, so if that's what you are thinking just remember that you can LIC. And I'm sorry if it sounds like I'm being all negative, but quite frankly the way I feel is that if *this* is what it's All About then someone better give me some medication or something. *Fast.* Because I totally Do Not See It.

Mary parades me around the crowd like I'm this trophy

she's just been awarded. Various people including Kathy and Athena turn and go Hi! in these super-bright voices, like all of a sudden we're best buddies or something. Meanwhile Al loiters behind us like a steward. We wind up at the corner of the room where the more popular kids have gathered like it's a VIP area or something. If you can't see it just imagine a scene out of *Carrie*. About half the guys are dressed in these oversized T-shirts with Che Guevara on, and they're all digging each other in the ribs, gulping from cans of beer and burping in a way that by comparison would make Homer Simpson look sexy. They're so not even worth wasting your eyesight on. Meanwhile half the girls are standing around against the wall trying to look like models. Instead it looks like they're waiting for life to happen to them or something. The other half are dancing with rest of the crowd, doing *en masse* homage to Beyoncé by waving their bits around like every roll of puppy fat is a gift from God (it's like, someone please bring back heroin chic – and like, *soon*).

It's really rocking, says Mary, who's obviously really proud because it's her party.

I'm like, Yeah, cringing all over.

After a bit of mindless banter with various loser nobodies Mary forces me towards the kitchen. Al's like, trying to make conversation with her, but Mary just brushes her away like she's a glob of dirt, and at some point or other she gets lost in the sea of insignificance behind us.

In the kitchen is Ian, who's this fitness obsessive. His head is being supported over the sink by Kristy, who's this total slut and who's making these cooing sounds like the sight him choking back his vomit is the prettiest thing she's ever seen. It's not even ten o' clock, so this kind of thing is even more stale than it ought to be.

Looks like Ian's had a bit too much, goes Mary, who's clearly got this talent for making like, redundant observations.

I'm like, Uh huh.

Mary gets me a bottle of beer and one for herself, and then sits on the counter and starts telling me the story of her life, like my sole purpose on this planet is to be fascinated by her. It's like, Pass the Valium. I try to at least nod along, but I keep getting distracted by the sounds of Ian's retching just a few feet away, and then the complete grossness of realising that it's actually, the sound of him and Kristy snogging. I'm like, Someone get me out of here, but then I realise what Mary is now saying to me. She's going, I've always kind of liked you, it's just that you're so aloof. It's hard for a girl to talk to you, you know?

She gives me this meaningful look, like I'm in any shade of doubt about what she wants here. Another blinding smile. Then she starts leaning in with her eyes closed. It's like it's happening in slow motion and I have this full-on urge to burst out laughing because it's like, total amateur's night. I don't do that though of course, 'cos I know that would be like scarring her for life.

Still, the sad truth is there's no nice way to let someone down so I'm like, I better go look for Al! like God's suddenly just given me this mission or something. Before Mary has a chance to like, open her eyes and realise I'm not there any more I'm running for it.

I fully expect to find Al hanging out with the nerds in Rejectsville and wanting to go, but I can't see her anywhere. I ask one of the nerds if they've seen her but they get so flustered from the fact that someone's actually noticed their existence I can't figure out what they're saying to me. It kind of makes you wonder why they bother – they all look

130

round with these faces like they know this is where they're supposed to want to be, but in reality it's totally obvious they'd be much happier at home deciphering algebra. They should just deal with it.

So I end up taking a tour. The place is massive, and it's a bit like a house of horror, like you get at one of those old-fashioned fairs or something, 'cos there's wrecked kids stumbling around like the undead and coming out on you unexpectedly from corners with soul-sucking, boozed-up eyeballs.

I eventually find myself in the bathroom where there's a whole tub of ice with a load of beer dunked in it, so I help myself to another one and sit down on the toilet for a smoke while I collect myself. All I can think is that Al must have taken off. But it's not like her, not without at least telling me, so I get out my phone to write her a text. I've already got one. It says U JERK I CANT BELVE U JUST DMPED ME LKE THAT. HVE FUN WTH THT BITCH! I send her one back saying OK LEZZER BUT WHERE R U? but after a minute I get a reply saying CNT!, so I figure she really has gone.

Then this like, vampire-style shadow falls across me and I look up and see Fabian is standing there in this totally wrong PVC coat. His hair is like, saturated with gel and spiked up so that it looks like he's had an accident with an electrode. I could swear he's also got eye-shadow on, and he's looking down at me like any minute he's going to try and suck my blood. It's like, Anne Rice overload.

He's like, Hey, how's it going?

I'm like, Are you stalking me or something?

He's like, I just came for the party, in this all defensive voice.

He goes to the bath and takes a beer which he tries to

131

open with his teeth. It doesn't happen so he ends up using his key-ring, looking totally shamed and annoyed.

Then he goes, Got a cigarette?

I'm pretty fed up, so I'm like, Go back to Psychosville.

He takes a massive mouthful of his beer and then spits it into the air. It kind of hovers there for a second, this pouch of fluid, and then plummets down and explodes all over the floor. A bit gets on my shoes which pisses me off because they're my Converse, which I had to save up for eons to buy.

I'm like, Isn't there a rock somewhere missing you being under it?

Fabian just ignores this. Wanna see something? he goes.

I'm like, No thanks, thinking he's probably gonna flash me, or worse still get out his knife and start waving it around like it's a trick or something. But instead he starts rolling up his sleeve. He goes all the way to his elbow. I'm like, looking, because you can't help yourself. It's like, an elbow, Wow. Then Fabian reaches across and plucks the cigarette out of my hand. I'm like, Hey! but before I can do anything he plants it on his skin. There's this little fizzling sound as the cigarette goes out. Fabian grimaces and then looks at me.

I'm like, mega-freaked. What the hell did you do that for? I go, sounding all shrill.

Fabian just grins like my reaction is a gift I'm giving him or something. Then he rolls up his arm even more and shows me the skin just below his shoulder. It's like, scar central. There's this whole mish-mash of thick white lines running through each other like someone's been playing noughts and crosses with a highlighter on him. It's totally whack.

I do them with razors, he goes, like they're supposed to be beautiful or something.

I'm like, You need assistance.

Fabian's grin reaches Cheshire dimensions. Wanna touch them? he goes.

I'm like, the definition of No.

He touches them himself. I look at the door and judge my chances. All these possibilities are racing through my head, like what if he breaks his bottle and tries to stab me with it, or what if he refuses to let me go until I've got like, a matching set of scars or something? It's a full-on situation and I don't know what I'm supposed to do. Probably I should try and talk to him about how scarring yourself for life is wrong etc., but I have no idea what to say. Besides, if he wants to scar himself he can go right ahead the way I see it, so long as he does it many hundreds of metres away from me. I remember how I was thinking about him when Jon gave me that E, and how sad I thought it was because he's screwed up. I don't think it's sad now – at least, not a good kind of sad.

I'm like, You should totally talk to someone. I try to say it sincerely, but Fabian's like, totally offended.

He's like, Fuck you. You're just like all the others. Just 'cos you're a faggot you think that makes you all special. But it doesn't. You're just another fucking white nigger like everyone else.

I don't quite get the white nigger thing, 'cos Fabian's white too so like, how does that work? But I guess with Nazi punks anything goes so long as it sounds good. Fabian suddenly has that crazy look in his eyes and I think, Well at least I tried, though I wish I hadn't bothered. I stand up and step slowly towards the door, half-expecting him to like, tackle me or something. But he doesn't. He just drops his head and then goes, Hey, remember those times?

I'm like, What times?

133

He's like, You know. When we hung out.

I'm like, Yeah?

There's this long pause while he studies his lap, and I think maybe he's forgotten about like, existing or something. But then he looks up at me with his crazy look and goes, We should hang out again sometime.

I'm like, Yeah, sure, thinking I'd rather hang out with Hannibal Lecter. I leave him there.

Once I've escaped from Fabian I decide it's definitely time to blow. Being exposed to a party of losers is one thing, but being exposed to Fabian's arm is quite another, and it's just too much. I need to go back home and like, purify myself or something.

The older guys who were on the porch are now sitting giggling on the stairs, and their eyes are like, totally ga-ga so you can tell they must be shrooming it. Me and Al tried magic mushrooms a few months ago after we managed to persuade this old hippy to sell us some in Camden. They must have been duds though 'cos we spent the whole evening after we'd taken them sitting in this juice bar and waiting for something to happen which never did. Or maybe he just hocked us the old Sainsbury's closed-cup variety.

I make a beeline for the front door, but before I can reach it this hand like, hoists me into the corner behind the coat stand.

Look, nobody can see us, goes Mary in this tense whisper that lets me know there's going to be no escape this time. How she didn't get the message before is like, mythical. But there's nothing for it.

I'm like, Listen Mary, I think you're a really nice person . . .

Any normal person hearing these words would know

134

right away what I was on about, but the thing with Mary is that all her brains are in her boobs. She takes it like, the opposite to how she should. She leans forward before I've even decided on how the next part should go and clamps her mouth over mine. It's big and warm and tastes of lipstick. But I go into shock or something, 'cos she takes me totally by surprise. I just stay completely still and press my lips as tight together as I can, though she has like, this demon tongue which keeps trying to force them open. Probably she's been practising half her life, because we're talking about a real muscle here. After what seems like a millennium she finally gets the message and stops kissing me. Then there's this long pause while she deals with the rejection.

She's like, I thought you liked me.

I'm like, I do. But not like that.

She thinks for a bit. You can practically hear the cogs grinding. Then she goes, Jaz, are you a gay?

Now I'm the one thinking. I don't know Mary that well or anything. I don't care what Fuck Face and the Tweedles say about me 'cos it's not like anyone ever listens to them, but Mary's pretty popular. She could like, do some damage. Still, since she's a girl and since she's pretty much guessed anyway I figure I may as well tell her. Plus I also figure it'll help her get over being rejected, which I think you'll have to admit is pretty decent of me.

So I'm like, Yeah, that's it.

Oh my God, she goes. There's more silence, although it's not really silence 'cos someone's wopped on some super-naff J-Lo track. I can just see them all in the next room bouncing their arses up and down to it. You'd think I'd just admitted I was a pedo or something the way Mary goes all silent. But then, like finally, she goes,

It's OK, I wish you'd told me, in this voice that's all sickly sweet and understanding, which is pretty much what I expected from someone probably born and bred on soap operas.

I'm like, Sorry.

She's like, It must be so hard for you!

Yeah. But it's OK, I go, acting all vulnerable.

She's like, If you want to talk about it . . .

It's like, what is it with people and talking? First Mum, then Fellows and now Mary. As if that's what being gay is all about. It's like, what is there to talk about?

I'm like, Listen, I gotta take off. You won't tell anyone, will you?

She's like, Of course not! as though the idea would never occur to her. But I'm not too sure. All of a sudden I have this image of her surrounded by her posse and Athena asking her in her Greek baritone, So how did it go? I can just see Mary going all silent and giggly, and then being prodded and whispering in this excited voice, Can you guys keep a secret? which is a bit like asking if you can float lead. Still, I figure there's nothing for it now, so I kiss her on the cheek to let her know how much I appreciate that she's stopped molesting me, and off I go.

On the way to the bus stop I send Al a text asking WOT THE HELL HPPNED TO U? but she doesn't reply, which is unlike Al. It dawns on me that maybe she's really genuinely mad at me for leaving her alone, which of course is totally unfair since I didn't even want to come and it was her own stupid fault for insisting on it.

Back at home I find Mum and The Nun in the kitchen. Mum's trying to do some paperwork at the same time as cleaning, while The Nun's reading her some essay in this impressively monotonous voice, like she's deliberately try-

136

ing to send her up the wall or something. Of course Mum's thrilled that I'm back before the agreed time, but I have this urge to talk to Grandma so I leave them to their excitement and go upstairs to find her.

She's in her room, the one which used to be mine, and she's lying fully clothed on the bed and snoring with her mouth open. It's pretty undignified really, plus one of her hands has fallen right into her crotch so it kind of looks like she's fallen asleep in the middle of having a wank. I don't want to wake her up but I don't go right away either. There's something really fascinating about people when they're asleep, especially Grandma. I look at her and I wonder what it's going to be like at that age. It's a pretty sappy thing to imagine, but you can't help it when you're looking at old people sleeping. I think about all the time in between being Mum and Dad's age and being Grandma's age, and it just seems so awful that all that time's got to even happen that I practically fall over and have to steady myself by grabbing hold of the bed. I look at her and I wonder if when I reach her age I'll just end up the same, all undignified and wishing death would just hurry up and come along and put me out of my misery. It's like, what's the point? I'd totally rather die suddenly when I'm young, even if it's in the middle of taking a shit or something. When I was younger I used to think about death loads, before I started thinking about sex (which is kind of like the opposite of death so it's funny how these things connect). It's never bothered me like it bothers other people though, the fact that you have to die, because unlike The Nun I'm a total atheist and I don't believe in hell or being made to pay for my sins or any of that other crap. The only thing that's ever bothered me was the idea of dying on the toilet or something embarrassing like that.

But I don't think even that bothers me any more 'cos it's not like you'll care about dying on the toilet and how it looked when they found you, or any of that kind of stuff, if you're dead.

16

First off, sorry for going off on a total sermon back there. I guess it's pretty hypocritical to go on about Mary and her soap-opera personality then launch into the queen of sappy speeches myself.

Anyway, this is like, what happens during the week. First off, at our next session with Higgs the whole E-xperience comes out and I'm expected to talk about why I did it and stuff, like it's this totally self-destructive thing rather than something that people do for like, pleasure. Fortunately Higgs doesn't seem to think it's such a big deal. In fact, he's much more concerned with Mum and Dad and how they feel about it. When Mum says something about how she's afraid of me turning into a drug addict Higgs acts all concerned and asks if she's ever considered one-on-one counselling, which she finds pretty shocking. He suggests to them that they try to remember themselves more, which sounds totally cryptic to me. But Mum interprets it as meaning she has to buy like, a zillion self-help books and start learning them off by heart. She starts coming out with totally surreal stuff like. You're only bad when I consciously believe it to be so, or I process everything I just don't proceed with it. Weird/bizarre/scary, I know. The Nun loves it though, and sits there at dinner going, That's just like what the Bible says! and quoting religious stuff right back at her.

Dad meanwhile just cooks like he's got an army to feed, which is pretty nice actually 'cos whenever you want a snack there's like a hundred delicacies in the fridge to choose from. But Grandma doesn't have her meals with us any more, so we take it turns delivering them up to her on a tray. She spends most of her time staring out the window with this daft smile on her face. It's really a shame, 'cos it's like she's lost all faith in reality and now the whole world is this one great big cosmic joke to her or something.

I try to give Al a call on Sunday night, and I get her mum, who manages to *look* false and frightened even down the telephone. She's like, Oh I'm afraid Alice is a bit busy right now. Perhaps you'll see her at school.

I have no patience with the Rutlands any more so I'm like, Can't you interrupt her? It's really important.

Mrs Rutland ums and ahs and gets off the line. Then Mr Rutland gets on and goes to me, Listen, Jarold, Alice is rather busy at the moment so we'd prefer it if you didn't call here. OK? like it's the most natural favour in the world he's asking me. I get super-pissed off but I bite my tongue and just put the phone down, 'cos it's obvious that if I insult them it's not gonna help matters. I end up sending Al a text saying WOT IS THE DEAL WTH U? but she doesn't reply. It's way worse than the last time we had a fight. It's like, I don't even know what I'm supposed to have done wrong here.

On Monday I don't bother going by her house and I don't see her at the bus stop either. I catch a glimpse of her in assembly though, so I guess her dad must have driven her to school in the end. She ignores me in this really obvious way. I think it's such a joke to ignore someone, 'cos it ends up being like, more effort than it

140

takes to just tell them to Fuck Off. But I decide Fine, if that's the way you want to play it.

In class it becomes clear right away what a mistake it was to own up to Mary about being gay. Everyone knows, I'm sure of it. It's like she sent them all an email or something. The way I know isn't because people are all sniggers and smirks, or calling me names. It doesn't work like that. It's more like everyone just avoids me, pretends not to notice me or catch my eye. I don't know why I even care, but I do. 'Cos after a while it becomes really quite frustrating.

Our class is always pretty full 'cos there's only one geography set at St Matthew's, so there's only ever two or three seats left unsat on. I'm one of the first to sit down and wouldn't you know I'm like, in the middle of them. A total billy, because no one wants to sit next to me. And as the class fills up it gets more and more embarrassing. You'd think I had scabies or something the way people pretend not to see the seats, and the thing is that kids are like sheep in this respect. Like psychic sheep. 'Cos they can't all have heard whatever Mary's spreading about me, but they kind of just *sense* something and because no one else is sitting next to me none of the others want to either. That's what kids are like. Actually that's what all people are like. They just copy each other. It's not like they do what they're told, because they don't need to be told, they just do whatever they think everyone else is thinking they should do. I bet loads of people even get married just because everyone else they know is doing it. I bet that's how Mum and Dad got married.

Of course Al doesn't sit next to me either, just raises her head till she's practically looking at the ceiling and walks right on over to the other side of the classroom and sits down next to Sam Gibbons, who's probably the only person desperate enough not to mind her sitting next to him. She buries herself in her textbook like it's the most absorbing thing she's ever come across in her whole life. I reckon that's pretty mean of her. It's pretty clear what's going on with me, so she could have at least given me a sympathetic look or something. She could have at least fucking sat down next to me.

So it's, like, paradise for juvenile delinquents, like something out of a nursery. But of course it bugs me. You can't help but be bugged when people give you the cold shoulder, even if they are a bunch of losers. It's like, what the fuck has Mary been spreading?

One guy, this jerk who's called Tony, which is a pretty fitting name since he totally looks like he should be in the Mafia, whispers something as he passes me to the other guy he's with, and I go bright red with shame. I didn't even hear what he said, but I've gone red. It's like I know it's about me, even though I don't. Paranoia, man. It's weird what being made to feel like an outsider can do to you. I wonder if this is how Sam feels all the time, since he's usually the one nobody'll sit next to on account of his super-sized head.

By the time Fellows arrives I'm like, totally thrilled to see him, even though he looks more than ever like he's on the verge of suicide. But I'm quite glad of that since at least I know things could always be worse.

All Monday I don't speak to Al, or anyone else for that matter. In English I do my usual trick of coming in super-late and leaving super-early to avoid any chance of a confrontation with Fuck Face. When I get home I hole myself up in my room 'cos The Nun's got her sisterhood round and they've practically taken over the rest of the house. I consider having a rub with Orlando or trying to

142

actually get some work done, but I just feel so depressed all of a sudden it's hard to concentrate on anything other than how shit life is. I start doing reps to try and like, replenish my endorphins, but I lose interest after the first two and give up and lie down and stare up at the ceiling. I feel totally out of it.

Kids are such a bunch of cunts. But it's not just all those losers at school, it's everything. I mean, when you think about it, my life is pretty awful at the moment, so it's not like I don't have an excuse for self-pity or anything. The whole thing with Jon ended like, as badly as it could have, Mum and Dad are taking me to therapy and my best friend's like, chronically mad at me for something that happened at some stupid party I didn't even want to go to. Being ostracised by a bunch of loser virgins is like, the final insult, that's all.

And it's lying here, feeling all depressed and shit, that I first get to thinking how much easier it would be if I just didn't have to deal with any of these hassles. Like, if I started again somewhere where fun was something people actually liked to have rather than something that should be avoided at all cost. I mean, why is it that everything has to be so fucking depressing? What's the point of doing anything? Do y'know what I mean?

Well, maybe you don't. No one else seems to. Anyway. Tuesday:

I wake up with a plan, which is to find Mary and make her tell me what she's been telling other people. I didn't sleep very well, and I kind of wake up all mad and angry, in this mood which I don't really get much, which lasts all the way to school. I actually see Al on the bus, sitting right up front, and she catches my eye. She gives me this look like maybe she's ready to talk, but I'm so mad this morning I

143

just look away and ignore her, which is totally childish I know but I can't help it.

By the time I get to school I've calmed down a bit, but I get all riled up again when I pass junior school. If you can believe it, one of the little shits runs up to me and shouts Rah! right in my face. He runs away before I can catch him and, like, dismantle him or something. I'll never recognise him again either, since all the molestables look the same and most of them haven't started developing like, proper faces yet.

First period is art, which I kind of simmer through. We're supposed to be painting these self-portraits, but I find myself doing a portrait of Satan instead. If you can believe it, when Mrs Bolsh sees it she actually compliments me on my 'sensitive and expressive nature' and holds it up for the class to see, like they're all supposed to copy it or something, which just goes to show that art these days really is what you make of it. But in a way I'm totally irritated by it, and I want to snatch it back off her and tell her just what I really think about stupid art class.

Come break-time I march around campus looking for Mary. I finally locate her at the top of the science ward hanging out with Ian, that puking/snogging cretin you may remember from her party. They're like, getting full-on chummy with each other when I arrive. In fact they look like they're about to snog, and both of them leap like, ten feet in the air when I shout, Mary! from behind her.

She's like, Oh hi, Jaz, in this weird voice which is both innocent and yet knowing. Ian smirks and looks away, so it's pretty clear she's told *him*. I'm like, Can I have a word or are you working at the moment?

Mary's so dumb she doesn't even get when she's being insulted, and Ian's even dumber, since guys who are regularly pumping down the gym seem to like, sweat their brains out or something (which doesn't say much for a whole bunch of those super-built gay men you see in Starlight either).

She's like, Sure, in this friendly voice.

I'm like, In private?

At this point Ian decides he's a factor. He's like, If you've got something to say why don't you go ahead and just say it?

I'm like, so incensed by this I practically decombust. Before I even know what I'm saying I go, Fine. Mary, did you tell everyone about me being gay or what?

There's this long pause. I may as well tell you here what a fatal mistake this is on my part, because Mary kind of looks like I've shot her or something, and Ian opens his eyes so wide they practically fall out of his head. Mary starts shaking her head back and forth faster than a spin-dryer. Ian kind of recovers and jumps to his feet. He's like, See you later, to Mary. He runs off down the stairs like he's been given an injection.

Mary's like, Why did you just say that? Don't you know Ian's one of the biggest loudmouths in school?

Normally it'd be like, So why the hell were you about to snog him? but I'm way too deep into being like, Oh Shit, to think of such things.

I thought you'd told everyone, I go. My voice wavers. It's much higher than I've ever heard it before, almost like Mum's when she goes supersonic but not quite so ear-splitting.

Of course I didn't! she says angrily. What kind of a person do you think I am?

She looks down the stairs and sighs like a mother who's disappointed in one of her children.

In any case, everybody'll know pretty soon, she goes in this voice like she's deeply regretful or something.

At this point I kind of flop against the wall and crumble to the floor. Mary looks worried and comes and sits next to the pile of body parts that I've turned into. She leans forward so that her massive tits are like, expanding towards me and then does the naffest thing on Earth. She reaches out and strokes my cheek. I mean, it's like, full-on Yuck – it just goes to show that no matter how low you sink, there's always a lower level to be sunk to.

She's like, It'll be OK, you know, in this ultra-mumsy voice. She's well into this role. Her whole chest swells. I swear, it seems to get bigger by the second, like one of those frogs with the inflatable necks. It'll be OK, she goes again. I just don't say anything because what the fuck does she know? Nothing, that's what. But Mary won't shut up. She keeps stroking me, like I'm a vagina or something. Then she goes, Maybe it's for the best. You know, you shouldn't deny it. You should be proud of it.

When she says that I can't take it any longer. There's this like, ocean of puke rising from my stomach, and I just can't stand Mary and the way she's sitting there stroking my cheek like something out of one of her fucking soap operas. I want to scream at her or punch her or something. In the end I just tell her all icily to go get a breast reduction and push her hand away.

Jaz! she goes, like she can't believe me, but I'm already out of there. And then, just because I can, I decide not to bother with the rest of school that day and so I take a bus into town and end up wandering around the Trocadero

146

watching the Japanese kids dancing on those video-game pads and pretending like I don't exist or something. I wander round Piccadilly and down inside the tube station too. I'm hoping there'll be someone to bum a cigarette off since I've smoked all the ones I nicked off Dad. But it's rush hour and everyone's just pushing against each other and fighting to get in or out through the gates, and it's like a full-on scrum, so I end up pressed against this poster. It's a horrible poster. It's got these two pictures of women. One of them is like, this goth, kind of cool, all white with black hair and clothes and silver piercings. The other one's all dressed in this dull grey suit with this blonde highlighted hairdo, looking totally boring, and is smiling out of the picture. There's a little note under each one saying that the goth is the lead singer in this band, and the other one's like, a bank manager. And it's the same woman apparently, 'cos underneath the photos there's this blurb which says, 'In just ten years your taste has improved and so has ours'. It's advertising wine. It's the most depressing fucking poster I've ever seen in my whole life.

Of course word gets back from the school to Mum and Dad that I truanted it, because even though I'm in year six you still have to be accounted for when the teachers do their stupid roll-call. Mum's waiting for me at home with a whole speech prepared about how I'm really sliding and how she can't believe I'm really her son because when she was my age she never had any of these problems I have. She's like, When I was a teenager we didn't have any money. When I got back from school I had to work, from six till nine o'clock, and so did all my friends. We didn't own a television! like television is all I'm about. I just run upstairs to my room and lock the door. At least that's to say

147

I push my drawers against it, since obviously I don't have a lock.

On Wednesday I wake up and try to fake a disease, but Mum's not having any of it. She doesn't even bother looking at me when I tell her at breakfast I don't feel well. She just goes, It's probably your conscience, and goes back to reading whatever the latest self-help rubbish is. Dad looks me over but shakes his head, like I've failed some kind of test or something, so I end up going to school anyway. I tell myself I don't care really. It's not like I have to or anything.

So this like, scene takes place in the exact same corridor where I wrote on the crappy molestables' collage. That's now been replaced with a bunch of dappy pictures of hand prints, and I'm standing there staring at them for the simple reason that I've got nowhere else to go. It's free study period but there's no way I feel like studying. Then I hear the word 'Poof!' coming from behind me and the next thing I know I'm facing Fuck Face and his goons. And Fabian's with them too. He's kind of hanging behind them, watching us with this total smirk across his face. I give him this look like I can't believe how low he's sunk but he looks back at me and his grin widens. He just shrugs like he could give a shit.

Fuck Face comes towards me. There's no hope of escape whatsoever. I figure I don't even care. But as soon as Fuck Face gives me this great push and I go flying back and hit my head on the board, I realise that actually I do, because pain still hurts no matter how shit you're feeling.

I'm like, Just go and afflict someone else!

I make a bolt for it, though it's totally pointless. This time old Fuck Face just grabs my arm and, like, rips it backwards. It feels like it's about to come off. I use my other arm to swing at his face, and I'm pleased to say I catch him with

148

a nicely pleasant clunking sound right in his teeth. He kind of reels backward for a second, but he doesn't let go of my arm.

Tweedle Dum goes, You're not gonna let that pass, are you? like Fuck Face needs any more encouragement.

Fuck Face balls up his comic-book fist and gives me one in the head, which I swear will ring for days. I'm like, totally seeing stars, and it doesn't help that when I go flying backwards I hit my head *again* on the board. It's like my skull is that thing that dangles inside a bell. I kind of slide down the wall like a lump of shit that's been thrown at it.

Fuck Face is like, You know what we do with poofters at this school?

He comes and stands over me and the Tweedles come and stand at either side of him. Weirdly, what with the light and all shining right down in my eyes from the window behind him, he looks kind of celestial, like God or something. The Tweedles actually look kind of like seraphs. But it's only because you can't see their ugly mugs is all, and the fact that my entire brain is like, totally pulverised.

Tweedle Dum, or Dee (I can't quite make out which one's talking), goes, Look, he's acting all hurt.

Just as Fuck Face is about to show me what they do, there's this flicker at his neck. I like, blink my eyes a few times and try to refocus. (Turns out I'm practically concussed here, by the way. It's lucky I don't die.) It's Fabian's knife I guess, 'cos I hear Fabian saying something and then I hear Fuck Face like, begging him not to do anything, with real terror in his voice. Then there's like, this total cry of pain. I kind of see some red on Fuck Face's neck but I don't really believe that Fabian's cut his throat or anything 'cos that'd just be daft. But then I hear the Tweedles shouting stuff, like Fabian's insane, and there's all this yelling and stuff and doors are opening up the corridor so I figure more people are coming. But I don't really see it, I just hear it, and over it all there's this beat in my head playing like a full-on techno track.

Then Fabian's like, kneeling beside me going, I got that fucker for you! I got 'im good. Won't be cussing you up no more! and I'm like, majorly Huh the what? because I can't even tell which side of me he's supposed to be on. Then there's the voice of some teacher who's like, clearing the way around me and telling people to get back and issuing orders and stuff. It's totally surreal, like finding yourself in a David Lynch film or something, only one that's severely out of focus.

Anyway, I end up sat in Fatty the headmaster's office while my brain resettles itself. The nurse, who's even fatter than he is, bulges in to see me and pokes me around and shines a little torch in my eyes. She decides there's no point in me going to hospital, which is typical of her because she's this total power-nut who just loves diagnosing pupils herself and hates sending them off anywhere else for, like, proper treatment. But pretty soon I start thinking halfway normally so I guess just this once she was right.

Fatty's got all these questions for me, but I can't be bothered with it so I pretend like I'm still dazed and he calls Dad to come pick me up.

Meanwhile Fabian's like, totally vanished. But he's in deep shit because he cut Fuck Face's cheek. Not badly – unfortunately – just a little nick. There's not even gonna be a scar there probably. But it was enough to scare Fuck Face. When I finally get to leave the office 'cos Dad's arrived he's sat outside in the corridor with the Tweedles, staring into space like he's traumatised or something. Tweedle Dum gives me this full-on evil look and whispers something into

Fuck Face's ear. But Fuck Face doesn't seem to hear him 'cos he just carries right on staring straight ahead as we pass by. He looks totally unhappy and it kind of makes you almost believe that inside every bully there really is a sappy little orphan waiting to get out or something. But even if that's true I don't care, 'cos he totally deserved it.

17

Dad's pretty sympathetic once I tell him I was picked on by homophobes. I kind of play up that part and leave out the bit about writing old Fuck Face Joseph's name above the cardboard cow in the molestables' collage, even though I know it's probably going to come out once he gets a grilling from Fatty.

It's cool in a way though, because he tells Mum and she gets all mad about it and it's kind of touching in a way, how mad she gets, especially 'cos she alternates between that and cooing over me and my head. She goes on though. All about how we're going to sue the school and imprison my bullies, and then later she comes up to my room and gives me this long talk about freedom, like I've earned the right to listen to this great philosophy of hers that she's been like, accumulating for all of her life. She obviously thinks it's a Special Moment, when actually it isn't. I'm touched though, and I feel kind of bad when I run out of patience and have to tell her I'm fine and to please leave me alone.

That night I get a call from Al. She's heard what's happened and is all hyper-apologetic. She's like, Jaz, I'm so sorry I can't believe it! I feel so bad. She goes on and on about how she feels guilty and how her parents have been hassling her and other stuff, and how she should never have ignored me and how it's probably some hormone kicking in or something which made her do it. Seriously, listening to her you'd have thought she'd forgotten she was talking instead of just thinking. After a while she starts asking me questions about what happened and telling me some stuff I don't know, like that Fabian's been expelled and Fuck Face has been suspended. Then she starts going on about her parents, and how they're on at her to buckle down and focus on her studies and stuff, and how much she feels like a slave at home. But the truth is I can't actually be bothered to even listen much. I mean, I suddenly feel so bored of it all. Not just her parents – of the whole school thing and everything else that's been going on. Of life, basically, if that doesn't sound too naff. Because it is boring, when you think about it. I don't know, maybe you don't. Maybe it's just my concussion or something. Then she starts going on about poor Fellows and how we still have this like, mission to get his jolly roger a good workout. But I'm just not interested. I kind of give her the silent treatment, I suppose. It's not 'cos I'm mad though. It's just that I can't be bothered. Finally she goes, Let's go to Starlight tomorrow night, in this super-excited voice, which I know is her way of *really* trying to make it up to me, but I just think to myself, What for? and that's when I get this sudden flashback of Fabian telling me about how people always just do what other people tell them to, and I think Yeah, it's totally true. Then I think to myself, Uh oh, 'cos Fabian's this total Nazi and that means that I'm basically agreeing with him, which means maybe I'm turning into a Nazi or something myself. Still, it *is* true, what he said, and even if he is a Nazi it doesn't mean he can't like, ever be right about anything.

I tell Al I've got to go and hang up pretty fast. Then I pay a visit to Grandma, who's sleeping, which is all she seems to do these days. That and stare out the window.

The Nun comes in while I'm there and demands to know

153

what I'm doing. She's like, totally jealous of all the attention I've got from the whole thing at school, and tells me that I should have some respect for the elderly and let her nap in peace.

I'm like, If you keep talking you're the one who's gonna wake her up.

The Nun's like, You know, you have no respect for other people. Sometimes I really think you might have psychological difficulties.

Normally when she says something like that without Mum and Dad around I'm like, flexing my finger muscles and getting ready to attack, but today I just ignore her. She seems kind of surprised by the lack of reaction, but after a good sesh of righteous tutting she wanders off again.

Then Grandma opens her eyes and says, George? which is really scary because that was Grandpa's name. For a minute I consider like, pretending to be him or something, just to make her feel better, but then she closes her eyes and goes back to sleep, thankfully.

The whole of the week that follows is totally boring, so I'm just gonna give you the broad strokes. Like at school, everything goes pretty much back to normal. Me and Al go back to sitting together, and nobody really says anything to me about being gay, since the whole Fuck Face thing has kind of made me into this walking spotlight. Except for a few brainless gym freaks, that is, who've obviously been pumping iron with Ian and who make like, puckering noises with their lips whenever they see me, which is like, sad beyond sad.

Mary keeps catching my eye in the canteen or wherever and giving me these meaningful smiles. She catches up with me at one point and tells me how sorry she is about it all and how she knows I was 'overwrought' when I said that thing about the breast reduction, which like, doesn't mean it wasn't still a valid suggestion as far I'm concerned. But I guess maybe it's nice of her to be understanding about it, even if it is totally sickly.

I keep expecting to get called to someone's office or something and get like, forced to cry while one of the stupid counsellors there holds my hand and says stupid things about my right to life like I'm an idiot or something. But Mum must have called the school and told them she had the situation under control because nothing happens at all. I'm pretty sure she called them up to demand they like, arrest Fuck Face or something for trying to kill me, even though I told her not to.

That's all that's notable really. There's no sign of Fuck Face, or Fabian of course, and the Tweedles sit at the back of English class looking like they've been, like deprogrammed. We're nearly off *Twelfth Night* now, and I can't wait. I can't stand the fact that we keep having to reread the final scene, where they all find out who's who and laugh about it and then all get married like that's supposed to solve everything or something. I can't stand Shakespeare full stop I've decided.

OK. There is one more notable thing, and it's pretty weird. It's just me. I'm clearly not my normal self. Don't ask me why, but maybe the whole banging my head against the wall kind of lobotomised me or something, 'cos I'm just not thinking right. It's like, I can't be bothered to crack jokes, or listen to lectures, or chat to Al, or get excited or do anything much of anything. At home the only thing I can think of to do when I get back from school is have a long bath and a wank, which is totally sad. Al keeps going on about going back to Starlight and eventually she manages to drag me there, but the whole evening is this total ordeal because I keep thinking about Jon and how that turned out and like, what's the point?

So basically I'm turning into a full-on manic depressive, and it's like I'm watching myself from outside and I can't be bothered to do anything about it. In our next session Higgs picks up on the fact that I'm even quieter than usual and tries to get me to talk about it. Mum tells him about the whole thing with Fuck Face and all this stuff about how it's affected *her*, and Higgs looks quite shocked and it's probably the only time I've ever seen him actually lose his computer cool and act like a human being. But I can't even be bothered with talking to him and so all the journey back Mum's like, criticising me for not being more accessible, until finally (and much to my surprise) Dad tells her that maybe she should lay off a bit, and she goes all silent and shocked 'cos she's not used to Dad like, thinking proper thoughts for himself. He gives me this look in the mirror and then smiles at me like he's on my side or something, which is so lame that I'm tempted to stick my tongue out at him – except that I can't even be bothered to do that.

I just keep thinking about stuff. Like Fabian, actually. I think about him a lot. I kind of wonder how he's doing, since he did save me from being like, murdered or something, and it seems kind of unfair that he got expelled for doing it. I keep thinking about those scars on his arm and thinking of him doing them to himself. Total whacko. And I keep remembering how we used to hang out together, before Al started at St Matthew's and back when he was less like, challenged. I guess he was always a bit of a freak, it just didn't use to bother me. Like he had this whole obsession with Tipp-Ex and used to paint the desks and chairs in class with it. And he once showed me how to smell glue, which was a total head-fuck but I'm glad I did it, because otherwise I wouldn't know what it was like, and I do have this weird memory of dancing round singing nursery rhymes with him from it. So I guess we did have good times, until he started going psycho and doing crazy stuff like threatening other kids with compass points and collecting dead insects. I wasn't really his friend any more when he chased Mrs Bolsh with the scissors, but I can kind of see why he might have done it, because it's just what I would have liked to do when she told me my self-portrait was all expressive and sensitive, when actually it was supposed to be Satan.

On Friday it all turns to shit. I have this like, encounter with Fellows. He's been shooting me looks all week like he's hoping I'll come and talk to him about the whole bullying thing, but finally he decides he can't contain the good advice he's got all stored up any longer.

After class he's like, Not so fast, Jarold, I want a word with you.

So I stand there like a dork while everyone files past me with these knowing expressions on their faces. It's blatantly obvious what this is going to be about, and it's like I'm trapped in one of those mega-lame films where the disillusioned student gets this magical pep talk from his aging mentor. Al nods at us as she passes like she totally approves. I pretend to scratch my head so I can give her the finger but I'm not fast enough and she doesn't see.

So, goes Fellows once everyone's gone, I heard about what happened.

I'm like, No. *Really?*

He either doesn't hear the sarcasm in my voice or edits it out with this special filter designed to protect romantic ideas from, like, reality. He's doing that thing where he gazes off past my left shoulder like there's this wonderful world full of green fields and butterflies there, instead of some brick wall with a map of the Congo.

He's like, I'm sorry. I'm so, so sorry.

What are you like, Apologiser-Man? I go, kind of jokingly. I just want to end this situation.

He doesn't hear this either. He just goes in this whimsical voice, One forgets how cruel the developing mind can be. When people don't understand something they become afraid of it, and that means they persecute it. You have to be strong and you have to be forgiving, Jarold. That's what it takes.

When he says this my whole depersonalised thing suddenly cracks. I'm suddenly like, ready to projectile spew at him. I mean, you can only be so strong and so forgiving before you can't take any more. So I'm like, Listen, you need to get laid.

This time he hears me. He's not too thrilled.

He's like, Jarold, I want to help you through this difficult time, but I find it hard to do so with your attitude. You have to—

At this point I lose it. It's like something breaks inside of me and there's this massive string of words coming out of my mouth like I'm not even in control of it. I'm like, You really want to help me through this difficult time? You really want to help? Then you can butt out and leave me alone! You can take your stupid ancient ideas and shove them where the sun don't shine!

Fellows is like, standing with his mouth wide open. His eyes are totally bulging out of his head like he can't believe what I'm saying. For a second I think maybe he's going to hit me again, and I think to myself, Good, for some reason. But it just makes me even angrier. I hear myself go, You're just a sad, wrinkled old fart who can't find anyone!

And then I run out of the classroom without looking back. Al's waiting for me outside but I just run past her and don't stop till I've reached Freedom outside. She catches up with me a minute later.

She's like, What the hell happened back there? He's *crying*!

I'm like, LIC GAS.

Al gives me this disturbed look, but I just shrug her off and go home. We're supposed to be doing something on Saturday but I can't be bothered so I end up spending the day in my room mostly staring at the wall.

So it's Sunday morning and we've just got back from another session with Higgs, in which Mum does all the talking and me and Dad sit there and listen to her going on about how much better she feels now that she's focused with all these books. She keeps on asking Higgs questions about them like he's written them all himself or something, and I'm sure that even though he doesn't show it he really just wants to tell her to suck on it.

Anyway, what I do is I decide to go and pay Fabian a visit. I know. It's like, masochism or something. But he did help me out and you can tell from the way he is that he's pretty lonely really. Like one of those guys who acts all like he wants the apocalypse like, right now, but secretly really wants to be liked and have lots of friends etc. (barf barf). But I guess everyone's some kind of a cliché when you think about it, and I feel kind of indebted to him or something. Plus he got expelled, so it's like, what's he even doing now?

I prepare myself for a full-on weird-out though. His parents are divorced and he lives with his mother, who was always pretty bizarre, I remember. She's this spiritual sculptress called Beverly, which is like, the worst name ever, even worse than Jarold if you ask me, so it's no wonder

159

she's bizarre. She used to let me call her Bev, but since I haven't seen her for like, years, I decide not to be too familiar and to call her Mrs Wrens, in case she wonders why I stopped hanging out with her son, 'cos mothers are like this whole different species when it comes to their sproglets, so maybe she hasn't figured out what a freak he's turned into.

So I go to his house, which is actually only about ten minutes on the bus from mine, which kind of makes the whole thing even weirder. You'd have thought they might have moved to some anarchist commune by now, the sort of place they might stand a chance of fitting in at, but they're still living there, 'cos I recognise the weird twisted sculpture things Bev used to do in the garden, which she once said were supposed to represent two people 'meshing together' but always looked more like upright turds to me.

Anyway, I let myself into the front garden and go past the turds, which are set up along the path like guardians or something, and I ring the bell. There's a long pause and I think maybe no one's home, but just as I'm about to try again and then give up, Mrs Wrens answers. She looks totally different to how I remember her, which is probably not surprising seeing as that was like, four years ago. She's all pale and thin, like she hasn't eaten for all that time, and she's wearing this oversized grey jumper which is a total fashion faux pas when you're, like, as skeletal as she is.

So I'm like, Hi Mrs Wrens, how are you?

She smiles this smile which is like, totally joyless, and looks at me for the longest time. I start to get this feeling like something's seriously up. Like maybe she hates me and blames me for getting Fabian expelled.

I've been expecting you, Jarold, she goes.

I'm like, Huh? because she says it in this quiet voice that's almost ghostly, like she's channelling a spirit or something rather than talking for herself. Then, all of a sudden, I know what's coming. I just *know*. It's like, this feeling of being sure about something that I can't really explain, but I want to do something to show that I know it's coming, 'cos somehow it's like if I can do that then it won't be true after all. I know that sounds totally fucked up, but it's the sort of feeling I get. It's the feeling I got when I came home last year and Grandma was in the kitchen and Dad took me to the side and said he had something very sad to tell me, which was that Grandpa was no longer with us. But of course there is nothing you can do really, 'cos you can't change stuff like that. So I just stand there like a dork and go, I'm here to see Fabian. Is he in?

Mrs Wrens looks totally startled and almost hopeful for a second, but then her face kind of smoothes out like a piece of paper and she smiles her smile again, which is like, the opposite of happy.

Didn't they tell you? she goes.

Tell me what?

He's dead, she goes.

I'm like, What do you mean? like there's another meaning to the word Dead. I hate myself for saying that, but I'm kind of surprised, so I just say the first dumb thing I can think of.

My Fabian's dead. He . . .

She takes a minute to get to it but she doesn't seem very upset to be honest. It's almost like she's trying to think of the best way of putting it, that's all. She doesn't cry or anything, she just looks perfectly calm, like she's describing the weather or something. Probably she's completely Valiumed up. She goes on, He killed himself on Tuesday evening. I thought they would have told you about it at school.

161

I kind of shake my head. This is full-on. My first reaction is to ask How? I don't want to be insensitive or anything, but I can't help myself and before I know it, it's slipped out there. Mrs Wrens doesn't seem surprised.

He was in the bath, she says. He cut the veins in his arms and . . .

Then these tears start silently dripping down her cheeks and it's awful. We both just stay, like, frozen facing each other, her with tears rolling down her cheeks and me gaping at her like a moron. Then this other woman appears who must be like, her sister or something because she looks exactly the same only taller. She puts her arm round Mrs Wrens' shoulders and gives me this look like she wants to say, Why did you have to come here and upset her?

Come along, Bev, she goes, all stern like it's her bedtime.

She goes to close the door on me but then Mrs Wrens turns back and calls back to me, Come round again, Jarold. Come back and see me . . . another time.

Then the other woman closes the door and I'm left there alone on the step for a minute, feeling more like a dork than ever.

Then I go home. I kind of trudge the whole way back with my feet close to the ground so that they hardly ever leave the concrete. It's a pretty cold day and I'm shivering but I don't even care. It's not because I feel guilty or anything about Fabian, you understand. Because I'm not retarded enough to go down that whole route where it's all supposed to be my fault blah-blah-blah. Because it's blatantly not. I didn't even know him, except for when we hung out like, four whole years ago. And if anyone was gonna end up dead at St Matthew's Fabian's like, the first person you would have thought of.

But that's not to say I don't care, because I do. It's not

nice when someone dies. Ever. At least, it shouldn't be, even if they're a complete Nazi when you think about it. I mean, even when Hitler died it must of been sad in a way.

When I get back home I do that whole thing of walking back and forth in the garden and I see The Nun's stupid tree and I just start thinking about how much I hate her and it, and the next thing I know I've kicked it down. Of course I get in seriously deep shit, because The Nun comes out at this point to tell me it's time for dinner and sees what I've done and like, starts having full-on convulsions. Then Mum comes out to see what's going on and sees the broken tree too and she erupts like a chronic case of zits, and I just stand there while she starts threatening to send me to this special farm for kids who are complete fuck-ups, where they make you stay silent for a whole week and do chores like digging dung until you're like, no longer a human being any more, because maybe that'll drum some sense into me. Then Dad comes out because of all the commotion and once he twigs as to what's going on he starts joining in with his feeble effort, so there's this full-on barrage of yelling like they're all competing with each other or something.

Funny thing is, though, I don't really hear anything. I guess it's 'cos I'm still a bit numbed-out by the whole thing with Fabian. But I don't know, 'cos I'm not really thinking about Fabian after I've kicked down the tree, or anything much. I just stand there and look at the house and I see that Grandma's watching all this out of the window and she's got this dreamy look on her face, and it looks like she's trapped and wants to get out, and I feel this total horror inside which makes me almost vomit up everywhere right there and then. Instead I just slowly walk up to my room, followed all the way by this like, entourage of yelling, and close the door behind me and shift the drawers in front of it.

I lie on the bed and stare up at the ceiling. I can hear The Nun sobbing in her room downstairs and I do feel kind of bad about it, but it's too late now. Probably she'll hold it against me for the rest of my life.

I must have lain there for a few hours but it doesn't seem like that long. Only next time I look around it's dark outside and I realise I'm like, in a famine. It's past eleven and nobody bothered to come up and make me come down to have any dinner or anything.

Anyway the house seems quiet enough, so I figure probably everyone's gone to bed. I get up and go downstairs to the kitchen to raid the fridge for some of Dad's food. But I stop 'cos in there I can hear him and Mum having this argument. I say argument but as per usual it's Mum taking out her shit on Dad. The weird thing is that they're doing it in whispers. It's kind of scary.

She's going, I can't take it any more. Every other day it's something new. He's out of control. There's something wrong with him.

And he's like, Maybe we *should* send him away for a bit. Do you really think it's a good idea?

And she's like, I don't know. I don't know anything any more. Sometimes I just wish he wasn't . . .

There's this pause and then Dad goes, It's not his fault, and Mum snaps back at him, I know that! Don't talk to me like I'm an idiot!

Then she starts hissing like air escaping from a balloon, and she starts coming out with stuff like, You don't care about this family! You're always just so distant! I'm the one who has to deal with all the crap Jarold throws at us. Well, I can't take it any more!

164

And Dad keeps going, What do you want me to do? What do you want from me? until finally Mum goes off the deep end and cries, Maybe a divorce!

There's this long, long silence.

Dad's like, I know you don't mean that.

Mum's like, Don't I? *Fucking don't I?*

Mum's another of those people who never uses the really bad swear-words, so when she does it's the same kind of feeling as when a teacher swears – all wrong, like you've entered this parallel universe where Walt Disney is evil and beige is like, the coolest colour.

In this tiny voice that sounds like it comes from a midget Dad goes, Perhaps we should take a holiday, just you and me?

Mum's like, Dream on! Christ, can't you even think for yourself? We've got a sick mother, two full-time jobs, not to mention the real problem, and you want to take a holiday! Wonderful idea! Pat yourself on the back!

Dad's like, Lois—

But there's the sound of her scraping back her chair and then she cuts him off by going, I never even wanted to be a mother. How did this happen to me?

Then there's the sound of her coming towards the door and I try to slide behind it but I'm not fast enough and she comes out and like, practically walks into me. She doesn't say anything though, she just looks at me. In her face it's like there's this look of complete disgust but also this weird satisfied look, like she's thinking, Good – now you know what I really feel. Then she clomps off upstairs. I stand there feeling all horrible, and then I peek into the kitchen and see that Dad's opened the door and is sitting on the back step smoking.

I decide to starve and go back up to my room where I call

up Al. It's weird though, because I don't even know that I'm doing it, or what I'm planning to say to her. I just press the buttons and do it. It's like something's taken control of me, so maybe it is shock or something after all.

Al answers right away. She's sounds like she's been crying. She like, wails down the line at me, Jaz! We're moving house! We're moving to Leeds! Oh God . . . Leeds! I can't go to Leeds . . .

I'm like, Huh?

Al's like, Dad got his transfer – *to Leeds!*

And then it's like something clicks in my head, just like that. It's obvious what we have to do here, it's the only option. I'm like, Listen Al. Do you want to run away?

18

So Jon's like, What the fuck is going on?

We're in the kitchen. Me and Al are holding our bags and standing there like a prison line-up while he patrols up and down like a sergeant. It's scary how much he reminds me of Mum.

I'm like, Listen, just chill, OK? We just need somewhere to stay for the night and we'll be right out of your way in the morning.

Jon's like, totally not listening, so it's just a waste of my even bothering really. He's like, Are you gonna tell me why the fucking police brought you here? What did you tell *them*?

He goes on and on and asks so many questions it's like, what do you want, an essay? Finally he calms down a bit and starts breathing like he's suddenly remembered it's something you need to do. The funny thing is he looks kind of cute when he's all angry, and I'm kind of a bit switched. But there's a time and a place and you can be pretty damn sure this isn't either of those things. Then Al lets out this massive stupid yawn, which is so big it looks like she's unhinged her jaw to do it. Jon suddenly notices her and goes, Who are you anyway? Is this your sister?

We're both like, the definition of no. It comes out in unison and then we both start laughing manically, since it is three o'clock and after the whole Death stalker/police experience we're practically hysterical. Jon kind of gives this smirk too, so you can see he's not totally absorbed by the spirit of being anal. He's twenty-two, so he's got maybe a couple more years before the whole concept of fun becomes like, totally alien to him.

He's like, OK, just sit down.

So we sit down and he makes some tea. We keep giggling though, every time we catch each other's eye. It's really bad, 'cos you can tell Jon's seriously worried about this. Finally he brings the tea over and sits down opposite us and goes, So you're running away from home, right?

Al's like, Of course not.

But I'm like, Yeah, because sometimes there's just no point in lying. Jon shakes his head in this way just like Dad does, and I'm a bit freaked by it 'cos being reminded of both your parents in the space of a few minutes by a guy you got off with is pretty weird. It's not at all pleasant, actually.

He's like, I can't believe you came here. Of all places.

I'm like, Sorry, all sarcastic because it's pretty insulting. It's obvious all he cares about is himself, not us, and plus he's still got all those age issues going on.

We can leave if you want, I go. I stand up and nod to Al to do the same. Her eyes go all wide like perfect circles 'cos the idea of going back outside into the ice age doesn't thrill her, but she stands up too. Anyway, of course we're only bluffing. Jon immediately waves his hands in the air like one of those symphony conductors.

Sit down, sit down, he goes, You're not going anywhere.

I'm like, Listen, we'll be out of your hair tomorrow morning, OK? We just need to spend the night here.

Jon's like, But what about your parents?

It's like, Hasslesville, because he won't let it drop, so I end up inventing this whole story about Mum and Dad and

168

how Dad beat me up for being gay and Mum told me she never wanted to see me again for the rest of her life. Jon looks quite impressed by the time I'm finished, and I must say I do a pretty good job 'cos even Al's looking at me like she's wondering if it's all completely made-up.

Jon's like, I'm so sorry.

He reaches across the table and takes my hand in this really tacky way. But the thing is, even though it's tacky it's kind of touching, because he thinks it's all real what I've told him.

I'm like, It's cool, forget about it.

Then Jon remembers Al again. He's like, What about your friend?

We both look at Al. Her face kind of wobbles for a minute and then she starts sobbing. I swear, Al can't act for shit but this time she does me proud. She just goes, I can't even talk about it! and Jon frowns very deeply but nods like he understands. He fetches a box of tissues from the side and gives it to her. She blows her nose like a trumpet and I ask again if we can stay the night.

He's like, Of course, but what you gonna do in the morning?

I'm like, Don't worry about it.

Jon gives me this long look like he's trying to figure something out about me. Maybe it's whether or not I'm lying, I don't know. I'm like, hardly even alive by this point, but I've got to say he's looking pretty sexy. His hair's all tousled and his robe is kind of open a bit so you can see his chest. It's got just a little bit of hair, which I reckon is a massive turn-on. I can't stand full-on gorillas – that would be like getting off with a mound of fur. But if they've got nothing then it's like they're a total baldy. Actually I'm a baldy, but I reckon I've still got a chance of growing some thatch yet.

Anyway, I'm like, returning his look and getting all aroused, and I'm pretty sure he's thinking what I'm thinking, but then this door opens and this other guy comes into the room and goes, What's going on? Who are these people?

This new guy isn't wearing anything except for his Y-fronts, and he's some rare species of gorilla, I'm telling you. It's like, sprouting from every pore. Al's majorly grossed out by it 'cos she jerks her head away like in that scene at the end of *Raiders of the Lost Ark* where they can't look at the light. Despite the whole bodysuit, he's not that bad-looking, this guy, though he's kind of mature. Jon starts explaining that we're friends of his and we're in a bit of trouble and need somewhere to stay. I think it's pretty decent of him to leave out the fact that we're runaways, but maybe this guy he lives with isn't the type who'd deal with it too well. He kind of gives me the eye while Jon's explaining. It's actually a bit gross the way he does it, 'cos he kind of licks his lips too, and even Al, who's normally like, dead to this sort of thing, notices it. She gives me a nudge and makes eyeballs like she can't believe how blatant he's being.

Jon's flatmate is called Buddy. He's cool with us staying the night, and even offers to help make up the living-room. But Jon manages to get him to go back to bed. Then he like, escorts us into the living-room where there's this couch that like, magically turns into a double. We both fall into it like dead people the second he's gone.

I wake up pretty early (like a couple of hours later), and there're all these birds singing outside and I've got a bit of a headache from it. Despite this, and the fact that Al's snoring away next to me like a phlegm factory, I feel kind of excited. It's like we're on the run from the law or something, and it's like anything could happen. Not that anything will, of

170

course, 'cos it's all mapped out. Al made sure of that. We're just gonna look for work and set ourselves up slowly, taking as long as it takes. We both left behind notes. It's pretty naff but that way they know we've not been kidnapped or murdered or anything, so Mum won't get the police to like, start scanning the whole country for our body parts. I didn't really say anything in my note, apart from that I was going, and thanks for everything, though I don't know what everything is, unless it was like, giving birth to me. I don't think I'll miss any of them – I reckon I got that out of my system that time with the E. Except maybe Grandma, even though she's a total vegetable these days.

It's weird to think about, 'cos they won't have even found the note yet. Mum'll find it tomorrow, when she wonders why I'm not standing to attention at breakfast alongside Teresa. The Nun'll be thrilled, I bet. She's always wanted to be the centre of attention in our house, so good luck to her I say. Maybe she'll even manage to convert everybody.

But I keep thinking back to that argument I overheard them having in whispers, and the way Mum looked at me when she saw me as she came out the kitchen. This like, chilling look. I mean, they were talking some pretty heavy shit, but she looked *glad* when she saw that I'd been listening. It's just as well I'm out of there really. I'm so sick of the way no one even bothers to stop and think that maybe I see things differently and maybe that's why I don't conform to every last detail around me.

I fall back asleep thinking about this stuff and when I wake up again there's this gorgeous smell of bacon, and my tongue practically shrivels up since I haven't eaten for, like, an era. Al's not next to me and there are mumbling sounds coming from the kitchen. I kind of leap to my feet and throw myself at the door, even though I'm only in my underwear, because Al's useless on her own and it would be just like her to tell Jon all this stuff he doesn't need to know. But Jon's not there, it's Buddy (dressed, thankfully), cooking this fry-up.

He's like, And good morning to you! looking me up and down like I'm for sale or something. Al gives me this weirded-out look.

I'm like, Hi, kind of embarrassed.

Buddy's like, Jon's gone to teach his class at the pond so I said I'd babysit for him.

It's not clear whether he's taking the piss or is just making an innocent joke, so I let it go. But Al looks totally suspicious.

She's like, Don't *you* have to go to work?

Buddy's like, I'm at work.

Al gives him this look like he could die screaming and she'd happily watch. Buddy seems kind of amused by her.

I work from home, he explains, I'm a website designer.

He's says what he does all self-importantly like he's expecting us to applaud or something, and he looks kind of peeved when we both just nod. I go fetch my T-shirt, since I'm feeling kind of on display, and Buddy dishes us out some fry-up each and we start eating like we've been raised on pellets all our lives. Buddy looks even more amused. He watches us – at least, he watches me. He's like, a total lech. Eventually it gets on my tits.

I'm like, Could you be any more obvious?

He acts all surprised, but he's not embarrassed. He's like, Can't help it if I like what I see, honey.

Al gives him this stare like she can't understand why God hasn't struck Buddy down yet, but I kind of like him for saying that. It's like, why shouldn't he be honest about it?

172

So I shrug at her and start talking to him. He's not so bad either. He asks us how long we're here for and if we fancy a trip into town later and maybe he can show us around. Al keeps shaking her head over and over like she's stuck in a time glitch or something, but I say, Yeah, that would be cool, and Buddy's like, All righty then!

The second we're alone Al hisses at me, What the hell?

I'm like, What? all innocently.

She's like, Can't you see he just wants to bone you! We should get out of here!

I'm like, Settle, petal.

Al's like, You settle! He's just wants to crack on to you! Sometimes you can be so *stupid*.

She's properly into conniption mode, and can't even sit still. She keeps biting her fingernails, and if you don't know what Al's fingernails look like then you should know that they can't get much shorter.

I'm like, Listen, I'm here for a reason, and that's because I'm sick and tired of being told what I can and can't do. So let's just chill and try to have fun or something.

I don't really see what she can say to that, but being a politicsy type Al's always got something up her sleeve. She's like, I just hope you don't end up old and alone.

I'm like, What the huh?

But she won't say anything else and I can't be bothered to push the issue. In fact, I'm like, Why is she even here if she didn't want to come? I mean, I'm glad and all that she *is* here, but at the same time it's like, Who wants to be dragged down all the time?

So Buddy drives us around Brighton in his Mercedes (I kid you not, I'm totally planning on becoming a website designer). It's pretty cool, 'cos we listen to the radio and see loads of stuff. It's just nice not to have to go anywhere or

173

anything, just to drift. He doesn't ask many questions either, just tells us all these things he knows. He knows the craziest stuff. Like that 90 per cent of men dribble when they ejaculate and only 10 per cent shoot (I'm like, Based on your experience or what?). He's a pretty witty guy it turns out, and by the time we get to the pier even Al's looking like maybe she's having a shred of fun.

The pier is something else. It's like, totally surreal – I don't know if you know it, but there's this rickety old roller-coaster on it that goes quite high. It's a pretty bizarre thing to have on a pier, over the sea. I remember once coming here on a holiday with Mum and Dad and The Nun back when she wasn't The Nun but like, normal. Me and her must of been about six or seven and Dad tried to persuade us to go on it, but we saw the faces of the people coming off, like the definition of I-want-to-puke, and both refused. Dad was like, Come on! but we were both totally negatory, and so he didn't go on it either and we just got our stupid handwriting analysed by the machines and then all sat on the pebbly beach next to all the other families who thought they would have this great day out just by being close to the sea. Totally lame.

So I decide I like, have to go on this roller-coaster. I figure I owe it to someone, since I didn't go on it that time. Don't ask me who, unless it's Dad. Al's not keen but she agrees when she realises the alternative is being left to stand and watch with Buddy, who she's still dead set is a total perv and who like, declares that he'd rather just jump off the pier than ride with us.

So we get into the carriage and pull the bar down and off we go. The carriage starts to rise, and Fuck Is It Scary. The whole track doesn't seem too stable, 'cos the carriage rickets this way and that like any second we're gonna slip and go falling through the sky. Brighton and the pier and all the beach with the families on it stretches out underneath us like one of those pictorial maps tourists are always looking at in Leicester Square. We get to the top of the first dip and then we teeter there for a second, like we're sat on the edge of the world. Suddenly whoosh, we take off at breakneck speed. It's like we're never ever gonna stop. You should hear Al, 'cos I swear she breaks the sound barrier. There's only two other people on it and they're screaming blue murder as well. I probably am too. You can't not scream because the carriages jerk so hard when you go round a bend that it *hurts*.

When the thing finally comes to a halt Al looks at me like I'm a spastic or something and goes, Are you OK?

I'm in like, total fountains. I have no idea why. It's like this disease or something, 'cos like I said I'm the sort of person who doesn't cry – though I bet you don't believe me since I've already cried quite a lot. Well, LIC GAS. I'm like, Yeah, a bit weirded 'cos I have no idea what I'm crying for either. It's just the whole feeling like being out of control, I guess. It's kind of liberating but it's kind of sad too and no, I don't know why that is. And if you think it's daft that I don't know, it's because it *is* daft, and at least don't be thinking I don't know *that*.

Al's like, Jesus, Jaz. We shouldn't be here. We should go back.

I like, recover in two seconds flat. I wipe my face with my sleeve.

Let's just go home, she says.

You're on your own, Sister, I tell her.

Her face becomes, like, this one big frown though, like she's Deeply Troubled. It's the sort of face you dread to see people making, 'cos you can just tell it means they're

175

developing an allergy to humour. Sometimes I just have no idea what's going on in Al's head.

Buddy's pretty amused when we get back to him. He has total fits over my hair, which he says is all 'Bart Simpsonesque'. I'm like, Whatever. I feel tired, as well as pissed off with Al, and I can't be bothered to follow him into the centre and look round the shops or anything. Buddy's pretty tuned in though, 'cos he seems to sense that the whole spirit of adventure has like, died a sudden death, and he says it's time to get back 'cos he needs to do some work. He gives my arse a pinch as I'm climbing into the car and then looks all innocent when I look at him. Al's like, right behind us and is majorly grossed out, but I'm cool with it 'cos it's like, hey, you are allowed to express yourself from time to time. The way I see it people don't do what they want to do often enough. They just do some alternative which they'd kind of like to do, which isn't the same thing at all, and as a result that thing isn't enough and they end up depressed and annoyed with everyone else around them.

Anyway, we get back and Jon's hanging out in the kitchen waiting for us. You can tell he's a bit pissed off that Buddy took us out. I think maybe he's jealous even, but he doesn't actually say anything. It's just this vibe he gives out. He doesn't actually seem to like Buddy much, 'cos neither of them say Hi or anything. He just goes to us, We need to talk. Then Buddy goes off to work in his study so we end up sitting there at the table with Jon. It's kind of awkward.

I'm like, So how was snorkelling?

I'm only joking, but Jon's like a closed register. He goes, It's windsurfing, like I'm this idiot who can't remember or something. Then he goes, Listen, you guys need to figure this out. I've been thinking about it and the best thing I can come up with is for you to go to the police. They'll put you in touch with a social worker or something.

He looks at us like he's just invented the answer to all our problems. Me and Al look back at him like he's a total moron.

I mean, for fuck's sake, we're not living in the sixteenth century here! he goes, When this kind of thing happens there's benefits and councils and all that crap that's been set up to help people out! To help out guys like you.

Luckily he doesn't sound like he knows anything about it, which is good 'cos if he'd been anything like Mum he'd have reeled off this whole list of things we could do probably, and I'd have had a hard time talking my way out of it.

I'm like, Listen, we've done all that stuff. Sometimes shit happens and there's nothing you can do. Trust me, we've *tried*. If we could just stay here for a few days . . .

I kind of make my voice go all pleading and desperate. I sound like a total prick but Jon still looks like he might be setting forth on a trip to guilt city. But then Al spoils it by saying, I don't know, Jaz. Maybe there is something we can do. Maybe we should just go home and try again.

Jon's whole face is like, exactly what relief looks like. I'm almost ready to kill Al for saying that, but she's making these eyes at me like she's a drowning woman or something.

Jon's like, I could even drive you if you wanted.

I kind of hate him for saying that. He says it so fast it's totally obvious he's desperate to get rid of us. He wasn't jealous that Buddy took us out today, he was just annoyed probably 'cos he thought we were settling in. I think back to him taking my hand last night and how I felt bad about lying to him. But some people just deserve to be lied to.

I'm like, I can't go back. I just can't. Maybe Al can work

177

things out with her *alcoholic parents*, but there's no way I can with mine. But it's OK, Jon, I can find some other place to crash. I understand that this is a hassle for you and I don't want to put you out or anything.

Al winces when I say that about her parents. I think it's a pretty funny joke, since it's easier to imagine Mr and Mrs Rutland deciding to go gay than it is to imagine them as alcoholics. But Al's sense of humour is well and truly like, over. There's this pause which lasts for eternity, in which there's like, whole bales of tumbleweed blowing through, and then Jon lets out this great long sigh which sounds a bit like trapped wind that's been stored up all day, only coming out the wrong hole. I mean, from the way this guy sighs you'd think I was asking him to donate a lung or something.

Jon's like, But surely you've got to at least call them.

I'm like, You're not hearing me. They don't give a shit. They think I'm the Antichrist. By being here and not there, I'm Doing Them A Favour.

Jon looks at Al.

Is it true? he goes.

I wait for Al to fuck it all up, but she suddenly develops this urgent need to go to the bathroom. She kind of brushes my shoulder as she passes in this way like she maybe meant to do it, like she really wanted to hit me or something. Left alone with Jon I decide to try some waterworks to see if that'll clinch it, but I can't seem to make them happen. I hate that about crying – you can never do it when you want to. At least I can't, though The Nun always seemed to have it under control.

Jon's like, Well, I guess you can stay here for now, but it can't go on. We've got to figure something out. You've got to go to the police and at least talk to them. You can't just

178

run away. I mean, have you even thought about your future? Jesus . . . Jon suddenly turns all pale like some thought has just occurred to him. You must still be at school!

It's like, issue central here. But he's looking kind of sexy again, and I start to wonder, despite myself. I mean, you can't not think about these things, so I go, I thought you liked me.

Jon's like, I do. I mean, I did – but now it's different.

He sounds kind of like he's backing out of it or something. Like he doesn't want anything to do with me on that front, which pisses me off, 'cos I know he likes me, 'cos of everything that's come before.

I'm like, Why? It's not illegal or anything.

Jon's like, Yeah. But it just *is*. I don't screw around with kids, Jaz. I can't do it. My dad left my mum for some guy half his age and it took me all my life to forgive him for it. And of course it didn't work out either, because all this guy was interested in was . . .

He trails off, probably aware of the fact that he's heading straight for the cheesiest outburst in the history of anything. He stands up and goes to the cupboard and opens it like he's suddenly remembered he had something in there he wanted to find. But all he does is clink the cups around like they needed to be rearranged or something. Then he goes:

I want to help you out. Really I do. I'll let you stay here, if it's OK with Bud. For a few days. But you have got to figure some stuff out. If you're not going home then you need to contact the police or someone. I mean, don't you have any relatives?

At this point an alarm on his watch goes off, which is lucky because if I had to answer any more questions I would have probably told him where to shove it and just shovelled

179

on out there and gone looking for a hostel. I swear some people just don't understand when to quit. Jon closes the cupboard and goes, Listen, I've got to get ready to go out.

I'm like, Oh. Where to?

It's not that I'm angling for an invite or anything, but Brighton is supposed to be the cool place to go out, and I've heard they're pretty lax about the whole age thing getting into clubs. And since we are his guests and all I guess I figure maybe he can give us some pointers or something.

But Jon's suddenly like, redder than red.

Actually . . . I've got a date, he says, looking at his feet like he wishes they would do more of the talking. I'm like, Oh and whatever.

He goes and I sit there feeling really shit, 'cos I kind of still fancy him and all even if it's not the whole butterfly-effect that it was when I first saw him. I get up and go into the living-room, where Al's sitting on the couch/bed looking like she's been infected with chronic unhappiness or something. She doesn't say anything to me, and I don't say anything to her. We both just sit there, and then I lie down. I don't mean to sleep but the second my eyes are closed that's what happens.

19

The next thing I know I'm being shaken awake by Al, and it's like she's been transformed into a totally different person. She's all excited and giggly. I swear it's like she's gone through some space warp to a parallel universe and swapped with an alternative version of herself.

She's like, Come on, you've got to get up, we're going soon!

I'm like, Huh. Going where?

To Bar None – Buddy's taking us, she goes, Come on!

There's this funny smell in the air. I notice that Al's like, dressed in her famous floral gown, and is holding a drink in one hand and also a spliff in the other like, totally ready to go. There's these clinking noises from the kitchen and Buddy's singing some naffo pop tune in this weird falsetto like Justin from The Darkness.

I'm tired, I say.

Oh no you're not! squeals Al in this massively OTT way like we're in a pantomime or something.

Are you going to get out of bed? she goes.

I'm like, I thought you hated him.

Al shrugs. She's like, He's not so bad, in this voice that makes it seem like *I* was the one who had reservations. Come on! she shrieks.

Suddenly I notice something about her that tells me all I need to know about this sudden change of identity.

I'm like, What's that's in your nose?

Al's fingers leap up to her nostrils and she giggles and runs to the massive ornate mirror Jon and Buddy have hanging in their living-room. She peers at herself and makes a few snorting sounds.

Ask Buddy! she goes like it's the coolest thing ever, I'm sure he'll give you some too!

I like, roll out of the bed and start rummaging around in my backpack for some better clothes. Al comes and plops the drink next to me and then hands me the spliff. Then she goes back to the kitchen and a second later I hear her distinctive laugh, which she could probably sell to a film studio as the sound effect for a foghorn. The idea of Al mixed with coke of the non-cola variety is a bit disturbing. I mean, we're talking about someone who normally gets wasted on cider and blackcurrant. But quite frankly I don't care. In fact, if it means she stops acting like someone's pissed on her grave I hope she spends the rest of her life in some kind of stupor.

I'm still kind of peeved that Jon just went out on this date. I mean, I know I've got no right to be or anything, I'm not a complete idiot. But still, I'm like, here, wide and open, so it's like, what's the deal? I don't care about feelings or anything though, don't get me wrong. I've just got a massive hard-on for him is all.

Anyway, so we troop out to this bar. It's not all that. I mean, it's pretty OK I suppose, way better than Starlight. It's got proper podiums and dancers and the barmen are all totally drop-dead. So are half the people here actually. In fact it's like a full-on orgy and there's nothing just OK about it. But I'm just not feeling it for some reason. I'm still sleepy and the spliff hasn't helped matters.

Al loves it. She practically creams like, multiple times. She keeps going, I can't believe how amazing it is here! like this kid at Disneyland or something. It's so not cool, but she kind of gets away with it. I never really noticed but the thing about Al is that she's kind of cute when she's excited, in a none-gross cute kind of way. I mean, she can't compete with anyone in here or anything, but she has this quality to her which is kind of sweet.

Buddy spruces up pretty well too. There's still all that fuzz but most of it's hidden under his shirt, and he kind of looks a bit devilish with his hair all slicked back. He seems to know just about everyone in the club, 'cos they all sort of swarm around him when we go in like he's this human magnet or something. Al like, stands next to him like a bodyguard, and pretty soon she's talking to everyone in the club as well, while I kind of end up at the sidelines. I don't know what it is, I've just got this lump in my throat. I kind of miss old Starlight a bit, even if it is like, right at the bottom of the coolness scale.

Buddy keeps buying us cocktails. It's just as well since between us we've got about enough money for one shot of something. I drink all these Long Island Iced Teas, which I've never had before but which are pretty tasty. I'm wasted pretty fast too, because when I go to lean against the bar I slip and catch my elbow. But it doesn't matter, 'cos no one's paying much attention to me anyway. They're all, like, standing on each other's shoulders trying to talk to Buddy.

After a bit I start to think I'm gonna keel. It's ultra-hot in this club and they start playing this Latino music, and everyone starts swirling around to it like their mission in life is to turn circles. Just watching makes me feel dizzy, and I end up like, clutching on to my stool for support.

Then Buddy appears from nowhere. It's well weird 'cos I could have sworn he was over the other side of the room –

he just comes up to me and asks if I'm all right, and suddenly I know what he's thinking. But he also suddenly looks kind of sexy. He looks into my face like he's so worried about me he doesn't care about anything else, and I tell him I'm fine and that I just need some water. Let's get you to the bathroom, he goes.

I'm like, Sure, 'cos it's blatant we're gonna be having a fumble. Thing is, I'm so wrecked I can hardly even see straight. I look back at Al but she's being chatted to on all sides by like, a whole gang of women in sparkly dresses.

In the bathroom, I get some water from the drinking fountain and feel a tiny bit better. The place looks like it's decorated with real gold. It's like the opposite of the dingy old toilets at Starlight, which look like someone shat and wiped the walls with it.

Buddy's like, So you want a line? and I'm like, Sure, even though I'm hardly still even vertical here.

We go into the end cubicle and he takes out this great big bag of powder and empties a bit on the toilet seat. Then he carves out two lines.

He's like, This is quality stuff. You dig?

I'm like, Yeah. Sure.

He takes out this rolled-up note which he has to practically hold and jam up my nose for me. But I eventually manage to do the line he's cut for me, and then we start kissing and his hands are like, touching me all over. I'm suddenly struck that I'm not sure I want to be here, 'cos close up he's not so hot really, and his breath isn't great either, which really is hell when you're trying to kiss someone. But it's too late to be saying No, and the coke gives me this buzz anyway, and I do kind of feel myself responding a bit.

Buddy leans close and whispers in my ear, Let's go back to the flat.

I'm like, OK, but only because I don't seem to have a free will any more. I'd have probably said the same if he'd asked if I wanted to take a dip in the urinal.

I feel bad about leaving Al. Even though I'm trashed beyond trashed I do think of her. But she's obviously having a great time and is clearly like, this novelty or something to all the people here, so it doesn't seem so terrible. I try to say something to Buddy about it though, that we should let her know or something, but he's like, She's a big girl, she'll get a cab back, and I'm like, Yeah. Which is totally forgetting that she's got no money or anything.

So we jump in a cab (there's like, an army of them waiting outside) and pretty soon we're back at the flat. Jon doesn't seem to be here, which is probably just as well 'cos I'm all over the place and he'd probably freak big time if he saw me fooling around with Buddy. I'm still not sure I want to be doing this, and I do make this like, token effort to like, grab hold of the kitchen table as we pass. But Buddy takes my hand and totally like, carries me up the stairs to his bedroom. Which is quite something. I think he kind of wants me to start admiring it, but I'm in no condition to start licking his ego, so instead I start kissing him, and he starts kissing me back like he wants to eat me or something.

The whole thing is a total Lynch-fest. It's not that different to when I was hit on the head really. It's like time isn't quite working like it's supposed to, because the next thing I know I'm on the bed and Buddy's got his clothes off, and I'm reaching down to take off mine and whoops, if they're not off already. Then Buddy's all over me. He's like rash, I swear. I can feel his stubble, like, everywhere. It's not even a turn-on, but you can't really tell someone to stop

185

when they're in the throes, so I just lie back and deal with it, and try to thrash about a bit too so he doesn't think I'm a total vegetable in the sack.

Then he does that thing to me which gays are, like, famous for doing. I'm not even expecting it or anything, and I don't even remember him turning me over or whether or not he even puts on a condom. But I remember the pain, because it's like a firecracker's gone off up there. Seriously, Nothing can prepare you.

Buddy's like, moaning, Oh yeah, oh yeah, oh yeahhhhh! like he's a cowboy or space cadet or something. Meanwhile it's like I'm being impaled. I grab the sheets with my fingers and dig my nails in, 'cos there's not much else for it. All of a sudden it totally makes sense why women in labour always want someone's hand to squeeze. I taste my own tears which are streaming out of my eyes like in total torrents.

How is it? Buddy shouts to me at one point. I'm like, Are you for real? but he's not listening, or else I don't say it out loud. He just doesn't ever stop though. It's like being humped by this machine. This really hairy machine.

The really weird thing is, as he goes at it, I start to not care about the pain. I mean I'm actually kind of glad that it's painful. I can hardly explain it, but it's kind of like I want him to hurt me. Like I want him to punish me because I feel like a bad person. I feel like a bastard to be honest. I don't know why, I just do. All these horrible feelings are swelling up inside me and I feel really frightened all of a sudden, like I'm a little kid who's lost in this big dark city, or something equally tacky like that. It's kind of like Buddy's fucking these feelings out of me, and even though it's painful, it's a good painful, because it's replacing those bad feelings with a pain you can actually like, *feel*.

I close my eyes, and then I have this image of Fabian and

186

me. It's a memory. We're in class together waiting for the teacher to arrive, like, back in Year One. He's trying get me to prick my finger with a compass point and exchange blood with him like they do with wounds in films in order to swear their allegiance to each other or something. I'm going, No way you freak! and Fabian's calling me a pussy and then stabbing his own finger. Then he sucks on it and grins at me. I see all this blood on his front teeth and his lips are all stained with ink from chewing his pen. He always chewed on his pen like it was a stick of gum or something. But this is where the memory stops being a memory and becomes like, this freaky vision, 'cos I suddenly find myself staring at the headboard of Buddy's bed and I can see Fabian's face, like, superimposed over the top of it. It's totally the coke and weed and alcohol combo, but it seems so real I'm like, the definition of disbelief.

I'm like, What are you doing here? to Fabian.

In between his pumps of pain Buddy shouts to me, I'm giving you the best fuck of your little young life, my dear!

It's like, whatever – all I can focus on is Fabian's face in front of me. He's still got ink all running down his lips and he's smiling in his own special freaky way. He's holding out his finger to me, but it's not just his finger that's cut. Instead his whole hand is covered in blood and it's like, oozing out of this gash in his wrist – it's a totally unfriendly apparition to be seeing. He's not saying anything but it's like he's still trying to get me to mingle my blood with him so we can be one and the same or something.

I'm like, You've got to be joking.

Buddy's like, Oh no, baby, this is no joke!

Then Fabian starts to fade away. As he does his face kind of stops smiling and looks really sad, like he's sorry to be going. I'm kind of sorry too, because I remember about how he's dead and how he attacked Fuck Face with his knife for me. The next thing all I can see is the headboard.

Then it kind of hits me that I have no idea what I'm doing here. There's this sound like someone shrieking and I kind of come to and realise where I am. Maybe it's the coke wearing off or something. But suddenly I'm ultra-conscious of what's going on – of the fact that I'm being screwed from behind by this guy in his room in Brighton. Of the fact that I've run away from all these problems at home. And that I've left Al alone at some club.

I start to struggle free of Buddy and turn my head and that's when I see Jon. At first I think it's just another vision, but if you've ever had one you'll know there's no mistaking actual reality when it's standing in front of you. He's stood there in the doorway with his mouth all stupidly open like he's catching flies. He looks right into my eyes and I look into his and then his whole face crumples up in disgust and he just turns around and stalks away. I want to call out after him but when I open my mouth all that comes out is this cry of sheer agony which has been building up for some time. Then Buddy lets out this Ahhh, which is exactly the same as the sound the doctor asks you to make when he checks out your tonsils.

There's more pain as he takes his cock out, and then he kind of flops over me in exhaustion and lies there on top of me. It's a bit like wearing a super-heavy fur coat.

He's like, Was it good for you?

I'm like, Get the hell off of me!

But he doesn't move, he just snorts and tries to wrap his arms around me. He's kind of surprised when I sort of do this backflip thing and send him flying off the bed. He lets out this yell 'cos he hits a table and knocks off this big glass bowl which lands on the floor and shatters into like, a zillion pieces. Right away I'm up and running back and forward like a speed freak, trying to find all my clothes and put them on at the same time.

Buddy's like, That was a fucking three-hundred-pound vase!

I'm like, LIC GAS.

Then I'm bounding out of the room and across the hall. I stop and take a deep breath. Then I knock on Jon's door. There's no answer so I just open it and go in. He's sat there on the bed rubbing some kind of ointment on his face. He keeps rubbing it so I kind of stand there like an idiot and then finally he stops and goes, So how *is* Buddy? in this totally bitchy way.

I'm like, Listen that was just a thing, OK?

Jon stops what he's doing and gives me this look like I'm a wilted turd or something. Then he heaves the mother of all sighs. He's like, Why don't you just go, OK? You don't have to explain anything to me, it's your life. Anyway I'm tired.

He goes back to rubbing his ointment. I stand there moronically like, trying to think of something to say back to that, but at this point Buddy appears at the door behind me.

He's like, a total state. He's wearing this black silk kimono with a dragon pattern on it, and his fuzz is like, spurting out through all the gaps. He's like, What the hell's going on? I can't believe you broke my Dynasty! Do you know how much that fucking thing cost?

I'm like, Send me a bill.

Buddy's like, Fuck you!

And Jon's like, Can you both just *leave*?

There's this windy pause and then Buddy throws up his hands in the air like a full-on diva and then whirls round and stomps back to his room. There's the sound of his door slamming. I feel weak in my knees and I find myself crouching on the ground. The world seems to be swimming and going dark for a few seconds. Then the dizziness passes and I find that Jon's crouched beside me.

He's like, What's wrong with you?

Listen, I hear myself go, We have to go and find Al. I left her alone at this club and she doesn't even know how to get back. And she's never taken drugs before.

Jon's like, You did *what*?

He totally can't believe I've just left my friend in the middle of some city I don't even know, especially what with her background of alcohol abuse. He's like, Give her a call!

This didn't even occur to me, so I take his mobile and try her number. There's this pause and then the sound of a phone ringing downstairs. I'm like, Oh shit.

Jon starts furiously pulling on his clothes and this is when I start to come clean about a few things. Like the fact that Al's parents aren't really alcoholics, and the fact that basically I've done nothing but lie to him since we've been here. I feel a bit sick while I'm telling him because he doesn't react or anything, just keeps on dressing and then turns and goes downstairs. I follow him down, still trying to explain, and then out of the house and around the corner to where his car is parked. The more I talk the more lame and desperate I sound. Jon unlocks the doors.

Get in, he says in this dead-sounding voice.

I'm like, Just listen a sec—

Get in, he cuts me off.

I get in and we drive off in silence. Then Jon turns to me and asks which club we're going to and I tell him. I feel like a total cunt, and my arse hurts like I've got a razor-blade stuck in it. We come to some traffic lights and while we're sitting there the silence becomes like, overwhelming, plus I can't stop squirming in the seat. Jon stares straight ahead and goes, You're some piece of work, you know that? I mean, what kind of a friend *are* you?

I don't say anything. It's true.

You know what? I was on a date tonight, and it was going really well. But I decided to come back because I thought . . . He trails off, like suddenly he's thought better of what he was going to say.

I'm like, Thought what?

He's like, Never mind.

At this point the lights change and we take off again. To cover the silence he switches on the radio, and we spend the rest of the journey listening to this soppy-voiced DJ telling callers how to unfuck their lives. It feels like an era before we reach the club. Jon pulls up outside and says he'll wait for me. I get out and go up to the door. They won't let me back in though. The bouncers, who are these guys who look like they've been brought up on a healthy diet of steroids for their whole lives, look me up and down like I'm a piece of shit with arms and legs. They actually think it's funny that I want to go in.

I'm like, My friend is in there! She's all alone.

They don't look too convinced by this. I try to explain, but they're not having any of it.

Go back to school, mate, says one of them and then laughs like he's so witty he's gonna pop a blood vessel. I want to hit him, but I don't, since this guy could probably take out Superman with his little finger. I return to the car and tell Jon the status. He looks just thrilled but he turns off the engine and gets out and goes up to the doors. The bouncers move to either side to let him pass right away, like he's Moses or something, and he disappears inside.

191

After about ten minutes I start to wonder what's going on and if maybe he's stopped for a quick one and a boogie inside. Just as I'm about to like, make a second attempt and, like, rush the bouncers or something, he reappears. He gets in the car and goes, She's not there any more.

I have this sick feeling all over now, like I'm seriously gonna throw up. I'm like, totally ready to convert, or anything so long as it'll bring Al back.

He's like, One of the barmen remembers a girl being really out of her head and asking him for directions to the pier, so we'll go take a look there. If we can't find her, we'll have to go to the police.

We take off once more. I'm leaking a bit now. In fact the tears are coming out of my eyes like I've burst a pipe. Jon looks over to me and heaves another classic sigh. But he reaches across and pats me on the knee (in a totally non-sexual way).

He's like, Look, she'll be OK. We'll find her.

We reach the pier and get out. There are a few couples wandering around and swigging from bottles even though it's freezing and the dead of night. Jon suggests we go in different directions up the road to look for her. I nod and start walking. The wind is back with a vengeance and after a few metres it feels like any second I'm gonna be lifted off my feet and sent hurtling into the sky. I pass this couple and some insane woman wearing this red top beckons to me and shouts out, Hey junior, how about a threesome? I don't even reply. I look back and the car seems like it's miles away, and there's no sign of Jon. I carry on for a bit but my heart's sinking like it's got a lead weight attached to it, and I picture how I'm going to have to explain to Al's parents that their only child's vanished for good. It's like there's no hope whatsoever. I'm tempted to just lie down with my head in the road and wait for some happy lorry to come and put me out of my misery.

But then, like some miracle (at least that's how it seems for a few seconds – I do still have *some* perspective), I look down at the beach and there she is. She's stood there right beneath me all huddled up and staring out into the sea like she's debating over how to drown herself.

I'm so thrilled to see her I don't even think about what I'm doing, I just put my leg over the wall and let myself drop. Then, about halfway through falling, I realise just how high up I was. I kind of crash back into Al's life shouting Oh shit! at the top of my voice.

She turns round and looks at me with her mouth hanging open. It seriously looks like I've just fallen out of the sky.

She's like, What the fuck are you doing here?

I kind of sit up and try and pull all my limbs back together. I can't quite believe I haven't broken anything. But I don't really care because I'm so happy to see Al again. I'm like, Looking for you of course!

Al closes her mouth and turns back to the sea. I stagger to my feet. Both of my ankles feel like they're sprained but I grit my teeth and like, hobble over to her.

I'm like, Al, I'm sorry. I really am.

Al's like, It's not fair, Jaz, in this faraway voice.

I'm like, What's not fair?

She's like, Why does everyone like you and not me?

I'm like, Huh? Are you having an Asian moment?

I don't mean it in a bad way, but apparently this is the total wrong thing to say because she whirls back at me with this face that's like, anger intensified.

Everyone just loves you, don't they?! she shouts, Everyone just falls over themselves to be your friend or to sleep with you or to whatever! No one does with me and it's not fair! Sometimes I hate you so much! You're so lucky and you have no idea! You don't give a shit about anyone but yourself and it's just perfectly OK for you!

I like, process this.

That's not true, I say, I *do* care.

Al's like, Sure. Right. I saw you leaving the club with *him*, you know.

Next thing I know I've stumbled forward and I'm trying to hug her. It's pretty confused, 'cos Al's this total hybrid of anger and neediness, and she practically has a fit trying to simultaneously hug me back and attack me. After a while though she calms down and we both just stand there.

Then I'm like, Listen Al, I gotta tell you something.

She looks at me. I can't hardly breathe though, I'm suddenly so out of breath it's not true. I start coughing in this way that seems like I'm being choked or something. Al pats me on the back in this totally useless, ineffectual way. In the end we both sit down there on the wet pebbles in the middle of the freezing cold to wait for my lungs to recover.

In between gasps I'm like, Fabian killed himself.

Al's like, What?

I'm like, It's true. I went round to see his mum and she told me about it. He did it last week, in the bath.

I tell her all about going to see Mrs Wrens, and then about what happened with him at Mary's party. And while I'm telling her this I feel this big sense of relief, like secretly inside I was feeling kind of responsible for it all this time. I know that's stupid, because I already said I wasn't or anything. But still I guess maybe the feeling was there, tucked away somewhere. You don't really know what goes on in your own mind, not with all those different levels and stuff and it's so good to be talking about it – to be telling Al,

I mean. I kind of kick myself for not talking to her before because she really listens and then she gives me this hug and says, That's awful, especially because you used to hang out together, and all that, and actually I feel kind of happy for a few seconds. That's the great thing about Al. She always knows the right thing to say when you tell her something like this. That's the reason I hang out with her, and none of those other losers that populate St Matthew's.

We sit there for a while hugging each other and listening to our teeth chattering away. Even though it's like, brutally cold and my arsehole still feels like it's been used as an ashtray or something, it's nice too. But in a weird way nice, 'cos I feel sad too. It's partly because of Fabian, but it's also because I suddenly know we're going back home. It's like, so totally obvious that's what's gonna happen.

Then I find myself giggling and Al starts giggling too, and I tell her about the Buddy experience, and then we have this total giggle-fest, and she shakes her head in this exaggerated politician kind of way and tells me it's my own fault for dumping her. I agree and then burst into giggles again. I can't stop, I'm like a trembleometer or something. Al says that she simply despairs of me. I'm like, Tell me about it, sister.

Then I suddenly remember about Jon and jump up.

I'm like, Shit!

Al's like, What is it?

I'm like, Jon! We came out to look for you! We have to find him.

We climb back up the wall and look up and down the road. There's no sign of Jon or the couple who wanted a threesome. We start walking towards where the car's parked. Thankfully that's still there, but of course the doors are locked so we can't get in. We're seriously starting to freeze here.

Al's like, Where the hell is he?

At this point you might have thought the evening couldn't have taken any more drama, but if you did you'd be wrong, because this is when the police car draws up beside us. If you can believe it, it's old Cross Eyes and The Bitch, who this time is in the driver's seat and is staring us down with a face that would melt plastic. She rolls down the window and goes, So what story are you going to give us tonight?

I'm like, We're just waiting to go home.

Cross Eyes is like, way behind his colleague and still focusing on who we are. When he realises we're the same kids from the night before his whole face lights up. He's like, Hey, it's Richard and Judy!

The Bitch's brow plunges towards her nose. She puts on the handbrake and gets out of the car. I fight an urge to run. She's comes over to me and stares right into my face like a search-beam. She's like, How old are you both? Have you two been drinking?

I'm like, No.

Al's like, No!

Cross Eyes gets out too and comes to look at us. We're both pretty sorry states. My trousers are torn and there's some blood from a cut where I fell which is splattered all across my shirt. Al's face has got dirt all over it from climbing the wall and we're both shaking away like turbo spin-dryers.

The Bitch looks at Cross Eyes and they share some kind of special police thought. She looks back at me.

I think you guys should come with us, she goes, in this voice that's like, the definition of an order.

I'm like, No really, we're just waiting for our friend to get back so we can go home. Really, that's the situation here!

The Bitch gives me this withering smirk. Cross Eyes sighs deeply and puts his hand on Al's shoulder and starts to guide her to the car. The Bitch does the same to me. Her grip is like a total vice, and my shoulder immediately like, deadens because of it. Then all of a sudden I feel this rushing sensation in my stomach and throat, and before she can react I'm vomiting all over her boots. She's not too happy about it.

Whoops! goes Cross Eyes, who's one of those types who always tries to make the best of a bad situation.

I like, kneel down and cough out some more sick. The Bitch doesn't try to touch me again, but busies herself with huffing and shaking the sick off her feet. I stare at the ground and try to will my insides to settle down. Meanwhile I can hear all this shouting and I realise Jon's arrived and is having a row with the police. Then I look up and The Bitch is looking down at me with this totally smug face, like she's just been proved right about something.

Let me guess, she goes, This must be your uncle.

20

Basically what happens is me and Al get taken to the station and given this whole series of warnings from this constable, which lasts for like, two whole hours. Of course the whole story about running away comes out – and how we're going back right the next morning – but nobody seems to care much about that. They're all far too busy competing with each other for the right to lecture us. All the while The Bitch patrols up and down like she's guarding us or something. Then, when it's finally over, we actually get told how lucky we are getting let off so lightly. It's like, yeah, *lucky us*.

Then it turns out Jon's been working on a lecture of his own all this time while waiting outside for us in the car. He gives it to us as he drives us back to the flat, really slowly, all this stuff about how just because you feel strongly about something doesn't mean you can just go ahead and do whatever you like blah-blah-blah. But it's not so bad as the constable's, and by the time we get back to the flat he's quite tearful and he tells us both that he's glad nothing happened to us and he'll take the day off tomorrow to drive us home. Al's like, That's so sweet of you! and he kind of sniffles and tells us to go inside while he sorts his car out. I turn round to Al and make a face that's supposed to mean she should beat it. She stares at me dumbly for a second, probably numb from all the lecturing, but then she gets it and goes in. Me and Jon sit there staring out the windscreen and not saying anything for a long time. It's like, my, what an interesting road.

Eventually I take the plunge. I'm like, Listen. Thanks.

Jon's like, Sure – no problem! in this ironic way like everything's so twisted even the idea of me thanking him is a total head-fuck. At this point I become aware of the fact that he really seems older than me, the way he's sat there at the wheel and frowning away the great-grandmother of all frowns.

I'm like, I'm sorry you cut short your date.

He gives this hoot of a laugh and then turns to me, and he's got this super-sage Gandalf-style expression on his face, a bit like the hero always gets at the end of the episode of some TV show where he's supposed to have come to a really important conclusion about life.

I'm not sorry. I'm glad, he says in this deep, mysterious voice. It's totally barfworthy, and I want to ask him, Do you even know what you're talking about? but I figure it's better to quit while I'm ahead. If he thinks he's learned something from all this then good for him. Hopefully it's at least something useful, like how to hold your breath or something. Anyway he still wants to 'sort out' the car, so I leave him to have his private moment or whatever and go inside to collapse next to Al on the sofa-bed.

In the end we catch the train back. Jon pretends to plead with us about wanting to drive us but the second I pretend to think about it he changes his mind. Thankfully Buddy isn't around when we leave, which is a major relief 'cos the next morning I'm sore from even thinking about It, not to mention sore from The Thing itself. At the station I give home a call and get Dad (luckily), who tells us he'll pick us up at Victoria. He's very curt on the phone and hangs up right away, which should have been a clue as to what was coming really. After that we have to say goodbye and it's totally awkward. If you can believe it me and Al both end up shaking Jon's hand.

There's major delays so it's not till evening that we actually get into Victoria. The train's really crowded, too, so we end up crushed in our seats opposite these total losers who're about the same age as us, and who spend half the time boasting who can spunk the furthest. It's like, how unnecessary?

When we arrive we go through the gates to find Dad and Al's parents waiting for us on the other side and looking thoroughly unhappy at having been in each other's company for so long. When she sees Al Mrs Rutland lets out this tribal scream that has half the station turning to look, and rushes to clasp her daughter to her bosom. Mr Rutland joins in, and they basically crush her to death while me and Dad make this sort of lurching gesture at each other.

When they've finally exhausted themselves the Rutlands turn to look at us. Mr Rutland takes a step forward and goes to me, You've got some explaining to do, boy! in this way that makes it quite clear he holds me totally responsible. Mrs Rutland gives me evils that are out of this world and adds, You ought to be ashamed of yourself! When I think about what could have happened . . .

Then, to my surprise, Dad's like, Hey, you can't put this all on Jaz. You should know it takes two to tango.

When we've all finished cringing from his metaphor Mr and Mrs Rutland stare at him like they can't believe what he's just said. I can't believe it either. It's like, where did the spine come from? Then Mr Rutland makes this like, growling sound. He takes a step forward and pokes Dad in the chest with his finger. He's like, Are you trying to tell me our daughter would have done something like this

200

of her own accord? It's your boy who made it happen! Him!

Dad's like, I hold Alice equally responsible.

Mr Rutland explodes. He's like, Are you calling us bad parents?! You're the bad parents! You're the one with the gay son, not us!

He pushes Dad and at this point Dad kind of loses it a bit too and pushes him back. Then Mr Rutland pushes him again and Dad goes stumbling backwards and almost falls. He stands up and glares at Mr Rutland. People all around have stopped to watch and it's like at any second they're gonna start shouting Fight fight fight. Mrs Rutland puts her hands on her mouth in this, like, total parody of horror. It's pretty obvious these people aren't used to these levels of excitement and aren't able to deal with them in like, a mature way.

Just as it looks like Dad and Mr Rutland are going to launch at each other gladiator-style, Al saves the day. She shouts out, It was my idea to run away!

There's total silence and then Mr and Mrs Rutland turn to her. Al nods. It's true, she goes.

I give her a What-The-Huh? look, and she gives me a look back as if to say, It's OK. I send her this mental thank-you, even though I kind of feel like maybe I actually should admit it was me because now she'll probably be punished for it. But then the Rutlands throw themselves at their daughter in this like, orgy of forgiveness, and start going on about how brave she is etc. It's like, some people really ought to just make their minds up.

In the car on the way home I'm like, You were pretty cool back there, to Dad, since it kind of seems like he deserves some sort of recognition or encouragement or something. But he just concentrates super hard on the road like I

201

haven't said anything. Then he suddenly goes, You've got some serious explaining to do when we get home, like maybe I thought it was gonna be a simple case of just walking in and asking what's for dinner. But I'm OK with it. I'm like, I know.

You would have thought, what with the fact that we could have died and stuff, that Mum would be waiting with her arms wide open ready to like, hug me for hours and tell me all about how she didn't care about anything that we've done so long as I'm all right. Well that doesn't happen. It's like, so the opposite. She's like a Venus fly-trap – she doesn't say anything as I walk into the kitchen where she's standing at the counter. Her face is totally unreadable. I go to give her a hug, and then, the second I'm within grabbing distance, she goes off like a hydrogen bomb. WHAT THE HELL DID YOU THINK YOU WERE DOING AS IF YOU HADN'T DONE ENOUGH ALREADY ARE YOU TRYING TO KILL ME THAT'S WHAT YOU WANT ISN'T IT YOU WANT ME TO BE DEAD WELL I WISH YOU'D NEVER COME BACK I WISH YOU'D HAD THE GUTS TO STAY AWAY AND I HOPE YOU FOUND OUT WHAT LIFE'S REALLY LIKE WHEN YOU DON'T HAVE SOMEONE PAYING YOUR WAY YOU SELFISH LITTLE ETC (totally depressing to listen to). At one point I manage to wrench myself free of her grip and she chases me around the room for a bit, but I'm much too fast for her and I put the table and Dad between us pronto. Dad meanwhile just stands there in the centre of the kitchen like this island of ineptness. It's like, explaining to do? As per usual *me* talking is the last thing anyone's interested in.

After about an hour (I kid you not) of sonic ear-busting, Mum's batteries finally start to run low. It's like she just runs out of steam mid-sentence. She kind of flops down at the table and sits there in this slumped position like the energy's been sucked out of her. Dad looks at her and I wait for him to say something to comfort her, but he doesn't, he just rolls his eyeballs around all over the place like one of those lizards that can move them in different directions.

What I'm thinking is, It's probably about time I gave them a proper apology. I mean, for real. I keep thinking about them arguing in the kitchen and how Mum looked when she saw me afterwards and the sight of Dad smoking on the back step all on his lonesome. It's not like I don't feel justified in any of the things I've done – I mean, life hasn't been easy for me of late and after the whole thing with Fabian I just felt like I had to get out of there. But I don't want Mum and Dad to be unhappy, and if all it takes is a simple apology and the I-love-you treatment, like I did that time with the E, then what the hell. They can have it.

So I go, I'm really sorry, all sincere and puppy-dog mode and then steel myself for the grossness of it. I'm like, I love you. That's why I came back.

There's this long silence. You're probably thinking there've been quite a number of terminal silences so far. There's more coming up, too, but this one happens to be the silence to end all silences. It suddenly feels like the world has just gone stark dead or something. It's like, the age of awkwardress. I feel my cheeks going all hot and red as I start to wonder why Mum and Dad aren't answering me and saying I love you back or something.

Finally there's this long hissing sound and it's Mum sighing the sigh that defines all other sighs. Then she stands up and even though she's trying to hide it I can see tears in her eyes. But they aren't tears because she's moved or anything by the whole puppy-dog thing. It's more like she's crying 'cos she doesn't believe me.

Then she slowly walks out of the room. I'm left with Dad. I would have thought he might go after her to comfort her or something, but he just stands there like a moron with a face like he's auditioning for an advert for Uncomfortable. I think that maybe I should tell him about Fabian, but somehow it feels like it would be wrong to use that as an excuse so I don't say anything, I just hang my head like I'm ashamed. I guess 'cos I am.

Then he goes, Happy now? and it's just about as bitter as Dad's able to get. He walks past me and I hear him going into the living-room. A minute later the sound of a football match playing comes from the TV.

I stand there on my own feeling totally low. Then I see that my bag is on the floor next to me still packed and everything, and all of a sudden I've got this urge to just leg it out of there. I could try a totally new city that isn't London or Brighton and see what happens there, I think. I could go to Manchester, or Scotland. But I don't. I tell myself that I've learned my so-called lesson. So instead I pick it up and go on up to my room.

On the stairs I run into The Nun, who's sitting on the top step and is all red in the face. If I didn't know she was incapable of feeling human emotions I'd say she'd been crying.

I'm like, Hi again.

She just looks at me. Even though I'm sure she's probably just gearing herself up to go all Regan on me, I feel this, like, tiny flicker of sympathy for her, because after all I did kick down her tree. To be honest I think I'd like it if she did go just a little bit Regan, 'cos at least it would be normal, and so far everything's been totally weird since getting back.

I'm like, Look I'm sorry, OK?

She looks at me for a second and it's like the Devil is debating whether or not to take control. But then, if you can believe it, it's like Teresa wins over. Instead of frothing at the mouth or something she just lets out this long sigh that's like an identical version of the one Mum did downstairs. Then she just turns away and goes into her room and closes the door. Not even a quick lecture on the power of prayer. And I know something must be seriously wrong here 'cos I'm actually *missing* Regan.

Upstairs I find Bilbo sleeping outside my door. He stretches out when I reach him and purrs a bit. It's nice to know someone's glad to see me, but depressing too, since Bilbo's only a cat.

The next day no one wakes me up to go to school, I guess because I'm supposed to be recovering or something, but it's weird because Mum and Dad both go to work and The Nun's at the convent so me and Grandma are the only ones at home. It's like no one even missed me.

I want to see Grandma but she's still asleep when I get up, so I go back up to my room and do some reps and then try and do a token hour of revision, but I can't concentrate so I send Al a text saying HOW R THNGS WTH PARNTS? I get one back pretty much straight away saying THERE ALL OVER ME LKE I NRLY DIED. U CAN FEEL THE TLC 4 MLES. CAN DO ANYTHNG NOW & THY WN'T MIND. Then we have this whole textothon and she tells me her parents are still determined that she's going with them to Leeds and she's like, resigned herself to it. Apparently they, like promised her the biggest room in the house they're buying and that they'd get her a bicycle, and then made her like, sign a contract or something saying she would give it a go. She's still kind of depressed about it though, so to take her mind off it we try and hatch a few schemes, like this one where Al's gonna come out as a lesbian to them just to freak them out (even though she isn't one. Yet).

I pay Grandma a visit a bit later on. She's sat up in bed doing some knitting, but when she sees me she gives me this massive smile and puts down her needles right away.

I'm like, Hi Grandma, just got back earlier on today, since Mum told me she told her that I've been staying at a friend's because she didn't want to her to be worried or anything.

So . . . you decided to come back then, did you? Grandma goes.

She says it in this totally crafty tone. Turns out she knows all about it, because she found my note before Mum did, only she put it back and pretended not to have seen it. I'm like, properly impressed, but Grandma's all like, whatever, like she's always been the coolest woman alive or something and she can't believe it's taken me this long to realise it. Then she reaches down under the duvet and produces this envelope like a conjurer, which she holds it out to me. Inside there's this letter and a brochure. The brochure's got all these pictures of this white Victorian mansion with a massive garden, with lots of geries dotted around and grinning these ultra-big grins at the camera like they've just got laid or something. The letter starts off 'Dear applicant, a warm welcome to Whitehart Homes in Kent . . .'

I'm like, What is this?

Grandma's like, It's my new home. I'm moving out.

Turns out she's been waiting in the queue for this like, luxury nursing-home for nearly a year now. She hasn't said anything 'cos she didn't expect to get in for at least another year, but someone dropped out (or more likely died or

206

something), and so now she's got a place. She beams at me. It's totally weird, 'cos it's like she's just got into university or something, only instead it's a nursing-home.

I'm like, Oh. Congratulations.

Grandma nods and folds the letter up carefully like it's this majorly important document, and puts it away again under the duvet.

I'm like, Do you really want to go then? Is Mum giving you such a hard time?

Grandma looks at me. It's pretty sad really, because even though I was annoyed when she first got here 'cos I had to give up my room, I kind of really like having her around. Not that she's been much of anything except a presence lately, but still. It's nice to know she's there.

Grandma's like, Unfortunately your Mum and I aren't much good for each other. But that's not the only reason. I want to be around other people my own age. I don't know anyone here. There's nothing for me to do except sleep.

She smiles a bit sadly, and picks up her knitting again.

Soon I'll be with your Grandpa again. But until then I just want a bit of comfort. I think at my age I deserve it, don't you?

I like, nod, but it's a pretty depressing way of looking at it. I mean, is that all old people do? Like, wait around until they can be with their other halves? What do you do if you don't have another half to wait for? You might just as well donate yourself to some clinic or something.

Grandma knits for a bit, and then goes, You know, *you're* not so different to your Mum as you'd like to think.

I'm like, Yeah, I guess we're both human beings, since that's the only similarity I can see.

She's like, When she was your age she ran away too.

I'm like, What the Huh?

She chortles for a second and goes, Well, I'm surprised that didn't come out.

And then she tells me all about how Mum was once this very troubled kid who refused to do what she was told and was always demanding stuff and losing her temper and stepping out with boys, and how poor old Grandma and Grandpa didn't know what to do with her. Eventually she ran off, but they set the police on her, which in those days you could apparently do with bloodhounds or something, and they brought her back and put her in this like, hospital, if you can believe it. Like, a mental hospital. It's pretty full on, and Grandma sits there in bed doing her knitting and telling me it like she's just talking about a nice holiday or something. It does kind of make sense though, since it goes some way towards explaining how Mum got to be so crazy. But after she's finished I'm like, Are you for real? since it's just possible Grandma's had another turn and is making it all up from la-la land.

Grandma's like, You know sometimes I have absolutely no idea what you're saying. Now, what I want to know is what you've been *doing* with yourself over the last three days.

For a minute I consider actually telling her, since the rest of the whole world practically seems to know about it and she does seem to suddenly have got a lot smarter than I've ever given her credit for. But then I decide not to. I don't want to be responsible for another stroke. In the end I just tell her about how Mum and Dad don't seem very happy to see me again and how I've like, disappointed them for the rest of their lives or something. She tells me to just give it time, which is pretty funny because that's what I told her to do once too.

I spend the rest of the day reeling from the revelations.

No wonder Mum doesn't get on with Grandma, even though it was a long time ago and all. But it's kind of fucked up. It doesn't make me all sympathetic towards Mum or anything, just confused, 'cos you'd think what with all that in the past she'd have been a bit more understanding with me over the last couple of months, instead of spewing acid every time I breathed. It's got to make you wonder. Like, when you think about how she is now, I mean. Once upon a time she was all sleeping around and running away, and it's like, What the hell happened? I kind of want to ask her about it but in the end I don't. When she gets home she doesn't say anything to me, just tells me what's for dinner and then goes upstairs for a lie-down. It's like she really doesn't care any more. Up until now I would always have been, Fine with me, but it kind of hurts a bit, this whole silent-treatment deal. I want to show her and Dad that I'm not the total spawn of Satan they've decided I am. But I just don't know how.

21

School the next morning is a total drag, but thankfully no one seems to know about the whole running-away thing, or at least they don't mention it. Right away I notice that Fuck Face is back and is hanging out in his usual spot at the back of class with the Tweedles. He seems quieter than usual though, like maybe he's even sorry about everything that happened, I think. He doesn't try to say anything to me. Plus he *has* got a scar from where Fabian cut him, which I hope stays with him for the rest of his life. He does kind of give me this weird look at one point, as we're leaving class, and Tweedle Dum whispers something his ear. But he can't do anything, even if he wants to, I think, since he's being watched closely after the whole bullying affair.

Nothing gets said about Fabian. I see Mary at break and ask her about it. She tells me that it got talked about in assembly on Monday, and Fatty made this big speech, which doesn't surprise me since he never misses an opportunity to go on about how much he empathises with us all for the tragedy of being like, teenagers. Apparently he was all on about how the system has failed yet another poor student and how we must all accept responsibility for it etc. He then asked for Fabian's friends to come forward and say something nice about him, but since Fabian didn't have any friends there was just this long awkward pause, which I reckon is pretty funny. But no one's talking about it or anything though, and so it's kind of like when something's suddenly gone but you're the only one who notices. And even I don't notice that much, 'cos it wasn't like we shared any classes or anything. But I do notice a bit. Just because of what I know.

Mr Fellows isn't in. He's off sick apparently, so instead we get lame-O Dr Dickhead who tells us to read the textbooks and make notes all lesson. I'm kind of glad, even though it's boring, 'cos to be honest I've been totally dreading seeing Fellows again. I feel pretty sorry about what I said to him last time, 'cos he was just trying to help and all, even if he was just doing it to, like, give himself a purpose or something. In fact, to be *completely* honest, I'm kind of worried about him.

Anyway, what's coming up here is basically totally freaksome, and I was thinking just to skip it and save you the hassle, but since we're here you may as well deal with it. I have to.

So after class I head off home. So far so amazing. Al's not with me though, 'cos she promised her parents she'd do, like, an extra hour in the library every day, which she invited me to join her in, but of course I was like, No. So basically I'm on my own – and don't think somebody hasn't noticed.

I turn the corner into the alley that leads down this side street to my stop and it's like something out of a Western. It's Fuck Face of course, with the Tweedles on either side of him, all stood there with their arms folded like this mutated version of *Charlie's Angels*. One look at their faces and you know this isn't going to be about kittens. I rapidly debate over whether to turn and bolt for it – I could just run right back down the street and like, throw myself in front of the school doors crying out for sanctuary or something. But I

don't run away, even though I could probably make it –
don't ask me why. I guess I'm just fed up. It's like, a facing-
your-demons moment. A total facing-your-ugly, disease-
breathed demons moment.

So I'm like, What the fuck do you want?

Fuck Face like, growls, You've got some explaining to
do.

Next to him Tweedle Dum sneers and goes, We just want
to have a little word, that's all, and Tweedle Dee's like,
We're not in school. There's no one to protect you now!

Then they all take a step forward at the same time, like
they've rehearsed it or something. Fuck Face's cheeks have
gone this weird shade of deep red, like he's been holding his
breath. He looks like he's about to go to war. It's pretty
frightening actually.

I'm like, Look, don't you have a detention to be in?

Tweedle Dum is like, Think you can get away with
getting old Joe here suspended, did you, faggot? He's
not too happy about that, is he? Not too happy at all.

Tweedle Dee's like, He's pretty mad about it in fact.

I'm like, You do know your nicknames are Tweedle Dee
and Tweedle Dum, don't you?

They ignore this. Tweedle Dum's like, There's no freaks
around to save you any more, *Jarold*. Did you actually
think you were gonna get away without a beating?

They all take another step. I swear it's like they're part of
a line-dancing class. It's too late to turn and run now.

I'm like, You're gonna be in deep shit if you don't just
fuck off!

Tweedle Dum's like, Oh I don't think so. Because you're
not going to be telling *anyone* about this little rendezvous of
ours. Not after we're finished with you.

Then he goes to Fuck Face, Show him your scar.

212

Fuck Face obediently turns his head and points. Actually the scar itself really isn't that bad, although it's definitely there. It's just this small line that like, runs an inch along the side of his jaw. I mean it's like, if I were him I'd be much more concerned about the way the rest of my face looked.

That's *your* fault, goes Tweedle Dum in this voice like the Snake out of *The Jungle Book*. Then he's like, to Fuck Face, Are you going to let this poof get away with that?

Fuck Face turns his head back and looks down at me. His forehead looms like the Centrepoint tower.

'Course he isn't, goes Tweedle Dum, He's not gonna let some faggot get the better of him, (to Fuck Face) He made a joke of you.

I'm like, Go buy yourself a soul! (Pretty lame, I know, but it's hard to be consistent with so many opportunities.)

You've got some explaining to do, says Fuck Face again in his super-gruff voice. They all take another synchronised step.

To be honest, if I thought there was a chance of actually pulling it off, I'd totally have a go at explaining. The trouble with someone of Fuck Face's mentality is that an explanation of anything would end up as just this total ordeal, not to mention the fact that you'd need to have the right props, like Lego and puppets and stuff. But it's pretty obvious he's not gonna be giving me the time to argue my way out of this. He takes another step forward all on his own, so he's, like, a couple of feet away. The Tweedles put these identical grins on their faces which kind of merge with Fuck Face's fuck face. Then I have this great surge of anger.

After all the stuff that's been happening of late I kind of made this decision that I was going to be like, this total pacifist and make an effort to actually care a bit more and stuff. But quite frankly there are times when things happen too fast for you to tap into being all Yoko. There are times when your body just jumps into action without you even having any say in the matter.

Before Fuck Face can reach out and like, Vulcan-death-grip me, I've done the one move you can pretty much always do and be guaranteed of a satisfactory result, which is to kick him in the gonads. I connect hard. Fuck Face's eyes bulge out Roger-Rabbit style and this sound comes out his mouth like a deflating whoopee cushion. He sinks to his knees. The Tweedles let out harmonious gasps of surprise.

Then I hear myself shouting. I must have gone all depersonalised again because the shouting seems all random and like it has nothing at all to do with me – except that I can hear myself doing it. I'm going, You total cunt! Don't you know Fabian's dead? Are you so fucking clueless you don't know what that means? When someone's dead! You're the one who should be dead! You! You! You fucking waste of space!

It's like, I know. Anyway, then (to everyone's amazement) Fuck Face makes this weird sound like he's snivelling. Like he's actually upset by the stuff I've been shouting. Like somewhere underneath that gorgeous exterior there's like, a sensibility or something. The Tweedles both look seriously disturbed.

Tweedle Dum is like, You're not gonna take that, *are you*? But he sounds totally unsure of himself, like he kind of expects the answer is going to be Yes, *actually*. I look at Fuck Face right in the eyes and it's like they're the total meaning of misery or something, and not just because of the pain. Then Tweedle Dee makes a decision – like, all of his own – and rushes me. He gets me in an arm lock before I have time to like, see him coming and repeat my kung-fu bollocks-kicking move.

It's OK, I've got him! he tells Fuck Face, all excited. He bends my arm back till it's like, unbearable, like any second now there's going to be this snapping sound and half my arm'll land on the pavement. I've got to admit at this point tragically I'm doing little more than whimpering like a total pathetic moron.

Go on! Take him out! goes Tweedle Dum.

Let him have it, adds Tweedle Dee just in case Fuck Face was still unsure of what to do. He twists my arm even further. I close my eyes and prepare myself for hospital.

Then Fuck Face lets out this roaring sound, and goes, Get the fuck off him!

I open my eyes. Suddenly Fuck Face is on his feet again. He literally rips Tweedle Dee off me (almost breaking my arm) and tosses him backwards. Tweedle Dee goes flying into Tweedle Dum, like something out of a comedy or something, and they both crash to the ground.

Fuck Face turns to me while they're picking their brains up and goes, I didn't . . . I didn't mean . . . I didn't mean it, in this voice that's wavering all over the place. And he's got tears coming out of his eyes like, For Real. I hear this sound of feet pitter-pattering away and look up to see the Tweedles making an exit.

I look back. He stands there panting over me with his mouth open so you can practically see the heart of all things fungi. It's suddenly totally obvious that this hasn't been about my demons at all. That like, all this time the Tweedles have been these two evil voices in his head, and that this has been a total McFly moment for Fuck Face. Meanwhile I'm like, hardly alive from his death breath, but I figure now's not the best time to say anything.

Do you think it's my fault he went and did himself in? he goes.

I kind of let this long pause go by. I'm totally tempted to say Yes, just to see if I can get him to like, perform some tricks or something out of guilt about it. But of course I don't. He's like misery in human form, so it would be pretty mean, and the peace stuff is kind of coming back to me now. It's funny to think he was feeling guilty about it too.

So I'm like, No, and he gives me this look like he wants to kiss me (the idea of which is gross beyond gross). He like, reaches out with both arms and it's blatant he wants a hug, but I've got no intention of getting any closer to The Source, so I keep him at bay by like, patting him on the shoulder in this totally retarded way.

Then he's like, You know . . . it's not like I haven't ever had . . . thoughts about guys before.

At which point I'm ready to suggest he goes and finds the Tweedles again. But I don't. Instead I have to endure some gush about him being all confused and insecure about himself (it's like, no – *really?*). Finally, to get away I fake an emergency dental appointment and tell him I'll see him in school. I make like to go.

Then I look back. Fuck Face still looks pretty unhappy, and I get this voice in *my* head, which is like, reminding me about Fabian and suggesting to me how bad I'm gonna feel if Fuck Face goes and tops himself now too, even though it's like, not even remotely likely. So I go back and kind of pat him on the shoulder some more and tell him to chill out and stuff.

I'm like, It's pretty cool that you're open-minded.

Fuck Face's expression totally morphs at this idea – that it's like, cool to be open-minded. He gives me a big yellow grin and then goes off to wherever losers go looking all pleased with himself. I'm left with the regret that I didn't somehow work in a bit about the importance of brushing your teeth.

216

So now I'm going to have to like, say Hello to him and stuff in school, which is totally lame. Maybe it's this wonderful thing for him, and now the whole direction of his life is all changed and he's gonna grow up as this caring, lovely Quasimodo type, I don't know. But I'm not sitting next to him in class or anything. That's like, For Sure.

22

The evening after the Fuck-Face incident is pretty grim, since Mum and Dad and even The Nun are still silent-treatmenting me. Dinner is just this parody of existence, since no one says a single word to me the whole time. It's like, hands up who wishes I wasn't born.

Anyway, school the next day is full-on weird. Firstly because when me and Al arrive Fuck Face comes towards us with this big smile on his face. He's all chummy and smiley, like we're suddenly his best friends or something, and when we go I notice he kind of droops a bit, like maybe he was hoping for more from us. I also notice that later on he doesn't sit with the Tweedles either – just on his own at the other side of the classroom 'cos there's no one else who wants to sit next to him. It's pretty sad really, since he's blatantly out of his depth. But that's what happens when you suddenly decide to stop being a bully and grow like, a personality. Who knows how long it'll last anyway.

Still, the main reason school is weird though is 'cos Fellows is back, and by the way there's a total shocker coming up here, so, like, prepare thyself.

Al spies him getting out of someone's car and going inside during morning break. I'm glad he's not at death's door, or gone insane from loneliness or anything, but I'm dreading the afternoon session when we have double geography period. It's destined to be like, majorly uncomfortable. In this like, effort to halfway appease him I tell Al we should maybe sit apart and she agrees and goes and sits next to Sam. I sit on my own at the front. I decide I'll try and speak to him at the end. I don't really see what I'm going to be able to say, apart from sorry, but I figure I owe him, so what the hell. Feels like all I do these days is say Sorry. Sorry for like, inflicting myself on the world.

Anyway, Fellows comes in right after the bell and straight away apologises for being late, as though anyone actually minds. But he looks all flushed, which is unusual for him, since ordinarily he's this kind of greyish colour. He gives me and Al a quick look but it's hard to read anything from it, and then he kind of stands in front of the whole class and opens out his arms like he wants to give us this massive big collective hug. Then he booms out, Good afternoon, people!

It's like he's on drugs or something. I swear if I didn't think it was like, impossible, I'd have believed the old codger had gone and got himself laid. I swivel round to see if Al has noticed. You can bet your sexuality she has. She's practically falling out of her chair. She obviously wants to whisper about it but she's got a fat chance of interesting old brainiac Sam.

Nobody can say anything wrong to Fellows all lesson. When he asks some wisecracker what the difference is between porous and igneous rock and they say Negligible he actually laughs, which is like, totally wrong. He even hums a bit to himself while we're all reading this chapter from the stupid textbook.

I take a long time putting my books in my bag so I'm the last out after class. When I look up I see that Fellows is waiting and tapping his foot up and down impatiently. I follow him into the corridor and stand behind him while he locks the door like I'm shadowing him or something. Fellows turns and looks at me.

He's like, Is everything all right?

I'm like, totally on the spot. Hey look, I go, I wanted to say sorry about what I said before.

Fellows looks at me for a minute like he's trying to figure out what I'm talking about, and I start to feel like the biggest moron on the planet. Then he seems to remember because he smiles and shrugs.

Don't worry about it, Jarold, he goes, I know what it's like to be your age. Your hormones are all over the place. It's quite understandable.

And just like that the whole feeling-sorry thing like, dies a violent death. But Fellows is starting to get into it now. He smiles at me and then goes, I heard about your little sojourn with Alice.

I'm like, Oh right, all icy now.

He's like, Don't worry, I'm not going to lecture you, I'm simply going to repeat what I've always said, which is that if ever you want to talk, I'm *there*.

Before I have the chance to puke in his face he heads off down the corridor leaving me all dazed by the like, vibes of positivity he's radiating. Al taps me on the shoulder.

Come on! she goes, We have to follow him!

And that's how we end up becoming Fellows' personal stalkers – trying to catch a peep of whoever's blowing him. Al says this other guy who was in the car this morning was the same age as him, and now she's positive this must be his boyfriend. I'm like, Grossness, but she thinks it's the most wonderful thing ever. She's gonna get like, a degree in fag-haggery pretty soon the way she carries on.

At first it's fun playing detective. Fun 'cos you know that

at any second you might get caught, and that's pretty scary when you're following your gay teacher. I mean, he could still have turned out to be a serial killer, which wouldn't have surprised me because sometimes it's hard to believe anyone can act so righteous and understanding all the time and not be like, murdering people on the side or something. But the fun of following him doesn't last. Once we get to his house it quickly gets boring. Turns out he lives in Shepherd's Bush too, which is handy, because after a few blocks I'm not in the mood for rushing over town just to see who he's shagging. Al's totally into the whole thing though, and keeps a straight face all through, whereas I'm giggling every few steps, since it must be pretty obvious to anyone else on the street that we're following him.

When he goes inside his house, I'm like, What now?

Al's like, We wait, like this is a stealth operation she's been planning for years.

So we do. We sit outside on a wall and wait. And wait. I'm like, totally over this whole scene, but Al doesn't let go easily, and it turns out to be well worth our sticking around, since an old red Volvo pulls up into his drive and this guy gets out, and that's when things suddenly fit together in my head, like when you guess the ending of a film or something. I feel like jumping up and shouting, Eureka! but I don't, because I'm not that far gone in the direction of uncool.

It's Higgs. He goes to the door and Fellows opens it before he's even had a chance to knock or anything. They start kissing like a pair of newly-weds, right there and then, which is not a pleasant sight, let me tell you. I mean, one of these guys is my teacher and the other's like, my therapist. It's like, I'm never gonna be shocked by anything in life after seeing this. And what's more, get this: I suddenly

221

realise it was Higgs who I saw at Starlight that night when I was hiding from Jon behind the jukebox.

Al's properly happy about it. She like coos, Isn't it sweet?

I'm like, still dealing with the info influx, at which point (and this is really stupid and is probably gonna make you hate me but I'm not gonna lie) I suddenly have the worst fit of sneezing known to man. It's all that time spent in the freezing cold in Brighton probably. Anyway it literally shakes the street, and every bird, beast and man turns to look. That comprises mostly of Higgs and Fellows. I'm, like, a deeper level of Oh Fuck. They like, simultaneously recognise me and open their mouths. I don't know what else to do, since me and Al being here is totally scuppered, so I end up giving them both a wave.

It's an awkward situation. We end up going in for tea and a chat. I mean, we could have run away, but I'd just die if Higgs brought it up in our next family session, and plus Al's really curious. It's like she's writing a dissertation on it or something.

It's kind of funny too. Inside Mr Fellows' house is just what you'd expect: square. It could only ever belong to either a gay man or an obsessive-compulsive tidiness nerd, or maybe both. We all sit round the kitchen table with these kitsch gold mugs of herbal shit. Fellows and Higgs slide their chairs together so they're like, practically sitting on top of each other and Fellows takes Higgs' hand, but other than that they don't make much of a display of affection, which I'm glad about because, frankly, I've already seen Quite Enough.

Higgs is pretty embarrassed at first but I get the feeling that Fellows is secretly kind of pleased we're here. He goes, Well, I hope you're both satisfied now.

Al's like, We're really sorry. We just wanted to see who you were dating . . .

Higgs is like, Humph, but Fellows is like, You may as well know that Henry here is my partner.

Higgs' face lights up, but he goes to Fellows, Mike – we've only just met! in this hushed romantic voice, as if he's Scarlett O'Hara or something.

Fellows is like, Sometimes you can just tell.

He's not talking to us. At this point it seems inevitable that they're going to start snogging again, so I'm like, deadening my senses in preparation for it. But they don't. Instead Higgs pulls himself together and goes, Well, Jarold. Is this going to be a topic in our next session?

I'm like, Are you crazy? which seems to please him. That's when I realise that I'm actually kind of glad he's a fag too, though my gaydar must be pretty way off, 'cos it's like, how come I didn't guess? But it makes me feel, well, validated if you must know, not that I'm the kind of guy who has a problem with what other losers think, because I really don't. But it's nice to see that you can still pull after forty, and maybe even stand a chance of happiness (even if it doesn't last – me and Al have bets on how long it'll be). I kind of like being here, sitting in this square kitchen and sipping tea, and being all young and inexperienced next to this pair of queer old boffs.

23

On Saturday we go to take Grandma to Whitehart Homes. She's got a lot of stuff, most of which has been stored in the garage all left over from her house with Grandpa. In order to shift it all Mum borrows an extra car from her practice, which is just as well because The Nun's friend Joan (alias The Witch) is along for the ride.

I come downstairs to help with the loading of the cars even though no one's bothered to ask me. Things are worse than ever with Mum and Dad now, like they don't even want to be in the same room as me, even if that means I don't do my chores. Like, yesterday I forgot to clean the bathroom though it was my turn, and Mum didn't say anything. At first I thought it was pretty cool, but then when I went in and saw she'd done it and still hadn't said anything I felt kind of disturbed.

Anyway I go outside to where all the ferrying is and straight away run into The Witch, who sees me and makes this muttering sound and then looks right in my eyes. She's like, Hello Jarold, Teresa told me all about what happened and I just want to remind you that the door to forgiveness is always open, all in one breath like she's been storing it up to say to me.

I look between her and The Nun, all stunned. Some of the things this girl comes out with are scary beyond the deep. Even Teresa looks a bit shamed by it, and busies herself with sorting out a pile of boxes on the back seat of Mum's car.

The Witch is like, You have to try to conquer your urges, Jarold. You have to try to think of the bigger picture.

I'm like, Just do us all a favour and have a wank.

The Witch smiles all serene, like this is just what she expected me to say. Say whatever you like, she goes, We both know who's going where.

Then she turns away and involves herself in fussing over Mum who's just come out the garage carrying this coat stand, basically acting like the second daughter she never had.

The Nun passes me and I go to her, Buy your friend a dildo or something.

I'm hoping she'll take this as a major insult and flip into Regan and then Mum or Dad'll have to intervene and it'll be just like normal, but instead she gives me this withering look like I'm a total lost cause and goes back into the garage for more of Grandma's junk. I want to say something about Joan's presence to Mum and Dad – since this is supposed to be a big-deal family thing, so why does *she* get to come along? But of course I can't now that they've like, given up hope for me as a human being. I've been trying to bear in mind Grandma's advice about just giving it time, but it's actually getting to be kind of painful here. I mean, did you ever see that *Simpsons* episode where Bart accidentally shoots a bird and Marge sees him do it and seems to stop loving him 'cos she thinks it was done on purpose? Well, it's like that. It feels like nobody really *cares* about me any more.

Anyway, to avoid more Christian terrorism I opt for Dad's bomb with Grandma while Mum, The Nun and The Witch take hers. Dad doesn't speak to me once throughout

225

the whole journey there, but he tries a bit of small talk with Grandma. He's really falsely cheery, and you can totally tell he finds the whole situation between Mum and her hard to deal with, like the fact that they don't get on and all that. He keeps pointing out how nice the weather's been getting, until it gets ridiculous, and finally even Grandma gets rankled by it and tells him what she's looking forward to is the peace and quiet of the countryside (like, hint hint). Dad gets the message and shuts up.

When we arrive Grandma acts all calm and queenly. The rest of us faff around pretending to think the massive white building she's going to be living in is really beautiful, when in fact it's gross and looks like a super-sized Barbie doll's house. We get greeted by this thin woman whose face is plastered with make-up and shown to the room, which is all the colours of a wedding cake.

We spend a lot of time assembling Grandma's stuff and then putting it in various different places all around the room while she gazes out the window at the garden outside. There's all these other old folk out there, so it looks like a bit of a convention. Then she turns round and interrupts The Witch midway through some self-righteous opinion about why the coat stand should go next to the bed, and goes, Who'd like to take a turn with me?

Mum sends us out with Grandma while she stays there with Dad to make sure the room's up to scratch, since with her everything's a potential lawsuit.

Outside Grandma looks up and down the lawn and sighs. George would have loved it here, she goes.

The Nun like, grabs Grandma in this choke-hold hug and starts cooing, Oh, you mustn't miss Grandpa, he's in heaven now and watching down over us, and so forth, while Grandma smiles in this pained way like she's being clenched by this well-meaning boa constrictor. When The Nun finally releases her she and The Witch both take an arm so Grandma's, like, literally being escorted down the garden. I kind of trail along behind like this totally unwanted mutation or something.

We keep walking for a bit, and down at the end of the garden behind the hedge there's this whole bunch of old biddies doing this routine of yoga or something in skin-tight leotards. It's quite a shocker, let me tell you. I'm like, Jesus, before I can even help myself. The Nun just rolls her eyes but The Witch finds this deeply offensive. She folds her arms and goes, *Actually* I think it's lovely that older generations still enjoy the benefits of exercise, really pointedly at me. Grandma gives her a look like she's just dying to say something about the benefits of sex as well, but she holds it in. Instead she suggests we wander over to the pavilion at the other end of the garden. The Nun's like, I think we should get back to help Mum and Dad, but The Witch is really into her role as Grandma's personal crutch and says she'll take her on while 'you and *him*' go back. Grandma looks just thrilled by this prospect, but she like, resigns herself and goes, Come along then, deary, in this ironic voice to The Witch, who leads her off like a victim of a concentration camp.

Back inside the doll's house we go down the hall to Grandma's room in silence, The Nun leading the way. We stop when we reach the door though, because from inside Mum and Dad are having this argument. It's pretty weird actually, 'cos even though you get used to hearing Mum shouting at Dad at home, she's always very careful not to lose her temper with him in public. She's going, Why can't you just support me once in a while instead of just always being so bloody quiet all the time? Why can't you make an effort to understand?

Dad's going like, I do make an effort to understand—

But as per usual Mum just shouts over the top of him so in a way it's a bit like she's having an argument with herself. She's like, No you don't! You think you do but you don't! You don't care, that's your problem! You just don't care!

And so it goes on. Mum's basically just flipping one of her apocalyptic rants and Dad's doing his usual turtle thing of just bearing it out and hoping she'll stop. Then from inside the room comes the traditional sound of sobbing, which means Mum's basically winding down now. But listening to it with The Nun, everything starts to feel hopeless for some reason. I mean, it's not like Mum and Dad were ever normal or anything, but somehow hearing them fighting while being with Teresa makes it seem different. It's like, what's the point of even bothering?

Do you think Mum and Dad are going to split up? she goes in this totally neutral voice.

She's looking at me with this funny look on her face, and it's a look I've seen on Grandma quite a lot, so maybe it's hereditary. I'm like, totally weirded out, partly 'cos I'm just not used to being spoken to by The Nun in any way that sounds even vaguely civil. But mostly it's because of what she actually says. Suddenly the idea of them splitting up seems like it would be a really Bad Thing.

I'm like, Who knows?

The Nun's like, Yes, who knows?

Which is a big deal 'cos it's like she's agreeing with me on something, which is something she never does even if it means going back on her religion. And what's really scary and totally unnatural in every possible way is that I actually feel this like, iota of affection for her, and I kind of remember that actually she is my younger sister. I kind of want to tell her it'll be OK or something. I rack my brains

228

for something to say, but in the end all I can think of is what I did to her stupid tree.

So I'm like, Listen, about your tree – if you want I'll help you plant a new one. We can dig up all the old roots and stuff and put it in the exact same place . . .

I trail off, partly because I've just realised how incredibly lame I sound, but also because The Nun's smiling at me. It's the kind of smile you don't very often see on someone like her. A sort of smart smile, like actually she knows what's what.

She's like, It's OK. Mum and Dad are getting me a horse.

She tells me that basically they're pouring all this money into co-sponsoring a pony at this local stable with her and a friend at school. I'm like, total state of suspended disbelief. I kind of want to get angry about it, but I hold it in. It just goes to show though what kind of a world it is, because you'd think that a tree like Rabbity's should be pretty irreplaceable. But in this life everything's got a value, and that's one thing The Nun's clued up on. I guess it's good for her.

She's like, I'm glad you came back, you know.

I'm like, Gee.

At this point The Witch comes clumping down the corridor towards us with her head held all high so her upper chin looks like this mountain ridge next to the rest of her face. She comes to a halt beside The Nun and goes, I've left your grandma talking to another pensioner. They seem to be getting on really well! as though Grandma is a code-name for this rare sociological experiment she's really proud to be taking part in. Then she glances at me and goes to her, Have you managed to talk any sense into him? like I'm not there or something.

I'm like, Fuck off.

The Witch is like, to me, I thought that was your speciality, and then she goes to The Nun, Is he planning on running away again? all smug.

She takes The Nun's arm and sighs like it's always them who have to pick up the pieces after the world's been blown to smithereens. Let's just hope if he does this time he has the sense to stay away, she goes like Superbitch.

The Nun looks at me and then at The Witch, all fastened to her arm like some exotic species of sucker fish. Then she's like, Joan this is a family matter so do you think you could mind your own business please?

The Witch's face like, melts. She looks like one of those aliens who's secret vulnerability has just been exposed, like a fatal allergy to the truth or something. She gapes at The Nun for a second and then goes, I'm going to wait in the car! She turns on her heel and clomps off. I'm kind of impressed but I don't say anything, and at this point Mum and Dad come out of the room wanting to know what we've done with Grandma.

Once we've located her we return her to the room and leave her sat by the window, in this new armchair that has all these buttons you can press to like, make it vibrate and massage you and stuff (I've a go and it's totally like being molested). We all line up to kiss her on the cheek and it's totally weird to think she's not gonna be living with us at home any more. Like, I can even take my old room back if I want it.

Just a minute, Lois, goes Grandma as we're leaving.

Mum hesitates and then waits so we all go out to the cars, which are parked right outside Grandma's window. The Witch is sitting inside Mum's company car with her eyes closed, probably praying or something. We've got a pretty clear view of Grandma saying something to Mum, and then we watch Mum nod her head really slowly. She takes Grandma's hand and holds it for a minute, and it's like they're actually bonding or something. Then Mum disappears and a second later she comes out. She's totally messy-looking, and I wait for Dad to say something nice to her. But he doesn't say anything, he just gets in his car and looks at me as if to say, Are you coming? so I climb in too, and off we go.

24

Okay, so this scene now is like, Full On. It's the next therapy session, and it's like, stellar weird. Mum and Dad are hardly even talking to each other, and now that Higgs is like, dating my teacher it's kind of like Fellows is somehow there in the room with us too. By the way, it's all complete schlock coming up – stop reading if you've got like, taste or anything. Either that or at least prepare your bucket.

We're all sitting in our usual places – me on the armchair, Dad and Mum on the couch and Higgs on the chair in front of his desk. It's actually kind of funny, 'cos the space between Mum and Dad on that sofa has grown and grown over our sessions, and now it looks properly stupid, like there's enough room for a trapdoor there.

Higgs is in flawless computer mode, which is probably pretty understandable. I mean, we've crossed a boundary outside of the therapy, and it's a pretty personal one at that. I didn't tell Mum and Dad about it of course, but I'm kind of terrified that he's going to. But he doesn't, thankfully. He just throws himself into his role and smiles this totally airbrushed smile and goes, So who'd like to begin? in this firm but very disinterested sort of way, just like a compassionate robot would sound. You can't help but wonder what it's like with him – *you know* (though it's a major freak-out to even consider it).

Anyway, there's this pause and I'm tempted to say something for once, since I kind of feel like this is my only chance to somehow make Mum and Dad actually listen to me. I've noticed that how it works is that Higgs usually lets me just sit here while he asks *them* the questions, and I've kind of realised that these sessions are actually totally about them and not about me at all. Me being here is just Higgs showing them that I'm a normal human being whereas they're the ones who are completely fucked. But the only thing I can think of to say is that I'm sorry, for like, the zillionth time, and I'm totally through saying sorry, since it's not like it changes anything. So in the end I decide not to say something, just to wait.

Soon enough Mum draws this deep breath which is usually the signal that she's going to launch into one of her major rants. I swear I catch this little jerking movement from Higgs, like he has this automatic urge to dive for cover under his chair or something. But then Mum suddenly stops short. Her face kind of sets in this blank, hopeless expression, like she's thinking, What's the point? She sighs and doesn't say anything. It's like, total Manic-depressivesville.

So we all sit there for like, a whole five minutes, just not speaking, and it's like an explosion of awkwardness. Then Mum looks at Dad and suddenly her face changes. She goes What's that? and then reaches into one of Dad's pockets and pulls out this packet of Marlboro Reds.

Dad tries to do one of those Oh-how-on-earth-did-that-get-there? reactions, managing to be as convincing as it's just about possible not to be. Mum turns the packet over in her hands like it's this omen or something.

She's like, You're smoking again?

Dad's like, Yeah, since the whole innocence thing blatantly isn't going to wash.

Mum's like, But . . . For how long?

And there's this sound of silence like you'd get in a graveyard, where it seems to roar or something, and she looks at Higgs like she's expecting him to do something. He doesn't of course, he just watches them, and then Dad suddenly blurts out, Lois – I just don't feel like I know who you are any more!

Higgs leans forward. This is Big. Dad always just sits there like a frightened child while Mum goes on and on about some stupid issue – like me. She can even go on an on about just how awful she felt when she forgot to pay a bill or something, which is like, who even gives a shit?

So with Dad actually like, stating an opinion all on his own about something, we're obviously covering ground here. But Higgs still doesn't say anything. He lets Mum react, which is a pretty clever thing to do. She looks at Dad and opens her mouth in this big O, but for once nothing comes out and so it just hangs there, like she's waiting for a dentist or something. After a minute it gets embarrassing and I'm like, this is too much, I shouldn't be exposed to this, but then Dad goes, I'm sorry.

Mum's like, How long have you felt this way?

Dads like, For years.

She's like, But why didn't you say something?

He's like, Because I couldn't! It's impossible to talk to you.

Mum's like, the definition of shock. She goes totally white and her eyes go all big and scary. She looks like the Bride of Frankenstein.

Higgs is like, Would you like a glass of water?

Mum ignores him and like, chokes a bit before going to Dad, Are you trying to tell me that you don't love me any more? Is that what you're saying?

Dad thinks about this. When you ask someone something like that and they think about it, it's never good.
Mum's in total spaz mode, and I actually feel kind of sorry
for her. I think about what Grandma told me about how
she was when she was my age, and I kind of think that
maybe you can still see like, a shred of that person now.
And if Dad says No it's like, probably going to destroy her.

So we're looking at him and it's like, No Pressure. Dad's
sweating buckets of course. It's like he's on *Who Wants To
Be A Millionaire?* – get this answer wrong and you've
blown it.

Finally he gulps and goes, I guess what I'm saying is that
I've always put your happiness ahead of mine. But I'm not
sure if I can do that for much longer.

I look at Higgs and suddenly notice that the computer
screen is down. He's practically wetting himself. He obviously thinks this is like, a major breakthrough, because
he's furiously scribbling on his pad without even actually
looking at it, as though he can't bear to tear his gaze away
from Mum and Dad. Of course you don't need to be a
therapist to know this is rocking the foundations of something called a marriage. That this is the works like, Big
Time. And I don't know if Dad's answer was what Mum
needed to hear, or if he's just injected our family life with
cancer, but you can tell that it came from the heart, which
means she can't really get angry with him.

So instead she sort of simpers, and starts looking round
the room as if searching for a portal that'll magically
transport her to safety or something. At this point Higgs
can't contain himself any longer. He's like, This is good,
this is very good, like he's talking about sex or something.
He goes to Mum, Tell us – how do you feel?

I'm kind of annoyed at him for asking her that, since it's

pretty obvious from where I'm sitting. She's got those same scared eyes that Dad usually has, and they look particularly pathetic on her, like she's wearing goggles or something.

Mum's like, I don't know, in this tiny, tiny pipsqueak voice. Higgs nods like this is just the answer he was hoping for.

OK, now comes the cheesiest part of this ride through soap-opera hell. Because before I even know what I'm doing I've stood up and gone and wedged myself in between my parents like a sandwich filling, and I've taken both their arms and I'm holding them like a three-year-old on a merry-go-round. I know. It's like I'm a traitor to something.

Mum looks at me and her face like, melts. She bursts into the Niagara of tears, and I look to Dad's face and see that he's having difficulty keeping the waterworks under control too. Pretty soon he gives in, and I may as well confess that I'm kind of leaking a bit here too. In fact it gets worse than that, because I then go, Please don't split up! in this terrified babyish voice. It's the sort of voice you can't fake but have to like, actually *feel* to be able to speak in (so there's like, no excuse).

So we all have this like, massive long bath and then finally we stop and Mum and Dad look at each other and smile all sappy like they've just survived Armageddon together or something. It's really gross, and has me trying to unwedge myself pronto. Unfortunately they've both taken this death grip on my arms, so I have to sit there and endure the gush that follows. It's like:

Her: Oh, Lawrence, I'm so sorry I wish I'd known you have to understand that I'm not perfect but that doesn't mean that I don't need you.

Him: I don't know what's happened to us but I know we'll work it out. I'm going to try harder from now on—

Her: I just hope you can forgive me if I've been too much—

Him: No, I hope *you* can forgive *me*—

Her: But there's nothing *to* forgive—

And so forth. Like, total barferia. It continued for a good ten minutes at least, but just remembering it is making me feel like, terminally nauseous. It's enough to make you believe in euthanasia for the emotionally challenged.

Anyway, Higgs is like, You've taken a really important step forward. I want you all to feel proud of yourselves, which is just about the dappiest thing I've ever heard. And since Mum and Dad are too busy admitting how wrong about everything they are to notice anything, I stick my tongue out at him. Higgs doesn't look too pleased. Thankfully at this point the session grinds to an end, concluding with Mum and Dad's decision to get marriage counselling (to which I'm not invited, thankfully).

And that's it for Mum and Dad. In fact, there's only one more scene, and it's not much of one. More like just something I go and do. But I'm going to give it to you anyway, since you've had everything else.

It's like, Sunday three weeks later. It's a pretty weird day, 'cos Al's just ridden off in this truck with her parents, Destination: Leeds, and I'm at this total loose end wondering who I'm gonna go out with now. I don't know, maybe I got infected by all the goodbye fever or something, since Al cried buckets and we both swore we'd text each other every day and it was all pretty emotional, but after she'd gone I got to thinking about Fabian. What I do is I decide to go back and visit Mrs Wrens. For some reason it seems like this thing I have to do, even if you can tell it's going to be all mushy, and I hate mushiness. But actually it isn't. It's surprisingly unmushy.

237

Mrs Wrens answers the door right away, like she's been standing right behind it waiting there for me since my last visit. She looks a bit better though, I'm glad to say. But you can tell she's been through hell, 'cos there's this look in her eyes which is different, like they've changed colour or something.

She's like, Hello, I'm glad you came by. I wasn't sure that you would be coming back.

She opens the door and we go inside and into the kitchen. There's newspaper all over the floor and bits of mud, and there's this lump of clay in the middle which looks even more like a turd than her other sculptures, the only real difference being that it's exceptionally large. Mrs Wrens says she just started doing sculpting again yesterday. She tells me that it's a cathartic thing to do.

We sit down and she makes some tea, and she starts off on one, telling me all this stuff about Fabian, stuff I had no idea about. Like she goes on about how his favourite thing to do when he was a tot was to try and stand on his head so he could see the world upside down, and how he kept falling over and hurting himself, but he never stopped trying to do it.

Right up until he died he was able to do a perfect headstand, she goes. Sometimes he would watch the TV doing it. Not many people knew that about him.

I certainly didn't. I sit there and endure some more parables about Fabian, and I'm almost tempted to contribute. But I don't, because the truth is even if he was nicest Nazi ever born, there's no sense in telling it to his mother, and if she doesn't already know about all that freaky stuff she probably doesn't want to. I guess when you remember people you don't think about them as freaks anyway. You think about them as individuals. At one point I tell her I'm surprised she can still like, live here and all, but she finds that kind of funny and laughs. She's like, It's just a house, not my boy!

She doesn't go on for long anyway. It's not like we're sat there for more than about twenty minutes or anything. And she doesn't ask me to do anything gross, like take a tour of his room or view the bathtub. She just seems content to chat a bit and seems really glad that I've come. I'm glad that I did it too, because it's like a kind of goodbye. I really mean that. When I get up to go she says, Don't you ever do anything as stupid as what my son did, Jarold. Because he *was* stupid. Terribly, terribly stupid, in this voice that's like regretful but all wise and old-sounding. It kind of annoys me that she keeps calling me Jarold, but I agree not to and then she shows me out and tells me if I ever want to stop by again I'll always be welcome. But I don't suppose I ever will, or that she really expects me to. But it's nice of her to say it. She's a pretty cool woman, so I hope she makes out OK, I really do.

And that's it. That's the last scene.

25

So like, epilogue:

Al's having a ball in Leeds. She thinks it's like, the definition of where it's at. She says it has tons of Character, whatever the hell that's supposed to mean. I kind of still miss her a bit, but I'm getting better at going out on my own, and I don't even mind that I don't always meet someone I like or anything. There's this new place I go to called the NY Plaza, which is so nothing as cool as it sounds but at least you can get in without having to pass an iris scan, and I've yet to run into old Fellows in there. It's like a nightmare or something of mine that I'm gonna run into him *and* Higgs one of these days.

Even though I'm no longer being psycho-probed by him I see Higgs all the time, because he's always sitting outside the school in his Volvo waiting for Fellows at the end of the day. He always waves to me, which is totally embarrassing. I still haven't won that bet with Al about them yet.

Mum and Dad have switched to marriage counselling and Mum doesn't yell quite so much these days, which is kind of a good thing – at least for your eardrums. Only instead of yelling she goes on and on about how much better things are now, and she's always touching Dad and stuff as if she's afraid he's gonna disappear on her or something. They both make a total effort with each other, and it's pretty false. Sometimes I'll come in the room and find them, like, bonding over books of carpet samples, and I'll be so grossed out I'll want to cut my wrists just to royally fuck up the whole operation. Even The Nun seems weirded out by it, though most of the time these days she's too busy fawning over her stupid pony down at the stable, which she and her friend have called Horsey, wouldn't you know it? Hey, maybe it's the only way for dysfunctional people to like, be together, so if Mum and Dad are really content this way then I guess it's OK by me.

We go to visit Grandma once every two weeks, on Sunday after Mum and Dad have had their therapy. We spend most of the time admiring the field of potted plants she's collecting in her room. On our last visit, while everyone else was off harassing the staff for cups of tea, she confided in me that she's still just waiting for another stroke to reunite her with Grandpa. She was all sly about it and she even gave me a wink, which is like, a totally weird thing to get from an old person. But I guess maybe it's kind of romantic that she's got a reason to look forward to dying though. Maybe.

Oh, I almost forgot, there's like, a follow-up to the whole Me and Jon saga. I saw him again in Starlight last time I went there. He came up to me, which I'm glad about because I wouldn't have had the guts to go up to him after what happened. He was all like, So how did it go? and I was like, Fine, blah-blah-blah. I was kind of surprised he came up actually, after everything, you know. Apparently he's got a boyfriend now and they're looking for a place of their own, which is nice I suppose. He was like, So if you guys are ever down in Brighton again and you need a place to stay . . . I was like, Cool, me and Al are thinking of taking a trip down there in the summer, at which point he kind of laughed nervously and went, Oh right, cool, in this totally unconvincing way, so I'm not holding my breath about that.

We do have plans to meet up again in the summer, though I'm really not sure if it's going to happen, 'cos apparently Al's having such a great time it's like the world outside of Leeds is just this pale imitation or something. In fact I haven't actually heard from her for over two weeks. We started off texting every night, but it kind of died out. Her last text was like, OMIGOD I'VE GOT A BOYFRND!!! if you can believe it, so I guess her time's all taken up with him. I bet he's one of those totally cheerless politics nerds who dreams of being an MP or something and has, like, legion issues in the bedroom department. She sent a picture of him with the message, and he's like, a total roly-poly.

So like, End of story. I told you not to big it up or anything. I'm not changed or some kind of a saint because of anything that's happened, I'm still just me and probably always will be, whatever *me* is. Maybe me is heartless, like that stuff Al said in Brighton, about just wanting to suck dick and not giving a shit about anyone else for my whole life. Then again maybe I'll turn out to be like Fellows and Higgs in the end and be all responsible and uppity and stuff. I bet Jon's gonna be just like that when he reaches their age. Or maybe I'll just become plain old dysfunctional like Mum and Dad (though the thought of that happening is like, the most depressing thing ever). Maybe I'll make like Fabian and just say, To hell with it all. In spite of what his mum said, it sometimes seems like he made a pretty smart move, though I know I probably shouldn't say so. But then you can't always go around saying stuff just because it's what you're supposed to say. That would just be stupid.

So here's the deal: I'm not going to give you some barfable moral or anything now, so just relax if that's what you were expecting. You can just take whatever you like from all this. Or else don't take anything. Or else LIC GAS.

A NOTE ON THE AUTHOR

Will Davis was born in London in 1980.
This is his first novel.

A NOTE ON THE TYPE

The text of this book is set in Linotype Sabon, named after the type founder, Jacques Sabon. It was designed by Jan Tschichold and jointly developed by Linotype, Monotype and Stempel, in response to a need for a typeface to be available in identical form for mechanical hot metal composition and hand composition using foundry type.

Tschichold based his design for Sabon roman on a font engraved by Garamond, and Sabon italic on a font by Granjon. It was first used in 1966 and has proved an enduring modern classic.